The Life She Regrets

A GRANITE SPRINGS NOVEL

Maggie Christensen

Cover and interior design: J D Smith Design

Editing: John Hudspith Editing Services

To good friend and fellow writer, Louise,
who helped me solve a plot dilemma.

Also by Maggie Christensen

Oregon Coast Series
The Sand Dollar
The Dreamcatcher
Madeline House

Sunshine Coast books
A Brahminy Sunrise
Champagne for Breakfast

Sydney Collection
Band of Gold
Broken Threads
Isobel's Promise
A Model Wife

Scottish Collection
The Good Sister
Isobel's Promise
A Single Woman

Granite Springs
The Life She Deserves
The Life She Chooses
The Life She Wants
The Life She Finds
The Life She Imagines
A Granite Springs Christmas
The Life She Creates

Check out the last page of this book to see how to join my mailing list and get a free download of one of my books.

Prologue

'I can't!' Ann Baird sobbed as she clung to Gus, their evening together spoiled. 'How can you expect me to leave Granite Springs? To leave Mum?'

Gus Thomas, the man she'd loved since she was a teenager, took her by the shoulders and kissed her on the forehead. 'It's our big chance, Annie. Can't you see? It's what we wanted, planned for – to get away, leave Granite Springs, build a life for ourselves. This company is going places. They're on the cutting edge of technology. It's an amazing opportunity. The salary's out of this world, and they've promised to find work for you, too.'

'I know all that, but it was before…' Ann drew back out of his arms, aware of how, in the past few months, her life had changed. Her father's death, followed by her mother's decline into a world of her own, had been devastating for her. Most of all, it had forced her to realise how much her mother needed her.

Gus sighed and pushed a hand through his thick chestnut hair, the hair Ann loved to run her own fingers through. His eyes clouded over, and his lips turned down. 'What about Susie? She lives here too, can't she…?'

Ann shook her head. She knew exactly what her older sister would say if Ann asked her to care for their mother. Susie was ten years older than Ann and had her hands full with three children under five. She'd tell Ann it was *her* responsibility, that it would be selfish of her to swan off overseas and leave Susie to care for their mother on top of everything else. Ann sighed too. How could she make Gus understand?

'But...' Gus drew her into his arms again and hugged her tightly.

Ann wanted him to never let her go. 'Maybe,' she said, 'once Mum is more settled.' But even as she spoke, she knew it was hopeless. The doctor had told her and Susie their mother might never recover from the shock of her husband's death, that the decline she was now displaying could be the first stages of dementia.

'You know that's not going to happen.' Gus's voice took on a bitter note. 'You told me what the doctor said. You can't ruin your life, Annie. We had such plans.'

Ann thought of the plans they'd made, the life with him she'd been dreaming of for over four years, all through his degree when they'd managed to steal weekends together whenever they could. She thought of how it felt to be in his arms, their naked bodies entwined. Then she remembered her mother, how she'd looked when Ann left her that morning. The normally cheerful woman had aged terribly in the past few months. She was a shadow of her former self. She needed someone. She needed Ann.

'I'm sorry, Gus, I can't leave her.'

There wasn't any more to say.

'They want me to start in three weeks,' Gus said. 'I should go. I've a lot to do before then.'

Ann watched the love of her life walk away. She wanted to call him back, tell him she'd changed her mind. But she didn't. She couldn't. Instead, she went back inside the house she'd grown up in, the house she'd now live in for the rest of her life.

One

Thirty-five years later

Ann often wished her life could be different. But there was no sense in harbouring regrets, in wondering what might have been. So, when those morbid thoughts threatened to overwhelm her, she kept busy. She'd pull herself up, remind herself she had a good life, and a good job. There were all the worthy causes she supported, her reputation in the community. But some days, it wasn't enough. This was one of them.

'Ann, can I have a word?'

Ann looked up from her computer, prepared to be annoyed at the interruption. But a smile etched her lips when she saw the intruder was her boss, Professor Nick Kerr, Dean of the School of Education at William Farrer University. Ann had worked here for the past twenty years, starting out as an administrative assistant before being promoted to her present position managing the Education office.

'How can I help you, Professor Kerr?'

Nick Kerr sighed. 'I wish you'd call me Nick,' he said, repeating what he had said many times.

She tightened her lips, knowing her insistence on using his title irritated him, but over the years she'd found sticking to a set of rules and principles was what helped her through the days.

'We have a situation I'd like your help with.' He ran a hand through his thick greying hair. He was an attractive man, but Ann had never felt anything other than respect for her employer. She'd been pleased when he and Kay Jackson had got together. They'd been married for several years now and, to Ann's surprise, Kay remained in her role as his personal assistant. But both seemed to be able to handle the situation, and the vice chancellor was in favour of the arrangement, so who was she to disagree?

Ann perked up. One thing she enjoyed about her role was the challenge some days brought. It looked as if this might be one of those days.

Nick's forehead creased. 'There's been an accident. It's one of the exchange students. She was on her way back from teaching practice when the motorbike she was riding ran into a wall. I'm not sure how serious it is, but she's been brought into Granite Springs Base Hospital. Damn fool to be riding on a motorbike!'

Ann knew how hard Nick had worked to have his exchange proposal accepted by the powers within the university. This was the first year a group of Canadian students had arrived to spend a year at the university, a cohort of William Farrer students having travelled to Canada. The program had proven successful – until now.

'Oh no! What would you like me to do?'

'Kay's been in touch with the parents, and the father's planning to fly here in a day or two. I'm not sure about the mother…' He appeared distracted for a moment.

Ann wondered if he was thinking of his own ex-wife who now lived in the north of Queensland.

Nick spoke again. 'I wonder if you could arrange accommodation for him. Dr Thomas. He'll most likely want to stay until his daughter is on the way to recovery, then perhaps take her back home with him. Not the sort of thing we wanted to happen.' He exhaled noisily.

Ann could see he was worried. This program was important to him. 'I can do that. I'm sure it'll be fine, Professor Kerr.' She knew what he was thinking. 'No one can hold you or the school responsible. I'm sure the vice chancellor and the senate will see that.'

'I hope you're right. I'm heading to the hospital now to see how the girl is, and if there's anything else we can do.'

'Okay. I'll get right onto it.'

Ann watched Nick leave. He must be thinking of his own two children, glad it wasn't one of them lying in a hospital bed.

Her daughter would be in her thirties by now. Ann had always imagined it would be a girl, a girl she'd call Annabel. She always wished she had a fancier name than plain old Ann.

When she refused to go with Gus, she knew it was the right thing to do, even though it broke her heart. What she hadn't bargained for was the discovery she was pregnant. It was too late to contact Gus – even if she wanted to. He'd already left.

In a panic, Ann had gone to her sister. To her surprise, Susie had been sympathetic, agreeing with Ann the news would deal yet another blow to their already distraught mother. She offered to help Ann arrange an abortion. It was the last thing Ann wanted, severing as it would her last link with Gus, and being against all she believed about the sanctity of life. Despite initially agreeing, she'd been unable to go through with it, backing out at the last minute, only to suffer a miscarriage a month later. Ann felt it was a punishment for even considering killing her baby and was consumed with guilt.

For a long time, Ann would gaze longingly at children who were the age her Annabel would be, wondering what she would have been like, if she would have been dark like her or have chestnut hair like Gus. And, as the years went by, Ann knew people saw her as unbending, even bitter. It was her only defence against the guilt and anguish she felt.

She picked up her phone.

*

'What's new?' Fran Larsen was Ann's good friend. She'd been Nick's PA until she went off to England to care for her sick mother, when Kay took her place. Now she worked in the School of Music and Drama alongside her new husband. Fran was the only person in whom Ann had confided her past.

'You haven't heard?' Ann asked, picking up her coffee cup. The pair were sharing their morning coffee break in the university café, something they often did. 'I thought you and Owen always had your ear to the ground.'

'Not this time.' Fran cocked her head to one side.

'There's been an accident. One of the Canadian students. Coming back from practice teaching down the coast. She was riding a motorbike and...'

Fran's face paled.

Ann silently cursed herself. How could she have been so tactless? It was a bike accident that brought Fran to Granite Springs, that changed her life. 'Sorry,' she said.

'No. I should be over it. I can't spend the rest of my life wilting every time I hear about a motorbike accident. One of the Canadian students, you say?'

'Cassandra Thomas. I've been booking accommodation at the new motor inn for her father who's coming over to be with her. A Dr Thomas. Some sort of bigwig in IT.'

'CAT.'

'What?'

'CAT. It's an international software company based in Canada. He's the owner, CEO, what have you. I thought you'd have heard of them. They specialise in CAD. CBI, and AI.'

'Now you've got me! Stop speaking in acronyms. What do you mean?'

Fran laughed. 'I thought you'd have come across those terms – Computer Aided Design, Computer Based Instruction and Artificial Intelligence.'

'Oh, of course. I knew that.' She laughed, too.

They were silent a few moments, sipping coffee, the babble of student voices and background music flowing around them, then Ann said, 'Cassandra Thomas. She's a lovely girl, bright and cheerful. I've seen her around when she comes to the Education office.'

'How bad is it?' Fran asked, her face still pale. 'Don't worry. I'm not going to faint on you. But I know how vulnerable bike riders are.'

'Nick says her condition is critical.' As she spoke, Ann reflected how natural it seemed to call her boss Nick when she was talking about him, while she found it impossible when they were face-to-face.

Fran's forehead creased. 'I hope...'

'We all do.' Ann said. 'But she's young and fit. Like you were.' Ann reached across the table to take Fran's hand. 'And you managed to recover and lead a full life.'

'Ye…es.'

Ann wished she'd kept her mouth shut. Why did she have to share the news about the accident? She should have known it would bring back bad memories for Fran who'd lost her boyfriend and her unborn child in the accident years earlier.

It was the loss of a child that had brought the two women together initially. They met when Fran first arrived in Granite Springs, when she was a patient in the Base Hospital where Ann volunteered. Then Fran had got a job at the university and they became workmates as well as friends. It was a friendship which had endured and become stronger over the years. Fran was one of the few people who knew the real Ann, the one she kept hidden under a façade of impersonal professionalism. She knew many thought her hard and cold. She'd heard what the young girls in the office said about her.

At first, after Gus left, after the miscarriage, her cool demeanour had been an attempt to maintain some semblance of normality. But, as time went on, it became part of her, and the pretence became the reality.

'Have you spoken with Dr Thomas?'

'No. My only task was to organise his accommodation. Kay's the one who's been in touch with him. He's due to fly in on the weekend. If he's as important as you say, I don't expect he'll be able to stay for long.'

'The mother?'

'No mention of her.'

'Maybe he's a widower. You'd think she'd come with him otherwise.'

'You would.'

The two women were silent again, Ann thinking of what she'd lost, the pleasure she'd been deprived of. She had no doubt that Fran was thinking the same.

'Anyway, I should get back.' Ann drained her coffee and pushed her chair back. 'Same time next week?'

'Why don't you come out to lunch on Sunday? I thought I'd ask Peta and Frank, too,' she said, referring to Ann's cousin, who recently moved to Granite Springs with her granddaughter.

'Thanks. That would be lovely.'

But walking back to her office, Ann reflected how, pleasurable though the day would be and much as she'd enjoy the company of the few people she could be herself with, she'd be the odd one out again. Maybe the girls in the office were right when they called her a dried-up old maid. But, after Gus left, she'd never been attracted to another man, never wanted to risk the hurt she felt as she watched him walk away.

Two

'You mean it, Gail? You really won't go? Cassie is lying in a hospital bed at the other end of the world and you can't leave your damn job?'

'It was her choice – and your tales of your misspent youth – that sent her haring off on the exchange to a university in a hick town in Australia. She's not dying, is she? And I doubt she'll want to see me anyway after her last outburst.'

Chris Thomas tended to agree with Gail's last statement. Cassie and her mother had been at daggers drawn for some years – ever since her parents split up. They were too alike. But whereas Gail's ambitions had resulted in her distancing herself from her family and pursuing what Chris called a false god, Cassie had chosen to do something more with her life. She wanted to see the world and to work with children. The opportunity to participate in this pilot exchange program was her way of furthering both those dreams.

Gail hadn't agreed, preferring their daughter spend the year closer to home – *her* home, which was several thousand miles away from where Chris lived in Vancouver. A massive argument ensued, culminating in Cassie's storming out in a flood of tears. Despite – or perhaps because of – her mother's disapproval, the girl had got her way and flown off to Australia last September. It was now January and, although Chris missed having her with him at Christmas, he'd enjoyed her messages about her first antipodean Christmas Day and the tales of Granite Springs which had brought back memories of his own younger days growing up in the Australian bush.

He put down the phone with a sigh. Gail wasn't going to change her mind. Somehow, over the years, what she saw as her high-powered position in the renowned glossy women's magazine had taken priority over both him and their daughter. Now, Chris could barely remember the woman he'd married. She was so changed from the lovely, vivacious girl who'd helped him forget, helped him learn to love again. The last time they'd met, at the airport to farewell Cassie, all he saw was the hard-bitten career woman she'd become.

Chris fired up his computer to google flights to Australia. Then he checked his diary. It wouldn't be easy for him to get away either, though easier now he headed up his own company. It was a far cry from his early days in Silicon Valley. Throwing himself into his new career in an attempt to forget all he'd left behind in Granite Springs, Chris had used his free evenings to enrol in a master's degree. That had led to a doctorate and a move to Canada where, still vulnerable, he'd met Gail.

Now, recognised as a world authority in his field, his life revolved around his company and his daughter. As soon as he heard about the accident, he knew he had to be there with her. He'd be lost without his beautiful Cassie. Even though he'd encouraged her participation in the exchange programme, he'd known he'd miss her dreadfully, and he had. But he also knew he had to allow her to spread her wings.

He couldn't understand how Gail could ignore her only child.

*

Dr Christopher Angus Thomas stepped off the plane and back in time. He hadn't been in Granite Springs since he left to take up the position with a large software company in the states thirty-five years ago. He'd never intended to stay away so long, but the death of his parents in a car accident in the year after he left, and his subsequent difficulty in arranging to return for the funeral, effectively severed all his ties there.

That and his rejection by his first love. If he'd thought there was any hope of their reuniting, nothing would have held him back. But Annie had made it quite clear her mother was her priority, and the old bag would probably live for years – just to spite him. Annie's mother had never been a fan of his, regarding his parents as beneath her. He didn't entirely blame the girl who'd been his childhood sweetheart – her sense of loyalty and family values were part of what he loved about her. It was the unfairness of it all that bothered him at the time. Just as they were about to spread their wings and start their life together, Annie's father died, and her mother fell into a trough of despair.

Perhaps if he'd managed to secure a job closer to Granite Springs, things would have been different, but the offer he received from the world leader in his field was too good to refuse. It hadn't occurred to him for an instant Annie wouldn't agree to go with him.

And now he was back.

He battled through a much larger crowd than he'd anticipated meeting in Granite Springs airport on a Sunday morning. He'd been gone a long time. He supposed he should have expected things to change.

Loading his case into the boot of a hired car, he headed into town. The main street didn't look any different. It was still lined with trees although they did appear taller than he remembered. He even recognised some of the shops. It was as if time stood still here. The town certainly hadn't received any sort of transformation. As he drove slowly along, he was flooded with memories, most of them good. He'd had a happy childhood and when, in his teenage years, he and Annie Baird had started dating, he thought his future was assured.

For several moments, he felt as if the past was coming up to meet him. He almost expected to see his younger self and Annie walking along hand in hand or with his arm slung around her shoulders, her face turned up to his. He felt a bolt of something akin to regret for what might have been if things had been different and wondered what had happened to the girl he'd known. Probably she was married and had sloughed off the dust of Granite Springs long ago. He didn't regret his life. He'd done well, made a success of his company, was what many would call wealthy. But wealth didn't necessarily bring happiness. He'd suffered many lonely nights thinking what if… Something he didn't regret was his lovely daughter. She was one thing he and Gail had got right. He couldn't wait to see Cassie.

This was new. Chris turned the car into the forecourt of an upmarket motel. Its white-pebbled façade and red tiled roof was more reminiscent of the California where he'd lived after leaving this town behind. *The Springs* was located on the edge of town and looked out onto broad acres. Walking into the reception area, Chris was greeted by calm green surroundings making him feel as if he was in a glade of gum trees. The theme was continued in the décor on the walls where paintings drew the eye to bush scenes straight out of his old poetry books. Whoever designed this, knew what they were doing. It was an oasis of peace for the weary traveller.

'Can I help you, sir?'

'Sorry. I was admiring the décor. I need to check in. The motel must be fairly new?'

'We opened just before Christmas. Your name?'

'Thomas.'

'Dr Thomas? I have your details here. If you could let me have your credit card and complete this form?'

While Chris was filling his details on the requisite form, the receptionist spoke again, 'Sorry about your daughter. I hope she makes a speedy recovery.'

How...? Then Chris remembered. He was back in Granite Springs. News travelled like the proverbial bushfire. 'Thanks,' he said.

He was pleased, once he reached his room, to find the same décor reflected in the walls and soft furnishings. He was impressed this part of Granite Springs really seemed to have changed, to have moved with the times.

After a quick freshen up, Chris's first port of call was going to be the hospital. He was desperate to see Cassie, to talk with her doctor, to find out her prognosis. The Dean of the School of Education had been good, had called him personally, and his PA, a lady called Kay, had kept him informed about the arrangements for his accommodation. He made a mental note to go out to campus to thank him personally. He'd be interested in seeing the campus, too. When he left, there had been no university in Granite Springs and no thought of one.

The Base Hospital hadn't changed. It was still the same red brick building it had been when he went there to have a broken leg seen to when he was around twelve. He barely remembered it, only the kudos of having a cast on his leg and the agony of having to forego playing sport for weeks till it healed.

Cassie was in ward eight in the surgical wing. Chris's heart started to pound when he entered the ward and asked which room she was in.

'Cassie Thomas?' The nurse, a tall young man whose topknot sat above an otherwise shaved head, smiled. 'You must be her father. She's been looking forward to seeing you.'

His words sent a wave of relief through Chris. He'd been worried Cassie might still be unconscious or in a coma. He'd been on a plane for the past couple of days and hadn't been able to get any updates.

'She's in room four. I think she's awake. She's still in a bad way. You might want to talk to her surgeon.'

'Thanks.' That was exactly what Chris did want to do. But first he needed to see his daughter.

Three

Sunday proved to be another glorious day. Ann dressed carefully in a pair of white pants and a blue striped shirt, realising as she did so her weekend outfits were no different from those she wore to work every day. Maybe that was something she should change, but it was difficult to change the habit of a lifetime. And they suited her tall slim figure. She brushed her short dark hair, peering into the mirror as she applied a smear of lipstick.

Despite her dislike of feeling the odd one out, Ann was looking forward to the visit. She'd only been to Fran and Owen's a couple of times before and loved the openness of the acreage where they lived. It would be good to see Peta, again, too. It was only six months since her cousin had arrived in town to escape from the drama of her daughter's death. At first, it had been strange to share her home, but she quickly became attached to Peta's granddaughter, Lily, after the initial shock of a child's presence in the old house.

But Peta had now moved on, too, to live with Frank Beattie. He was a good man, one Ann had known all her life. He, and his father before him, owned The Bean Sprout Café on Main Street, which had been one of her and Gus's favourite haunts.

What had brought Gus into her mind today? He belonged in the past, a past she tried not to think about, but a past which had shaped her, for better or worse, into the woman she was today. Maybe it was the thought of spending the day with two happy couples that had brought back the memory of the tall, handsome young man with thick chestnut hair. But Gus wouldn't be a young man any longer, any more than she was the lively young woman full of the joys of life he'd fallen in love with.

Ann was so busy with her thoughts, she reached the turn off to The Haven before she realised it. Driving down the lane, she could see the goats Owen was so proud of roaming around the paddock and looking curiously at her car. She could also see Frank's little blue ute was already parked by the house.

She got out of the car and took a deep breath. It was so peaceful here, apart from the raucous noise of a cloud of galahs flying in to land in the neighbouring paddock and forage in the dry grass.

'Auntie Ann!' A small blonde figure emerged from the house and ran to greet her with a hug. Lily was a lovely child. No one should have to suffer what she had at such a tender age, but she'd proved resilient and gradually returned to the happy little girl she was today.

'Lily!' Ann returned the little girl's hug, glad she'd managed to get over the fear of becoming close to children. At nine, Lily was a delight. It had been a blessing when Peta accepted Ann's invitation to come to Granite Springs when her daughter, Lily's mum, was brutally murdered.

'I thought I heard your car.' Fran, followed by Peta, joined them with hugs all round. 'Come in. I was about to open a bottle of wine. The men have gone down to check on the neighbour's alpacas. Frank isn't familiar with the breed and was curious to see them.'

Ann followed the two women inside to where a black cat was curled up in a rocking chair by the Aga. As they entered, the creature lazily lifted his head, opened his eyes and regarded them warily, before resuming the nap they'd interrupted.

'Take a seat,' Fran said. 'Don't mind Stormy. He'll probably disappear when we start talking. He prefers his own company.' She opened the fridge and took out a bottle of white wine.

Sure enough, at the sound of the fridge door, the cat stirred again and, with a baleful glance at the fridge closing, leapt from his perch and padded out of the kitchen. Lily disappeared to follow him, calling, 'Stormy!'

The three women settled down to enjoy refreshing glasses of wine and chat about the accident to the Canadian student. Ann had no further information, but Fran had managed to discover the girl had borrowed the bike from another student in an attempt to get back to Granite Springs in a hurry.

'I think there was a boy involved,' Fran said, taking a sip of wine. 'The things we women do for love.' She chuckled and Peta joined in.

Ann felt awkward. She'd been in love once. But her family ties were too strong to deny and she had let Gus go. This was another reminder. *Why had the past come up to haunt her today, after all those years?* She gazed out across the paddock to see the two men walking back. 'Here are Owen and Frank,' she said, relieved to be able to change the subject.

The arrival of the men brought a breath of fresh air. They were full of praise for the alpacas they'd admired on the neighbouring property.

'You should see them, Peta,' Frank enthused. 'They're much tamer than Owen's goats.'

'I have.' Peta chuckled. 'Remember I told you I met Jo Ford when I was new in town, and Col helped me with all the legal stuff last year. I've been to Yarran several times.'

'Of course you have.' Frank gave her an affectionate look.

'Watch it, Frank.' Owen went to the fridge and came back with two cans of beer, handing one to Frank. 'You need not only to listen to what your woman says, but remember it, too. As I've learnt to my shame.'

Fran picked up a tea towel and threw it at him.

'See what I mean?' he asked, catching it deftly.

Ann winced. She hated being privy to this sort of affectionate bickering which seemed commonplace with many couples. It made her want to disappear down a crack in the floor. 'Excuse me,' she said, 'I need to...'

'First on the right off the hallway,' Fran said.

Once in the hall cloakroom, Ann grasped the edge of the sink, closing her eyes. Why had she come? She suspected this would happen. First the memories which dredged themselves up from the depths of her past, then this overt demonstration of affection. She didn't blame them. Both couples were obviously happy. She was glad Peta had found Frank. She'd had a hard life. Ann suspected it had been harder than she was willing to talk about. She'd been shocked with the change in her cousin when she first arrived in Granite Springs.

But Peta now seemed to have recovered, apart from the occasional clouding of her eyes when she thought no one was looking. Ann was glad for her. But she couldn't subdue the tinge of regret that she hadn't been the one to help in Peta's recovery.

'Now you're back, we can have lunch,' Fran announced when Ann returned.

Glad of the opportunity to be of use, Ann offered to help.

*

After lunch, the whole party was persuaded by Owen to take a walk along the lane. At the gate, they were about to turn in the direction the men had walked earlier when Lily asked, 'Can we go to see the horses?'

'Sure. This way.' Owen pointed in the opposite direction, and the group sauntered up the lane till they reached a paddock where three horses were grazing peacefully. 'This is where Magda and George live,' he said to them. 'She's been here forever, but the house is relatively new. Her old one was lost in the bushfire we had a couple of years ago, but she's a wily old bird and didn't let the loss of her home faze her. In fact, I think it may have given her a new lease of life. It was after she moved back that she and George got together.'

Another couple! Ann remembered the gossip when the well-known retired solicitor and former director of Granite Springs Choristers revealed he and Magda were a couple. Ann had been at the lighting of the town Christmas tree when the elderly pair danced together in the street, confirming the relationship everyone had suspected for years. Magda was a masseuse and rumour had it, she could make accurate predictions about the future. Fran had told Ann how Magda foresaw her relationship with Owen.

But Ann had no time for such rubbish. She'd never felt the need for a massage, despite Fran's encouragement and advice it would help her relax. She didn't need to relax. She preferred to keep busy. It stopped her thinking too much.

As the group approached, the horses galloped across to the fence, jostling with each other in an attempt to be first to secure the titbits they seemed to expect.

'Sorry!' Owen opened his hand, palm up. 'Nothing for you today.'

Lily sidled up and stroked the nose of the nearest animal. 'It feels so soft, like velvet,' she said, jumping back with fright when the horse snorted.

There was the sound of laughter behind them.

Turning, Ann saw the woman she knew to be Magda standing there with two greyhounds.

'Don't be afraid. It's Lily, isn't it? I remember you came to visit with the twins. I think I know all of you except...?' She sent an enquiring look in Ann's direction.

'Ann Baird,' Ann replied, wondering why she'd always felt threatened by any mention of Magda Duncan. She was just an old white-haired woman, albeit livelier than most and with a wicked twinkle in her eyes.

'Of course,' Magda said. 'You're Peta's cousin, the one who persuaded her to come to Granite Springs. You're to be congratulated in helping her find her destiny.'

A shiver went down Ann's spine. There it was – the reason for her misgivings about the woman. But Magda hadn't finished.

'Your journey has yet to be completed. There will be a reminder from the past, a chance to put right something you regret. Don't let the opportunity escape. It could bring you great happiness.'

What utter nonsense. But Magda's words sent another shiver down Ann's spine.

All the way back down the lane, and all the way home, the words echoed in Ann's ears, until she forced herself to think of something else.

Four

Chris's heart contracted at the sight of his daughter lying there, her eyes closed, her face as white as the pillow she lay on. She was hooked up to what seemed to be a mass of equipment which bleeped and hissed – the only sounds in the room. There were two drips feeding into her left hand.

'Cassie,' he whispered, moving to her side. There was no response. He picked up her hand and squeezed it gently, fearful of hurting her.

He heard a movement behind him and turned quickly. It was another nurse – an older woman this time.

'Mr Thomas. I'm Marilyn. I'm the team leader on the ward. Your daughter is in good hands here. She was awake a few minutes ago but tends to drift off. She suffered concussion, and I'm afraid her leg has been badly crushed. Would you like me to contact someone from the surgical team?'

'I would.' Chris couldn't take his eyes off Cassie who lay so still, looking nothing like the spirited, enthusiastic girl he'd seen off at the airport only a few months earlier. He realised the nurse was still there. He turned. 'Is she... will she... She'll be all right...she'll recover, won't she?'

'We're doing all we can. It was a bad accident.'

Chris pushed back a lock of hair falling over his brow. 'I can't understand how it could happen. Cassie doesn't have a motorbike.'

'I'm afraid I can't help you there. Perhaps the university...?'

'Of course.' He'd go there next. The dean might be able to shed some light on how this all came about. He shook his head, just as Cassie stirred.

'Cassie!' he repeated, turning back to her bed. With his free hand, he pulled a chair closer to her bedside and collapsed onto it. 'I'm here, my darling. I'm not going anywhere until you're well again.'

'Dad!' Cassie's voice was weak, but there was a hint of a smile in her eyes telling Chris she was glad to see him.

Chris heard the room door closing and knew the nurse had left.

Cassie's eyes closed again, but her hand was still in his. He dropped his head onto the bed, his eyes beginning to fill with tears.

He didn't know how long he sat there, but his muscles were aching when he heard a cough behind him.

'Mr Thomas?'

Chris looked up to see a short woman with a wild mop of dark hair, wearing a set of blue scrubs. She looked as if she had just walked out of the operating theatre.

'I'm Bree, one of the surgical team which operated on your daughter.'

Chris blinked. He carefully released Cassie's hand and stood up. Now he was faced by the surgeon, Chris wasn't sure what he wanted to ask. The woman seemed to understand. No doubt she was used to talking to people like him. He felt traumatised by everything that had happened since he received the phone call to tell him Cassie had been in an accident.

'Why don't we go into another room? Cassie is asleep now.'

Chris turned his head to see his daughter's eyes were still closed. He allowed himself to be led out of the room and into another which was vacant apart from two blue, upholstered chairs.

Bree took a seat and motioned him to do the same. 'Mr Thomas...'

'Chris,' he said automatically.

'Chris, I'm afraid your daughter has suffered severe trauma. She received a blow to the head, which, despite her wearing a helmet, resulted in concussion. Also...' Bree's forehead creased, '...her left leg has been broken in several places and badly crushed. There's been damage to the nerves, muscles, blood vessels and tissue. We've done an initial repair, but she may need further surgery if...'

'But she's going to be all right?' Chris interrupted. He couldn't bear to think otherwise. He wanted his lively daughter back again. Why had he ever encouraged her to take part in the exchange programme? Because Gail was right. As soon as Cassie had begun talking about it, about how she wanted to see the town he had grown up in, and wasn't this an amazing opportunity, he had actively encouraged her to participate.

Bree hesitated. 'We're doing all we can. We hope to save the leg, but it'll be a few more weeks before we know for sure or how much movement she'll regain. It may take months for her to heal.'

Save her leg? Weeks? Months? Chris rubbed his forehead and shook his head. He squeezed his eyes shut, a heavy feeling in his stomach. He had flown to Australia without any real plan, but his intention was to take Cassie back home with him. He'd thought perhaps a few days, weeks perhaps, but this...

When he opened his eyes again, he saw Bree gazing at him with concern. She handed him a cup of water which seemed to have appeared by magic. He grasped it and gulped greedily.

'I know it must be a shock.'

Shock? That was putting it mildly. For the first time, he wished Gail was here to share his grief.

'So, what happens now?' Chris could feel reaction setting in. He took several deep breaths to calm himself.

'We monitor her, schedule another surgery when we think her body can cope with it. Then we wait.'

'There's no...' He let his voice trail off. Of course there was no other option. He had to trust the doctors knew what they were doing, but he had to ask. 'Is there anyone else... from Sydney maybe...?' He knew he sounded desperate. He felt desperate. It was his little girl they were talking about.

Bree drew herself up and squared her shoulders. She clearly wasn't accustomed to the expertise of Granite Springs Hospital being questioned. 'Our surgeons are highly qualified and highly skilled. The consultant in charge of Cassie's case also holds an appointment at Canberra Hospital and is often called in to consult in trauma cases in Sydney and Melbourne. Just because he is based here doesn't mean your daughter is receiving substandard care.' She bridled, all her former friendliness disappearing.

'I'm sorry.' Chris drew a hand through his hair. 'I didn't mean... I don't know what I'm saying... Cassie...'

'I'm sorry.' Bree unbent sufficiently to give a brief smile. 'I do understand. You want the best for your daughter. Believe me when I say she couldn't have any better care. We do have a process which we adopted from Queensland – it's called Ryan's Rule – whereby, if you're concerned about the care she gets, you can demand a second opinion from another medical team. But I assure you…'

'No, I'm sure you are doing all you can.' Chris bit his lip. 'I'd like to go back to see Cassie now.'

'Of course. You can stay with her as long as you wish, and I and other members of the team are always happy to talk with you.'

They walked out together, Chris returning to spend the next hour sitting by Cassie's bedside, only leaving when darkness began to fall.

He dreaded the call he must make to Gail to tell her of Cassie's condition. Maybe the knowledge of how serious it was, would force her to put concern for her daughter above her job for once.

And first thing tomorrow, he'd be back. Then he'd visit the university to see if he could discover why Cassie had been on the motor bike in the first place.

Five

Unusually for her, Ann spent a restless night. Magda's words had made more of an impression than she had liked. While it was easy to dismiss them as the ramblings of an old woman, Ann knew of cases where her predictions had been accurate. Fran was a case in point. But, she reasoned as she stood in the shower, the hot water bringing life to her tired body, the woman's words had been vague. They hadn't even been predictions, merely a few well-worn platitudes. They certainly weren't worth losing sleep over.

Sitting in the kitchen over her breakfast of a mashed banana on a slice of wholemeal toast accompanied by a cup of strong coffee, Ann was able to put things in perspective. Magda had caught her at a vulnerable moment. She'd had those weird memories popping up and was feeling slightly awkward with the two loved-up couples. Now, in the light of day, with the morning sun beaming in through the window, and a pair of kookaburras cackling their morning chorus on the back fence, it was easy to dismiss the old woman's words.

It was the beginning of a new week. The students would all have returned from their practice teaching placements ready for the start of the new semester, and the Education office would be especially busy. There would be reports to collate, course outlines to be typed up, and course materials to be stacked ready to be picked up. Ann wondered why the lecturers didn't type up their own materials. Some did. They all had computers. But several – mostly the older male staff – still regarded it as beneath them to do what they saw as menial work. At least it provided continued employment for her own cohort of staff, mostly young women at the start of their careers. They moved on with increasing rapidity these days, as they found more exciting opportunities, usually far away from Granite Springs. There weren't many like Fran and Kay who brought more maturity to their work and remained loyal to their employer. Ann was one of those, too, having been with the university since it opened and worked under three deans in the School of Education.

When she reached the campus, it was to see groups of students already milling around gathering in groups in the previously empty courtyards and lazing on the lawn. Ann loved it when it was like this – a hive of activity. And she'd come to love the students, too, putting aside her own regrets and enjoying their carefree attitudes to life.

She was walking toward the Education building when Nick and Kay caught up with her.

'Thanks for organising the accommodation for Dr Thomas,' Nick said. 'Kay checked with *The Springs* and he arrived yesterday. I plan to contact him today to see if there's anything we can do.'

'Is there any news about his daughter?'

Nick pulled on his beard. 'I haven't contacted the hospital today, but when I spoke to them yesterday, I couldn't get much out of them apart from the standard, "She's as well as is to be expected". I'll have Kay try again today. I'm sure her fellow students will want an update.'

'Can you let me know if you hear anything more? We can perhaps put up a bulletin board outside the office. There'll be a lot of students coming in today to check timetables and such like. I imagine the other Canadian students will be particularly concerned.'

'Good idea. Can you see Ann's kept informed, Kay?' he turned to his wife.

'Will do. Do you want me to contact Dr Thomas?'

'No, best I do it.'

By this time, they'd reached the building and went their separate ways, Ann into the main office and Nick and Kay up the stairs to where the dean's office and that of his PA were located.

The morning flew past for Ann with only a few minor crises, one when a young girl on her staff managed to get a sheaf of papers stuck in the photocopier, one when a student dropped a cup of coffee which spilled all over the reception desk and one when a junior lecturer wanted to complain about his timetable. It was a typical day.

Ann was coming back from eating lunch at one of the tables in the courtyard when she saw an unfamiliar figure ascending the stairs to Nick's office.

*

Chris was a wreck. Despite the comfort of the motel bed, he hadn't slept a wink. Every time he was about to drop off, he had visions of Cassie, wondering how she would cope with the loss of a leg. She was just at the beginning of her life. She didn't deserve this. But who did deserve to be in an accident? They happened all the time and, from what he'd read, most of the victims were young people in their early twenties.

Cassie turned twenty last September.

Entering the office at the top of the stairs, he was greeted by a cheerful dark-haired woman.

'You must be Dr Thomas,' she said with a smile. 'I'm Kay Kerr. I'm so sorry about your daughter. I'll tell Nick you're here.'

Kay, that was the name of the woman he'd spoken to before he left home. 'Thanks.' He knew there was more he should say, but the visit to the hospital earlier had drained him Combined with lack of sleep, it made him feel as if he was functioning on autopilot. There was no change in Cassie from yesterday. She was still doped up to the eyeballs and unable to communicate much. Even though the nurse he spoke with said it was normal and there was nothing to worry about, Chris couldn't help feeling anxious.

The call to Gail hadn't helped. He'd lost his temper with her again when she hadn't shown any concern at the news their daughter's condition was still critical and she might lose a limb, and had refused point blank to come to Australia. He fumed when he remembered how she'd snapped at him. 'It's the magazine's first issue for the year, Chris. I can't possibly come now. Anyway, Cassie always was a daddy's girl. It's you she'd want there, not me.' He could almost see the sneer on her face as she uttered those words.

Although Gail always put more effort into the magazine than she did her family, Chris knew how she resented how Cassie did prefer to go to him with her troubles and achievements rather than her mother.

She didn't understand Chris's business either, had never tried, merely seen it as a meal ticket to fund their luxurious lifestyle while she climbed the career ladder in her chosen field.

'Dr Thomas.' The tall man with a shock of thick greying hair and a trim beard held out his hand. 'I'm Nick Kerr. Come into my office. Tea? Coffee?'

'Call me Chris. And coffee would be most welcome.'

'Kay?'

'I'll see to it.'

Inside the large office, Nick took one of two seats by a low coffee table and gestured Chris to take the other.

Chris sat down with a sense of relief. He hadn't realised how tense he was till now.

Kay had followed them in and was busy with a Nespresso machine in the corner. When she had made two coffees, she placed them on the table and left, closing the door behind her.

'I'm sorry we had to meet under these circumstances,' Nick said. 'I can't tell you how devastated we are at what happened to Cassandra. You've been to the hospital, of course. They won't give us any information.' He picked up his cup and put it down again.

'It's not good, but I have to trust the doctors,' Chris looked down at his feet, then picked up his cup and took a gulp of the welcome beverage. 'What I can't understand is why she was on a bike. Where did she get it?'

'Ah!' Nick pulled on his beard. 'I may be able to help you there. She was one of a group of our students who were sent down the coast for practice teaching. As you can imagine it's a sought-after placement at this time of year. When we heard of the accident, we instigated an inquiry and interviewed the rest of the group. They finished up in the schools on Friday and most drifted back on Saturday and Sunday. From what I hear, the Friday night was a bit of a celebration. But it seems Cassandra…'

'Cassie.'

'Sorry, Cassie… was in a hurry to get back to Granite Springs. We haven't yet been able to find out what – or who the attraction was.

Students are pretty wary about giving too much away. But we did discover one of the others lent her the bike so she could be back on Friday, rather than waiting for a ride on Saturday or Sunday.'

Chris tightened his lips. *A boy. There had to be a boy involved.* 'The student who lent her the bike – can I talk with him? I presume it is a guy.'

'Steven Wilcox. I can have Kay arrange for you to meet him. He's devastated, of course. He realises he should never have let her ride it. It was quite irresponsible of him.'

'Cassie can be very persuasive.' Chris knew that to his cost, remembering all the times she'd managed to wrap him around her little finger. 'He's not to blame. And she's ridden a bike before – but a trail bike, not a road bike and not on a main thoroughfare.' He dragged a hand through his hair. He was beginning to get a picture of what happened. It was just like Cassie to do something like this, never considering what the consequences might be, never considering the fallout for everyone else who was involved – her parents, the university and the boy whose bike was now a tangled mass of metal. He picked up his coffee and took another gulp.

'If there's anything we can do…' Nick seemed at a loss. 'I have two of my own. My daughter is around Cassie's age. I know how wilful they can be. But it doesn't excuse young Steven. He has to accept some responsibility. I have to say he was most contrite when I spoke with him.'

'And he's lost his bike.' Chris fell silent for a moment. 'I would like to meet him – and compensate him.'

'That would be most generous. I don't imagine he's expecting anything from you. He'll be insured.'

'Of course.' Chris fell silent again, remembering how Cassie had loved her trail bike, how they both enjoyed riding together on the lake trails close to home. He was jolted back to the present by Nick's voice.

'I hope you're comfortable at *The Springs*. It was the best we could do. I'm afraid Granite Springs doesn't have much in the way of top-end accommodation.'

'It's great, thanks. Anywhere would be good. I only need a place to sleep, though I didn't get much of that. I'm just trying to get my head around how long it's going to take Cassie to recover.'

Nick's expression was one of sympathy.

Chris finished his coffee. 'I'll get out of your hair. Thanks for taking time to see me.'

'Of course. I wondered...' He drew his eyebrows together. 'Kay and I would like you to come to dinner with us. I imagine you'll want to spend most of your time at the hospital, but you need to eat. It can be so easy to forget to take care of yourself in these situations, and you'll be no good to Cassie if you get sick, too.'

Chris was about to refuse. He didn't come to Granite Springs to socialise. Then he realised Nick was right. It was kind of him. 'Thanks. It's good of you.'

'Great. Kay will let you have our address. Would seven suit?'

'Thanks,' Chris said again. Seven would be perfect. By that time, the hospital staff would be keen to see the back of him and settle their patient for the night. Hopefully tomorrow would see some improvement in Cassie.

Six

Ann awakened on Tuesday to remember it was her day off, the one day each fortnight she could spend as she pleased. She loved the feeling that she could choose exactly what she wanted. Weekends weren't the same. Everyone had them. This one day was special. It was hers.

But it didn't mean she spent it lazing around the house. In typical fashion, even these days were carefully planned. It was the day she fulfilled what she saw as her civic duty, when she delivered books to a couple of housebound ladies in her role as a Friend of the Library, then spent four hours as a volunteer at the Base Hospital. After a quick breakfast and tidy up, she set off for the library where she picked up her books, then headed to Eden Gardens to deliver them.

Ann started doing this after her mother died. The older woman moved into the nursing home when it became too difficult for her at home, when even Ann's dedicated care failed to provide sufficient support as her mother sank further and further into her own little world. Ann still harboured guilty feelings she hadn't been able to keep her at home. This, combined with the guilt she still felt about the death of her unborn child, sat heavy on her, heavier some days than others.

But today wasn't one of those days. The sun was shining, and she had the day to herself, though she was having dinner with her sister in the evening. Susie and her husband had only returned to Granite Springs a few months earlier after spending many years in England, and the older woman seemed determined to make Ann's life a misery. Of course, Susie wouldn't see it that way. She'd say she was only doing what a big sister should, trying to help Ann make the best of herself, become more social, meet more people. By people, she meant men. She appeared to have taken it upon herself to find a husband for what she regarded as her spinster sister. Did anyone even use that term anymore? Ann wondered what poor man Susie would have scared up for tonight's dinner. There weren't many unattached men in their age group in Granite Springs, and those few were, like Ann, happy to remain so.

After a lovely chat with her ladies in Eden Gardens, both of whom expressed their gratitude for the books Ann had selected for them, Ann made her way to the hospital in time to enjoy a sandwich with a cup of coffee in the café before beginning her duties. She closed the book she'd brought along to read while she ate, tucked it into the tote bag she was never without, and headed for the volunteers' staff room where she donned the royal blue tunic which was her uniform for the afternoon.

'Here you are, Ann. On time as usual.' Wendy, who coordinated the volunteers, always greeted her this way, making Ann wonder if others weren't as punctual as she was. She took her tasks at the hospital seriously, knowing how important the volunteers were to patients and visitors alike. The volunteer was sometimes a visitor's first contact in the hospital and for the patients, they provided a welcome break from the daily routine of what could seem a never-ending series of tests and procedures.

Ann gave a tight smile.

'I wonder if you could take over the delivery of flowers today. The florist is flat out and asked if we could assist.'

'Of course.' Ann was always happy to help in any capacity, but usually found herself allocated to the meet and greet role, which entailed her standing just inside the main entrance to direct visitors and steer them in the correct direction. Delivering flowers would make a pleasant change and allow her to meet some of the patients.

'Wow!' Ann exclaimed as Fiona loaded a particularly large basket of blooms complete with a *get well soon* balloon onto the trolley. 'These are spectacular. You've outdone yourself here.'

'They do look rather good, don't they?' Fiona, who had run the florist outlet here at the hospital for as long as Ann could remember, stood back to admire her handiwork. 'The email said she wanted something really special and money was no object. It's for the student who was in that bike accident. I'm not sure if she's well enough to appreciate them.' Fiona's forehead creased.

Ann helped her load the rest of the orders, picked up the list of recipients along with information about which wards they were in and pushed the trolley towards the bank of lifts, her nostrils filled with the delightful fragrance of the bouquets she was about to deliver. This was certainly going to be a pleasanter task than dealing with anxious relatives, though that task did much to help expiate her guilt and keep her on an even keel.

The delivery of the first few arrangements were soon completed to patients in the maternity wing. Whereas, several years ago, such visits would have been anathema to Ann, today she took pleasure in seeing the new mums with their bubs, all delighted to receive their flowers and, in some instances, chocolates and balloons.

Ann checked her list and headed for the lifts again to go to the next level where the surgical wards were located. The first two were easy, to patients recovering from minor surgery. Some were already ambulant and greeted her as she pushed the trolley along the corridor. It was good to see them hobbling along, some with crutches, others with walkers.

Only one more to deliver. Ann had left the basket for Cassandra Thomas till last. She was curious to see the girl she remembered as one of the prettiest of the Canadian group who always seemed to be the centre of a lively crowd. On the few occasions Ann had seen her, the girl had been well-mannered and polite, which was more than she could say for many of the other students, some of whom seemed to consider the Education office staff were only there to make their lives more difficult.

'For one of ours?' one of the nurses asked when Ann trundled the almost empty trolley into the ward, stopping at the nurses' station.

'For Cassandra Thomas. It says room four. Can I...?' Ann raised one eyebrow, unsure if she should take the basket into the girl's room. She was aware that, unlike the recipients of her earlier deliveries, this patient was still in a critical condition. She waited for a response.

'I don't think... Oh, here's her dad, now. Perhaps he'll take them.'

Ann turned to see a tall man walk out of the nearest room and close the door behind him. For a few seconds it was as if time stood still. There was a ringing in her ears, she felt the room spin around her. She was frozen, unable to move or speak.

The stance was the same, the face was older, more wrinkled, the chestnut hair was still as thick, but faded. It couldn't be, but it was. Gus Thomas, the man she'd thought never to see again, the man she'd tried so hard to forget, was standing in front of her looking just as stunned as she felt.

Seven

Chris couldn't believe his eyes. It was Annie, his Annie, looking exactly as he remembered her. Even her hairstyle was the same. His heart began to race. He caught his breath. 'Annie?'

'It can't be…' she said, the colour draining from her face. 'Gus?'

He hadn't been called Gus for decades. It took him back to his teenage years, years when he'd thought he had the world on a string and he and Annie would fly off together into a bright new future. But life had a way of bursting their bubble.

When he arrived in San Francisco, fresh from the Australian National University, he was definitely the new guy on the block. On his job application, he'd had to give his full name, duly typing Christopher Angus Thomas into the form. As a result, when he arrived, he was introduced to everyone as Christopher which was soon shortened to Chris. He didn't bother to correct them. He felt like a different person there where no one knew him. Gus Thomas became Chris Thomas. It was as if he took on a new identity.

Annie was looking as if she'd seen a ghost, and he didn't feel too hot either. He'd thought his first love was long gone from Granite Springs. What was she doing on his daughter's ward?

'What would you like us to do with these, Mr Thomas?' the nurse asked. 'We can't put them in Cassie's room.'

It was only then Chris noticed the enormous basket of tropical blooms, a large red balloon sticking out the top. He didn't need to look at the accompanying card to know this was from Gail. How could she imagine throwing money at a flower arrangement made up for her absence at her daughter's bedside? His lip curled in disgust. 'You can leave them here. Perhaps Cassie might like to see the balloon when she's feeling up to it.'

Then he realised Annie was clutching the handle of the trolley. Did she work here?

'You... *you're* Dr Thomas?' Her eyes widened. 'Cassie's father?'

'Guilty.'

Her face was still as white as a sheet and she looked as if the only thing keeping her upright was the trolly which she was holding onto for grim death.

'You've had a shock.'

He'd had a shock.

'Let me get you to a place where we can get some tea.'

Annie allowed herself to be led to the lifts. Pushing the trolley, she followed him in without speaking. The lift started to descend. Neither spoke. What they had to say to each other couldn't be said in a moving lift.

When they reached the ground floor and the lift doors opened, Annie found her voice. 'I need to return this.' She pointed to the trolley. 'The café's over there.' She nodded towards a doorway through which Chris could see groups of tables and chairs.

Chris waited till she joined him, and they walked into the café together before choosing a table in a quiet corner. 'Won't be long,' he said.

When he returned carrying two cups of tea and a packet of sweet biscuits, Annie had regained some colour. Her hands were on the table and she was twisting her fingers together. She was taking shaky breaths.

'Drink this. It'll help.' He emptied two sachets of sugar into both cups, and took a gulp from his, grimacing at the sweetness. But it did seem to lessen the shock he was still experiencing.

Annie clasped her cup in both hands and took a sip. She grimaced too. 'How...?'

'I live in Canada now and I've been called Chris since I left. It was easier at first, then I became used to it. Gus Thomas disappeared a long time ago.'

'I'm Ann now. No one's called me Annie since Mum died.'

'Ann.' He looked at the face he remembered, the face that had filled his dreams for so long. She'd always be Annie to him. 'You're still here.'

Annie nodded and took another sip of the sweet tea. 'Cassie's a lovely girl. I'm sorry. You must be worried about her.'

Chris was taken aback. This tightly wound woman making polite conversation wasn't the Annie he remembered. It was as if someone had taken the lively Annie of their youth and replaced her with this cardboard cut-out called Ann.

He drew a hand across the top of his hair, ruffling the thick waves, no longer the chestnut Annie used to run her fingers through. The memory sent a jolt through his stomach. 'What are you doing here? I didn't expect...'

'I live here. Oh, not at the hospital.' She gave a wry smile at his obvious surprise. 'In Granite Springs. I volunteer at the hospital. That's what took me to the surgical ward.'

'You don't work at the hospital?' He couldn't get his head around the fact he was sitting there trying to make polite conversation with the girl he'd left behind all those years ago. He should be hugging her, but the Annie sitting opposite him didn't look as if a hug would be welcome. Not from him. Not from anyone. She looked as if life hadn't been kind to her, as if she'd suffered. It made him want to know what had happened after he left. What had changed the lovely girl he loved into this tense woman who seemed ready to fall apart?

'No. The university. I booked your accommodation.'

Chris gazed at Annie in surprise. If she'd booked his accommodation how hadn't she guessed his identity?

'Nick only told me it was for a Dr Thomas from Canada. How could I have known it was you?'

'Of course you couldn't.' This was awkward. How could he get through the barrier she was putting up between them? It was like talking with a stranger. But over thirty years had passed – a lifetime. Perhaps they *were* strangers.

*

Ann knew she wasn't making it easy for him. But it was hard for her, too. How boring he must think her. She didn't want to talk about herself. Seeing Gus brought all that guilt and regret to the fore again. She couldn't come to grips with the fact she was sitting here, drinking tea with the man she'd spent her life trying to forget, the man she'd loved to distraction but had allowed to leave her, the man who had fathered her unborn child.

She almost choked remembering the tears she'd shed, the sleepless nights, how she'd tried to tell herself it was for the best. She'd almost succeeded. But now, faced with the older version of him, the protective barriers she'd spent her life building around herself threatened to collapse.

She could do this. It had been a shock to be confronted by her past. But he was only here for a short time to see his daughter. Ann remembered what Fran had said. Dr Thomas – it felt strange to call him Chris, but perhaps it would make it easier if she didn't think of him as Gus. Her Gus – was a bigshot. He owned an international company. He wouldn't want to spend any more time than necessary in Granite Springs. After all, he hadn't seen the need to come back in the last thirty-five years. He had a wife back in Canada, a daughter he'd be taking home as soon as she was able.

Ann lifted her head and pasted what she hoped was a smile on her face. 'You're an important man, now. You've done well, Dr Thomas.'

'Annie. Don't shut me out like this. There was a time when we meant everything to each other.'

For a moment, she almost weakened, then she remembered all she'd gone through and was consumed by the guilt that never completely left her. It wasn't Gus's fault. She was the one who'd rejected him. But it didn't feel like that. 'A big IT company,' she continued. 'I hear you've become famous. It even has one of those clever names designed to confound the unwashed. What does CAT stand for?' She wasn't really interested to know. But she had to say something to get her through this awkward meeting.

Chris laughed. 'There's nothing clever about it. It's my initials – Christopher Angus Thomas. You probably didn't know that when I was at primary school, a group of kids discovered my full name and teased me about being a cat. It sounds funny now, but at the time, I felt humiliated and cursed my parents.'

Ann looked down into her cup and tried to hide the smile that threatened to spoil her carefully constructed expression, designed to give nothing away. She wasn't going to let him see her weaken.

'How is your daughter?' she asked to change the subject.

Chris grimaced. He leant his elbows on the table and steepled his hands in a familiar gesture. 'Difficult to say. They won't know till later if she'll be able to keep her leg. It'd be a huge blow. Cassie's always been so active.' A bead of moisture appeared in the corner of one eye, making Ann want to reach over and wipe it away.

Instead, she asked, 'Does your wife plan to join you?'

To her surprise, he grimaced, his lips tightening. 'Gail? No, she won't be leaving her high-powered career to sit at her daughter's bedside.'

'Oh!' Ann was sorry she'd asked. There was something going on here she didn't understand.

Chris didn't explain.

Ann surreptitiously checked her watch. She was supposed to be on volunteer duty. Wendy would be wondering where she'd got to. She should have finished delivering flowers some time ago and returned to her usual routine.

'Sorry, I'm keeping you. I wanted to make sure you were all right. Seeing you like this, it made me think about the past.' He rose to leave. 'Annie, I'm here in town for a bit, until I know Cassie is going to recover, until I can take her home with me. Can we meet again?'

Ann looked at him, at the only man she'd ever loved, at the face which had filled her dreams. But he wasn't hers any longer, hadn't been for over thirty years.

Time had stood still for her. But it hadn't stood still for Gus. He'd built a business, married, had a daughter. He'd moved on with his life. He hadn't waited. Ann shuddered. Is that what she'd been doing – waiting, waiting for his return?

'I don't think that's a good idea,' she said.

Eight

The last thing Ann wanted to do tonight was to have dinner with her sister, but she knew how Susie would be if she rang to apologise. She sighed as she renewed her makeup, tidied her hair and slipped on her blue linen dress. She frowned at her image in the mirror, a tiny part of her wondering if Gus thought she had changed. She stifled the unwelcome thought.

Ann had hoped her sister's return would mean the two could become close again, but she'd quickly been disillusioned. Susie had always put herself first, considered Ann foolish for remaining in Granite Springs when their mother died, and accused her of being tied to the memory of her first love.

Now she and her husband were living in their renovated home which, in her sister's words 'oozed character'. Susie chose to mix with what Ann's mother had always referred to as 'the country set'. She'd joined the Country Women's Association and swanned around town as if she came from landed gentry. They had nothing in common.

But she was her sister and she'd been there for her when no one else had. Ann would always be grateful to Susie for that. She picked up her bag and went out to the car.

Ann's little Kia looked out of place beside the BMW, Range Rover and Lexus parked outside the elegant Federation home, its red brick exterior giving only an inkling of the heritage charms inside. She didn't recognise the Range Rover and sighed, assuming it belonged to Susie's latest attempt at matchmaking. Would her sister never give up?

'Ann!' Susie air-kissed her at the door – another annoying habit she'd developed overseas. Submitting to the greeting, Ann walked into the long hallway where the ten-foot pressed metal ceilings and ornate cornices always made her feel like she was stepping back in time. She had to admit Peta had done a good job for Susie, recreating the ambiance of earlier days while ensuring the original features blended seamlessly with modern comfort.

'Come and meet everyone,' Susie gushed, leading Ann into the formal living room where a group of people were standing by the window, the women with glasses of champagne, the men with what looked like whisky.

Ann did a quick head count. She was right. The stranger, gazing at her with undisguised curiosity, was clearly the one Susie had invited to meet her unmarried sister. The poor man. He no doubt wished himself elsewhere, too. The other two couples looked familiar. Ann had met them on previous occasions, occasions which had been as dull as this one promised to be.

'You know Ros and Andy, and Jemma and Bob, of course, and this is Sam Walker. He's recently bought the old heritage property on Oatlands Road and is the new editor of The Granite Springs Advertiser,' Susie said archly.

Susie's husband, Adrian, handed Ann a glass of champagne which she accepted gratefully, then looked up to see an amused pair of deep blue eyes and a cheerful grin. 'So, you're the sister Susie's been talking about.' Sam said. 'You and your sister don't look alike.' He gazed from one to the other, from Susie's well-coiffured blonde hair and her expensive red cocktail dress to Ann's tidy dark, greying locks and simple, blue linen dress. 'Pleased to meet you.' He stretched out his hand.

'Likewise.' Ann took his hand, noting the firm handshake. Well, at least he was a bit better than the last few Susie had tried to foist on her. The evening might not turn out to be too bad, after all. At least it might take her mind of her encounter with the past.

Seated next to Sam at dinner, the evening passed quickly. He proved to be an interesting companion, leavening the conversation of the others with anecdotes of his attempts to juggle management of his acreage with his role at the newspaper. It appeared he wasn't originally from the land but had always wanted to own an acreage. It wasn't clear to Ann what had prompted this recent purchase or if he was divorced or widowed – all of Susie's victims were one or the other. Ann seemed to be the only person Susie knew who'd never been married. Perhaps that's why she felt the need to *fix* her sister's life, to have her join the club of married couples.

The evening finally came to an end.

As Ann was walking down the driveway to her car, she felt a presence behind her. Turning, she saw that Sam, who had been chatting to Adrian when she left, had walked up behind her.

'I hoped to catch you,' he said with one of his disarming grins.

Ann stopped in her tracks. She didn't need this.

'When Susie said she wanted me to meet her unmarried sister, I thought…' He pushed a hand through his thick dark hair which was fading to silver wings above his ears. 'I thought you'd be… Hell, this isn't coming out the way I intended. What I'm trying to say is, I enjoyed your company at dinner and wondered if we could do it again sometime.'

'Dinner at Susie's?' Ann couldn't help herself. He looked so awkward trying to wriggle out of what no doubt had been his interpretation of Susie's description of her.

'No, I mean dinner, just us, somewhere in town. There seems to be a few good restaurants here.'

'Oh, I don't think so.'

He looked surprised. 'Was my company so terrible?'

'No, but…' Ann bit her lip. He wasn't like the other men Susie had tried to pair her with. None of them had accosted her on the way to her car. They had the decency to get her number from Susie and call her when she had time to work out a believable excuse to refuse their invitation, if indeed an invitation was forthcoming. Most were as happy as she was to forget the evening and get on with their lives.

'Well, why not take pity on me? I barely know anyone in town and it's not a lot of fun eating out on my own. You told me you do a lot of volunteering. Look on me as another part of your community service.'

Ann couldn't suppress the smile that came to her lips. Against her better judgement she found herself giving him her number and agreeing to have dinner with him. They didn't set a date.

They walked out to the kerb together, Ann unsurprised when Sam headed for the dark red Range Rover. It suited him, had the same outdoorsy aura he did. Despite herself, Ann had a sneaking suspicion she might enjoy having dinner with Sam Walker.

But once she arrived home, all thoughts of Sam Walker disappeared, forced out by the memory of her shock meeting with Gus.

For thirty-five years she'd resented him for leaving her, conveniently forgetting it was she who had sent him away. Why did he have to appear in her life again? Why now?

Nine

'Dad?'

Chris moved closer to Cassie's bedside to see her eyes open. He'd spent most of the day there, sitting on a hard chair watching her sleep, as he had done the previous day. 'I'm here, sweetheart.' He took her hand in his and stroked it, praying she'd recover.

'What happened?'

'You were on a motorbike. Don't you remember?' He tried to sound neutral, not disapproving, while still wondering what the hell she'd been trying to do.

'Oh!' She tried to lift her head without success. 'I wanted to get back to…' She tried again, her head lifting slightly before dropping back onto the pillow. 'What are you doing here?'

'Where else would I be when my favourite daughter has been trying to kill herself?' Chris tried to sound nonchalant but knew he hadn't succeeded.

'Mum?'

'She's busy. The January edition, you know.' He couldn't keep the bitterness out of his voice, but thought he saw a faint smile on his daughter's face. 'How are you feeling?'

'Sore. Everything's sore. My leg?'

'You made a bit of a mess of it, but it's going to be fine.' He mentally crossed his fingers. 'You were in a hurry to get back?' He needed to know why she had been in such a rush, why she couldn't wait to return with the others.

This time there definitely was a smile on her face. 'Miles,' she muttered before closing her eyes again.

Who the heck was Miles? Chris remembered thinking there was a boy involved. Was it this Miles?

At dinner with the Kerrs two days ago, he'd tried to find out more about what had led to Cassie's decision to return early to Granite Springs, but Nick Kerr hadn't managed to discover anything further. Similarly, Chris's conversation with Steven the day before had failed to provide the information he wanted. The young man had only repeated what Chris already knew – Cassie had been in a hurry to get back and had begged to borrow the bike, assuring him she knew how to ride it and had a licence. Neither was the complete truth.

'Who's Miles?' he asked. But Cassie was asleep again. Chris fumed. But now he had a name. Glancing at the now peaceful face of his daughter, he left her room and made his way to an area set aside for visitors. It boasted a couple of coffee tables, several soft chairs and a water filter. The area was empty. Chris sank down into one of the chairs and took out his phone. Nick Kerr had been most insistent he call if he needed any help.

His call was answered immediately.

'Good afternoon. Dr Kerr's office, Kay speaking. How can I help you?'

Kay's gentle voice had a calming effect. 'Hi, Kay. Chris Thomas here.'

'Chris. How is Cassie?' Kay's voice was tense.

Chris imagined her wondering if he was calling with bad news.

'No change, though she is communicating a little better. Thanks for asking. I have a question for you. She mentioned a name – Miles. I'm guessing he might be the reason she was in such a hurry to get back. I don't have a surname, but I wondered if you know of a student called Miles?' He held his breath.

Kay didn't answer immediately, then, 'It's an unusual name, but no one comes to mind. Can you leave it with me, and I'll check with our office? I'll call you back.'

'Thanks.' Chris cursed himself as he ended the call. It would be Annie who she'd talk to, Annie who was in charge of the office. Why didn't he think of her? It would have been the perfect opportunity to contact her, the opportunity he'd been trying to find. Her image had been sitting in the back of his consciousness ever since seeing her again. She'd been so cool, hadn't seemed like the same person, but he knew his Annie was still there, hidden under the façade she'd constructed. What had happened to change her so much? He had to find out. But Cassie needed him right now. There would be time enough to work out what to do about Annie later.

Slipping his phone back into his pocket, Chris walked back to Cassie's room and peeked in. She was still asleep.

'Why don't you get some fresh air? Cassie will probably sleep for a couple of hours now.'

Chris looked up to see Marilyn gazing at him, a look of concern on her face. In the few days he'd been here, she'd become like an old friend. While he didn't want to leave Cassie, Chris knew she was right.

'When did you last eat? Have you had any lunch? You'll be no good to Cassie if you get sick.'

Chris didn't answer. He'd eaten breakfast before leaving *The Springs* this morning, if you could call the sweet pastry and cup of coffee he'd hastily consumed breakfast. He suddenly realised he was hungry and checked his watch. It was way past what might be considered lunchtime. 'You're right,' he said. 'Can you call me if Cassie wakes and asks for me?'

'Of course.' Marilyn smiled.

Chris exited the lift, intending to make for the hospital café, but felt the need to get away, to go to somewhere new, away from all the reminders of sickness and sick people. He headed outside, almost surprised to see it was still a glorious day even though it was early autumn, the sun shining on his back as he made his way across the car park.

As he drove slowly into the main part of town, memories came flooding back. There was the riverbank where he and Annie used to walk hand-in-hand, the sign to the Botanic Gardens where they had their first date, the café where they'd drunk innumerable cups of coffee. They were all still there. He felt an ache for everything he'd left behind.

The café drew him like a magnet. He was surprised The Bean Sprout still existed, Old Charlie who owned it back when they were young must be long gone. But Chris seemed to recall there had been a son a few years younger than Chris and his mates. He parked the car and pushed open the café door to be greeted with the welcome aroma of freshly brewed coffee.

After ordering his usual macchiato with a delicious looking spinach and feta calzone accompanied by salad, Chris found a free table in the back corner of the café. He glanced around to see the place was busy, clearly a popular lunch spot, even though it was past most people's lunchtime.

It was filled with memories, even though the café had obviously been modernised and there was no sign of the old jukebox he and Annie loved. He remembered the iced coffees in summer, the warm orange juice in winter, the Saturday afternoons whiled away in the back corner, not far from where he was sitting now.

His musings were interrupted by the delivery of his meal by the same dark-haired woman who'd taken his order.

'New in town or passing through?' she asked with a bright smile.

'Just visiting,' Chris mumbled, unwilling to share his reasons for being in Granite Springs with a stranger.

The woman peered at him. 'Have you been here before?' she asked. 'You look vaguely familiar.' She waited.

Chris sighed. He'd been afraid of this, though why he didn't know. It wasn't as if he'd left under a cloud. He'd left to go on to bigger and better things, to make something of himself. He wouldn't be where he was today if he'd stayed in Granite Springs. But was that a good thing? Seeing Annie again had turned his world on its end. He didn't know what to think.

'I grew up here,' he said shortly.

'I knew it!' The woman stared at him again. 'Let me think. If you grew up here, you must have gone to Granite Springs High. Frank and I were there in the late eighties, early nineties. You?'

'Probably before you.' Chris picked up his cup signalling the end of the conversation, but the woman wasn't so easily deterred.

'I'm Marie. Frank and I have run The Bean Sprout for what seems like forever, but really only since his dad passed away. You remember Charlie Beattie?'

'Of course. Everyone knew Charlie back then.' So the café had stayed in the family. He could see a big dark-haired man behind the espresso machine now. He must be the Frank she referred to. He looked not unlike old Charlie.

'That's Frank,' she said, following his eyes, then seemed to get the message. 'Enjoy your lunch and I hope we see you here again.' She drifted off.

Chris did enjoy his lunch, but as soon as he had finished, he was eager to get back to the hospital. He wanted to be there when Cassie awoke again. He wanted to find out about this Miles. And he wanted to speak to the surgeon again to find out what further surgery his daughter was to undergo. Only then, could he take time to pursue his interest in Annie Baird, to discover what had happened to his first love.

Ten

It was two days since Ann had come face to face with Gus and she needed someone to talk to, someone who would understand. The only person she could think of was Fran. Fran knew about her past, but would she really understand Ann's confusion and disbelief that her old flame was in town, that he was the Dr Thomas they'd discussed only a week earlier?

As she already had an arrangement to meet Fran for lunch, Ann determined to ask her advice. Even though she'd refused to see Gus – or Chris as he was now called – again, she found it impossible to get him out of her mind. Knowing he was right here in Granite Springs, staying at *The Springs*, only a short drive away from where she lived, sent shivers up Ann's spine.

No matter how hard she tried, Ann couldn't dismiss Gus's image. Seeing him again brought it all back – all the joy, all the hurt, all the guilt. But the joy was uppermost. Over the years, she'd tried to paint herself as a martyr, having given up the possibility of a lifetime of happiness for her family. The time she had with Gus had taken on a golden hue, a halcyon period where time stood still. When she pictured Gus, it was as he was back then.

It had been a shock to see the older version of him, the faded hair, the lined face. But his eyes were the same, they crinkled up in the way she remembered. And his mouth, the lips which had kissed her with such passion, which had uttered words of love. It was still the same too. He'd filled out, no longer the tall lanky teenager she'd fallen in

47

love with. Gus was now a middle-aged man. But he still held the same attraction for her, an attraction she couldn't deny, no matter how much she wanted to.

The morning passed swiftly, giving Ann little time to consider what she as going to say to Fran. As she made her way across campus to Banjo's, she was having second thoughts about saying anything.

'I've ordered already,' Fran greeted Ann, as she slid into the seat opposite, 'Today's special is melting goats cheese layered with eggplant, pumpkin and capsicum on rye topped with pesto and served with salad greens and balsamic vinaigrette,' she read from the backboard menu.

'That sounds yum. I think I'll have it too. Won't be a sec.' She headed to the counter to place her order, then returned to join her friend.

'How are you?' Fran asked. 'Busy morning?'

'Hectic.' Ann proceeded to share some of the morning's dramas with Fran, comfortable in this familiar exchange of news. 'You?' she asked when she had enumerated the challenges of the office.

'Same old stuff. I don't know how Owen manages to do it, but it's the same chaos at the beginning of every semester. You'd think I'd learn. I live with the man, after all.' She gave an exaggerated sigh and grinned.

Ann felt the familiar dull ache she always did when Fran talked of Owen with such affection, but today it was overlain with something she couldn't identify. 'I met Cassie Thomas's dad.' The words spilled out unbidden.

'You did?' Fran was interested. 'What's he like?'

It was a natural thing to ask, but it gave Ann goosebumps.

'He's... I recognised him.'

Fran's eyes widened.

'He's...' Ann fiddled with her cutlery and wished their meals would arrive to save her from what she knew she had to say. 'He's Gus.'

Fran appeared puzzled.

'Dr Christopher Thomas and Gus – the man I sent away all those years ago – they're one and the same.'

'But...'

'I know. He changed his name, or had it changed for him. I'd completely forgotten – if I ever knew – his full name is Christopher Angus Thomas. Though...' she drew a hand through her immaculate hair. '…even if I'd remembered, I doubt I'd have made the connection.'

'Where did you meet him? Did he come here – to the university?' Fran gazed around as if expecting him to suddenly appear.

'At the hospital.' But Ann suddenly remembered the back view of the stranger walking up the stairs to the dean's office. He had been so close. 'You know I volunteer there on my days off. It was surreal, seeing him standing there.' She shook her head as if to dismiss the image her words conjured up.

'And?'

'There's no *and*.'

To Ann's relief, their meals arrived before Fran could ask anything more, and they were silent for the next few minutes while their meals and coffee were served. But the respite didn't last.

'How did it feel – seeing him again? It's been what?' Fran picked up her cup and took a sip of coffee.

'Thirty-five years. It felt…' Ann considered, '…odd, decidedly odd. It was such a shock.'

'Mmm, it must have been. But…' she waved her fork in the air. 'Did you… did he…?'

'It was over thirty years ago, Fran. A lifetime.' Ann tried to sound as calm and collected as she normally did, to follow the pattern she'd perfected over the years. But her voice shook.

Fran understood, as Ann knew she would. 'It must have felt weird. Did you… do you still find him attractive? No, don't answer that, it's none of my business. Unless…' She raised one eyebrow.

'Oh Fran!' Ann almost broke down, the tears she'd been stifling for two days welling up. She brushed them away. 'He wanted us to meet again. I refused. How could I do anything else? He's married. His daughter is lying in the Base Hospital critically ill. What purpose would it serve to relive the past?' She took a sip of coffee, then raised her eyes to meet Fran's. 'But I can't stop thinking about him.'

She looked down at her untouched plate of food, picked up her fork and poked at the carefully prepared dish. She'd lost her appetite.

'Aren't you curious to know what he's been doing all those years? I would be.' For a second Fran's eyes clouded, and Ann guessed she was thinking of her own lost love. But Fran's case was different, her first love had died. And she'd managed to move on.

But Ann was stuck in the past. She flinched at the realisation. She had never admitted it before, not even to herself. It was as if, when Gus left, Ann wanted to retain the memory of that part of her life, the part when she'd been happy. And she'd done it by refusing to change herself. Even the house she lived in was exactly the same as when she'd grown up there.

About to deny it, she realised Fran was right. Ann was curious. But while she would like to know when and why he'd moved to Canada, when he'd met his wife, what she was like, why she hadn't come to Granite Springs with him, if he had any other children – the list went on and on – she knew seeing him again was the wrong thing to do. It could only end in more heartache.

Fran's next words made her flinch again. 'He's in Granite Springs. You're not going to be able to avoid him forever. You should agree to meet him, get it over with, then you can put him behind you.' She peered across the table at Ann. 'You never have, have you? You've never forgotten him.'

Ann blushed. She shook her head, refusing to meet Fran's eyes. All those years she'd held onto the memory of what might have been. It had made her the person she was today, the bitter old maid her younger staff mocked when they thought she was out of earshot, the woman who'd refused to countenance another relationship. Had she made a rod for her own back? Had she been stupid to imagine there was only one man she could love?

'I met someone at Susie's,' she said to change the subject.

'Another dud?' Fran grinned, willing to be distracted, and familiar with Ann's accounts of her sister's attempts at matchmaking.

'Actually, no.' Ann remembered how easy Sam Walker had been to talk to. 'Sam Walker is the new editor of The Granite Springs Advertiser. For once, Susie lined up someone who is almost decent.'

'What a fluke. You meet someone who might spark your interest just as your old flame comes to town. No doubt about it, Ann. Fate certainly seems to have it in for you.'

Ann shook her head. 'I didn't say I was interested in him.' But she was glad she'd managed to divert Fran from speculation about Gus – *she supposed she should start thinking of him as Chris, but the name didn't sit well on her tongue. He was Gus to her, always would be.*

Lunch over, and as Ann walked briskly back to her office, she thought about what Fran had said. Perhaps she should see Gus again, put to bed once and for all the old attraction she felt. Perhaps it was time for her to turn her life around, to look to the future instead of living a life of regret.

Eleven

Chris had been in Granite Springs for over a week and had spent every day at the hospital with Cassie. Every time he looked at the cage over her shattered leg, he wanted to weep but he knew he had to stay strong for his daughter.

Gail still refused to travel to Australia. He didn't know why he continued to call her with updates on Cassie, given her lack of empathy for what their daughter was going through. It was one thing to have given up on their marriage, to have made her career her priority. But Cassie was her daughter, the baby she'd carried in her body for nine months before giving birth to their beautiful girl.

Gail had never been reconciled to the fact their daughter favoured Chris with her auburn hair and pale skin, or to what she called Cassie's idealistic view on life. Throughout her pregnancy, she'd pictured a tiny version of herself, a daughter she could dress up in all the frippery she loved and who would want to emulate her – or so she said. Cassie was a disappointment.

For him, Cassie was his reward for trying to forget Annie. She was everything he remembered of the girl he'd left behind in Granite Springs, the child they should have had together. Sometimes, he found himself pretending Cassie was their daughter – his and Annie's. He knew it was stupid. There had never been a child. He had married Gail.

At the time, it seemed the obvious thing to do. They met soon after Chris arrived in Canada, soon after he set up CAT and it looked as if it was going to be a success. It had been winter, he remembered. A cold winter's night. He'd been invited to an art display and had almost stayed home. Only the promise of meeting some useful contacts had drawn him out of his cosy studio apartment overlooking the ocean.

And there, blonde and elegant, wearing the sort of dress he'd always associated with movie stars, was Gail. She had sashayed up to him, evincing interest in the abstract painting he was trying to make sense of, taking him unawares.

In the beginning it was she who'd pursued him until, flattered by her attention, he found himself captivated by this beautiful woman in whose arms he managed to forget.

*

Chris walked in through the wide glass doors of Granite Springs Base Hospital, feeling almost as if he belonged there, stopping as he did every morning to pick up a coffee from the coffee stand before heading to the bank of lifts.

His finger automatically hit the button to take him to the surgical floor and Cassie's ward.

'Hi, sweetheart.' He bent to kiss her forehead, seeing her smile up at him. 'It's going to be another warm day out there. I'd almost forgotten what it was like in Granite Springs.' He pulled the chair closer to the bed and took a sip of his coffee.

He picked up the book he'd been reading to Cassie for the past few days and opened it at the bookmarked page. *The Dry* was Cassie's choice, by an Australian author he'd never heard of, and Chris was thoroughly enjoying the tale of murder in the Australian bush. Reading aloud to Cassie was fun, too. It reminded him of the times he'd read to her when she was a young child. Gail had always claimed to be too busy so, to his delight, he had been the one to have the pleasure of putting his daughter to bed and reading her a story.

He was reaching an exciting part of the story when he was interrupted. One of the nurses was standing in the doorway.

She cleared her throat noisily, then spoke. 'Mr Thomas, if I could have a word.' She hovered expectantly.

Sighing, Chris closed the book and laid it on his lap. 'Yes?'

She gestured towards the corridor.

With an apologetic glance to Cassie, and a 'Back soon, sweetie', Chris followed her out.

'What is it?'

'Dr Young will see you when she's finished her rounds. She'd like you to wait in the visitor's room.'

'Good.' Chris had been trying to arrange a meeting with Cassie's surgeon for the past few days, but Bree Young was evidently in high demand, either in theatre or caught up in some other activity that precluded her being available. 'When will that be?'

'I can't say. I just wanted to be sure you'll be here.'

'I'll be here till you throw me out.' Chris grinned, but the nurse had turned away. He went back into Cassie who was looking worried.

'What was it, Dad?'

'Nothing to worry you.' He took his seat again and picked up the book. But before he opened it, he took Cassie's hand. 'Your surgeon has finally deigned to see me after her rounds today.' He felt her fingers tighten in his.

'Will she be able to tell you if they're going to do more surgery, when I can get out of here?'

'I hope so.' Chris bit the inside of his cheek. Cassie had improved a lot since he arrived, but she wasn't out of the woods yet. There had been talk of further surgery when her body could withstand it. He was becoming impatient for news.

Cassie looked dubious. 'I just want to be able to move around again. Miles...'

There it was again – the boy's name. Chris still hadn't been able to get Cassie to tell him who Miles was and why she had been in such a hurry to get back. 'Don't you think it's time you told me about him?' He turned the book over in his hands.

Cassie looked up at him, her eyes wide, and gave him one of her sweet smiles. 'Miles is... Miles. We met soon after I arrived. He's studying music – he's a brilliant musician, Dad. You should hear him on the sax. He was playing in a concert in Canberra and I wanted to get back for it. That's all.'

That's all? What kind of explanation was that? 'And where is he now?'

Why hadn't he rushed to her bedside if he was so important to her?

'He's on tour. He got a place with the Canberra Symphonic and they're touring Australia. It's a wonderful opportunity for him. He hasn't even finished his degree yet. His professor helped him with the audition tape and has given him time off. He didn't know about the accident till I was able to text him. He was worried when I wasn't there.'

Finally! Chris was glad Cassie had decided to confide in him. It had all been about attending a concert. 'He's important to you?' he asked, fearing the answer. She wasn't his little girl any longer.

'Very. You'll understand when you meet him, Dad.' There was a glow in his daughter's eyes he hadn't seen before. Then they clouded. 'But you'll probably be gone by the time he gets back.'

'Perhaps not.' Chris stood up and went over to gaze out the window. The room had a view out onto an oval he remembered, one where he and his mates used to play cricket. It was empty at this time of day. Cassie's words hit home. He needed to know what her future held. If Cassie wasn't going to be able to travel for some time, where did that leave him? Chris knew he couldn't leave while she was in hospital, but he had a company to run. He couldn't remain in Granite Springs indefinitely.

Twelve

'Are you sure about this, Ann?' Stella the stylist who had been Ann's hairdresser for years looked at her dubiously.

Ann regarded herself in the mirror wondering if she'd taken leave of her senses. It was as if seeing Gus again had flicked a switch in her brain, making her realise she'd been living in the past ever since he left. It was time for a change, and she'd decided to start with her hair, to change the sleek chin-length bob of her teenage years and branch out. The style and the silver streak Stella had suggested rather than trying to hide the encroaching grey wouldn't be much for most people, but for Ann they were a huge step out of her comfort zone.

She nodded. She was sure, even if she didn't know exactly why she was so eager to make this change right now.

As she walked out of the salon, she tentatively put a hand up to touch the new style, the jagged ends of the new shorter cut making her wonder if this had been a mistake. As she walked along, she kept glancing at her reflection in the shop windows she passed. Was this really her?

So far, she'd ignored Fran's advice to make the effort to see Gus. She knew he'd be at the hospital, but when she saw Gus again, she wanted to be prepared. She wasn't ready yet.

Anyway, she straightened her shoulders, tonight she was going to dinner with Sam Walker. After hearing nothing from him for over a week, he'd called on Wednesday to invite her to dinner at The Riverside tonight. She hadn't agreed immediately, unsure if she wanted to be seen at Granite Springs' top restaurant on a Saturday evening with the new editor of the local paper. Then common sense had prevailed. It would have been churlish to refuse. She remembered what Fran had said, remembered her decision to change.

Hence the visit to the hairdresser this morning, but had she gone too far? Then, deciding she might as well go the whole hog, Ann turned towards Eve Tait's boutique. She stood staring into the window, seeing as if for the first time the display of colourful autumn outfits interspersed with hats and necklaces designed to tempt prospective customers. Did she have the courage to go in?

'Ann, I didn't expect to see you here. And don't you look nice. Love the new hairstyle.'

Ann felt a tap on her arm and turned sharply to see her cousin gazing at her in surprise.

'Peta.' Ann's hand went up to her hair again. 'You don't think it's…?'

'It's lovely. Makes you look younger.'

'Thanks.' Peta's words made Ann wonder what she had looked like before, if Gus had been relieved they hadn't stayed together, if his wife… There was no point thinking like this, in torturing herself by imagining what Gus's life was like.

'Are you going into Eve's? She won't be there today. She's taken her girls and Lily out to her mother's place. Lily is excited as there is a new baby alpaca for them to cuddle. I was going to The Bean Sprout to see if Frank needs any help. They can be busy on a Saturday and an extra pair of hands in the kitchen is often welcome. Why don't you come with me? We can have a coffee before I get started.'

Glad of the excuse to avoid shopping for a new outfit she had no real need for, Ann agreed and accompanied Peta along the road to The Bean Sprout. It wasn't somewhere she normally frequented, preferring one of the town's other cafés on the rare occasions she chose to go out for coffee. The Bean Sprout held too many memories. It was where she and Gus spent their afternoons after school was over. Gus used to joke they and their friends kept old Charlie Beattie in business.

For years, Ann had managed to avoid the place. But now her cousin was living with the present owner it was difficult to find an excuse that would make sense. She could imagine Peta's amazement if Ann told her it brought up memories of her teenage years she'd prefer to forget. After all, she'd remained in Granite Springs. The whole town was filled with memories.

'Hi, honey!' Frank came out from behind the espresso machine to give Peta a hug. 'Hello, Ann. We don't usually see you here. What can I get you?'

Flustered, Ann took a few moments to reply, giving Frank time to ask Peta, 'Your usual cappuccino?'

Peta nodded and smiled.

'I'll have one, too.' Ann looked around the café. Not a lot had changed. Frank had modernised the place, and the jukebox she remembered had gone. No one had jukeboxes these days. *It was a pity*, Ann thought, remembering all the fun they'd had, taking turns selecting tunes and dancing around to them. But that was a long time ago, another lifetime.

She realised Peta was talking to her. 'Sorry?'

'There's an empty table by the window. Why don't you grab it while I check what's going on in the kitchen and let Marie know I'll be there to help in a bit?'

Ann took a seat at the table Peta indicated, thinking how odd it was Marie still managed the café with Frank. Although not frequenting it, Ann couldn't help knowing the café's history. There were few secrets in Granite Springs. Frank and Marie took over the café soon after their marriage and ran it together for years until the marriage broke down. Now, although both were in new relationships, they still worked together, seemingly amicably.

'Two cappuccinos.' Frank delivered their coffees just as Peta returned and slid into the seat opposite.

'Thanks, honey.' She beamed up at him.

To Ann's surprise, this overt show of affection didn't affect her in the usual way. Instead of feeling awkward, she felt… She wanted someone to look at her in the way Frank looked at Peta. She swallowed and picked up her cup to hide her embarrassment.

'What's been happening?' Peta asked. 'I haven't seen you since we were out at Fran's. What prompted the new hairdo?'

Ann touched her hair again. She was beginning to get used to the way it felt. 'Nothing really.' She wasn't sure which question she was answering, perhaps both. She couldn't tell Peta about meeting Gus again. She'd never told her cousin about him. 'Well, I am going out to dinner this evening. But it's not really a date.' As soon as she'd spoken Ann wished the words back.

Peta's eyes lit up. 'A date? Oh, do tell.'

'Not really a date,' Ann repeated. 'It's one of Susie's matchmaking attempts. Sam Walker. He's the new editor of the Granite Springs Advertiser.'

'Oh, I heard there was a new editor. It's time I tried to get another article in the paper. Maybe you could give me an introduction?'

'Maybe.' But Ann doubted it. She had no intention of seeing Sam Walker after tonight's dinner. And from what she knew, Peta's interior design business was going from strength to strength. She had no need of Ann's help to promote it. When her cousin arrived in Granite Springs in the middle of last year, she was reeling from the death of her daughter at the hands of her son-in-law. But she hadn't allowed her grief to deter her. She'd created a new life for herself and her granddaughter, Lily, here in Granite Springs and started up *Forrest Interiors*.

Ann knew grief still overwhelmed Peta from time to time, but now she was in a relationship with Frank Beattie, she had found contentment. Frank was a good man who clearly loved both Peta and Lily. Ann was happy for her.

'I have to go.' Peta glanced around. 'The café's getting busy.' She drained her coffee and stood up. 'No need for you to rush away. Take your time.'

But Ann rose, too. She had no desire to sit there surrounded by memories, memories she'd successfully managed to stifle until faced with the past in the form of Gus Thomas.

*

As Ann expected, The Riverside was packed when she and Sam walked in. Unwilling to have him pick her up at home, she'd insisted on making her own way, choosing to meet him outside the restaurant. Now she was wondering if the evening had been such a good idea after all, seeing the curious looks being directed at them as they made their way to the table Sam had reserved.

She took her seat with a sigh of relief, trying to make herself as inconspicuous as possible.

'Seems to be a popular place.' Sam gazed around the large room as a bevy of young people giggling and carrying gaily wrapped parcels trooped through to disappear upstairs. 'What's up there?'

'I believe there's a function room.' Ann had never been in it. She'd only been to The Riverside on a couple of occasions, the last one when Peta shouted her a meal as a thank you for having her and Lily to stay. It didn't feature in the life she chose to live.

'Mmm. Must remember that for when I want to throw a celebration.'

Why was she here? Ann nodded to several people who smiled across at her, recognising their curious glances at her companion. He had arrived in town so recently, many people didn't know the new editor of the local paper. What did they think? She lowered her eyes to focus on the menu.

'Wow! A great selection. Have you decided?' Sam asked, peering over his menu with a friendly grin.

Ann hadn't. She'd been too busy worrying about being the focus of gossip. Two of the people she'd nodded to were on the university staff, while another worked at the library. Flustered, her eyes fell on an item in the middle of the page. 'I'll have the signature salmon dish,' she said, closing the menu.

'Good choice. Think I'll go for the wagyu steak. Do you prefer white or red wine?'

'Either.'

The waiter arrived and Sam placed the order, choosing a bottle of pinot noir to accompany their meal.

By the time their food arrived, they had already started on the wine, and Ann was feeling more relaxed. She'd forgotten what a good conversationalist Sam was. He kept her entertained with tales of his life when he travelled the world as a journalist. She barely needed to say anything.

What Sam didn't reveal was his reason for choosing to take on the role of editor in this small country town. While the inhabitants were proud of Granite Springs, considering it to be a thriving regional centre, it was an unusual choice for someone who was in the habit of travelling to the world's trouble spots.

Ann was about to ask him what brought him to Granite Springs when she saw a familiar figure enter the restaurant and shrank in her seat. What was Gus doing here?

'Something wrong?' Sam turned to glance in the direction Ann was looking.

'No, nothing.' She felt sick, her stomach was doing somersaults. 'I'm sorry, I…' she rose, tossed her napkin on the table and headed for the ladies.

Once there, Ann took a deep breath and stood, hands on the edge of the wash basin, gazing into the mirror, her breathing ragged. She must stop doing this – retreating to the loo when things became awkward for her. Tonight, the reflection was one of a stranger, the new hairdo turning her into someone she didn't recognise. What had possessed her? Who was she trying to impress? Certainly not her companion for the evening.

'Are you all right?'

Ann turned to see a stranger looking at her rather oddly. She must seem like a mad woman. 'Yes, thank you.' She ineffectually patted her already immaculate hair and washed her hands before returning to the restaurant.

Sam appeared to have barely noticed her absence. 'I ordered coffees,' he said with one of his grins. Did the man have any other expression?

'Thanks.' Ann slid into her seat with a sly glance toward the other end of the room where Gus was now seated, fortunately with his back to her. She breathed a sigh of relief. Coffee was exactly what she needed.

'I see there's to be a special parade in town for Saint Patrick's Day on Tuesday. Being at the paper means we get advance notice of every event in town,' he said somewhat apologetically. 'It might be fun to go watch it – and maybe call into the RSL afterwards. They're putting on a special lunch for the occasion.'

Ann winced. She wasn't ready for this. *What had she said or done to give him the impression she'd be up to spend more time with him so soon – if at all?* Yes, he was good company – and an interesting companion, but she wasn't looking for a companion. Fortunately, she had the perfect excuse. 'I'm sorry, I do my volunteer work on Tuesday.' Ann knew she sounded prim, but she was telling the truth and Tuesday was the day she'd earmarked to waylay Gus and settle matters for once and all.

She wasn't exactly sure what she intended to say to him, or what she expected him to say to her. But maybe she could get an answer to the questions that had been bothering her ever since they met again and put him out of her mind forever.

Thirteen

Chris blinked at the sight of Annie leaving the restaurant followed by the tall, dark-haired man whose hand seemed to fit snugly into her waist as he shepherded her out. He should have known. She was an attractive woman. Of course, she'd be married, probably with children, maybe even grandchildren. Chris winced. They should have been his.

He didn't think she'd seen him and although tempted, he didn't make any attempt to make himself known to her and her husband. Chris caught sight of the man's face as he exited the restaurant – a good-looking man, a veritable pillar of the community, no doubt. It didn't make Chris feel any better to think she had married well, that the man she'd chosen to replace him had remained with her in Granite Springs. Chris didn't recognise him. He must be a newcomer.

He quickly finished his meal, the lamb dish he'd been enjoying turning to ashes. Why was he so upset? He hadn't come back to Granite Springs with any expectation of seeing Annie again. In fact, if asked, he'd have said she was the last person he expected to meet. But they had met, and that meeting had forced him to regret his choice. Because he'd had a choice. He could have stayed, chosen a different life – one which would probably not have brought him the success and wealth he now possessed, but which might have been happier.

'Coffee sir?' A waiter arrived to remove his plate and stood looking at him expectantly.

'No thanks. Can I have the bill?' Chris knew he wasn't going to get much sleep, and coffee would only make things worse. What he needed was a strong drink to dull the pain of seeing Annie with another man. He knew he was being foolish. He had no claim on her. What they had was over long ago – thirty-five years ago. But seeing her again had awakened the feelings he'd kept hidden all those years and he'd hoped… What had he hoped? They could pick up where they left off? He gave a grim smile as he paid his bill and left the restaurant to go back to the motel.

On the way, he stopped at a bottle shop to buy a bottle of whisky. It wasn't his usual tipple. He normally eschewed hard drink. But tonight, he needed it.

Back in his room, Chris poured a large measure of scotch into a glass and tried to make sense of his feelings. Was it being back in Granite Springs in addition to seeing Annie that had brought on this sense of nostalgia? He found himself reminiscing about the past, about the years when he and Annie had been together, when life had seemed so simple. He remembered their first date, the afternoons bunking off from school together with much giggling on Annie's part, the long summer days spent by the river and their school formal when she looked like a princess. Then, there were the years when he was at university, when they lived for the weekends into which they tried to fit all their pent-up emotions, spending as much time together as possible; the nights squashed in the back seat of his old ute or, if the weather was warmer, lying in the paddock together, the blades of dry grass tickling their nakedness.

When did everything change? Why did they have to grow up?

*

Chris groaned as the sunlight hit his eyes next morning, the sound of church bells reminding him it was Sunday. The whisky hadn't helped. He'd stayed awake drinking and watching some hideous old movie on television till he'd finally drifted off to sleep in the early hours.

He headed for the shower, hoping it would make him feel better, and cursing himself for being such a self-indulgent fool. The cool water cascading over his body did help, as did the black coffee and toast which was all he could stomach for breakfast.

A blast of fresh air hit him as he walked towards the hospital building from the car park. Over his sparse breakfast he'd decided to put Annie out of his mind and concentrate on getting Cassie well again. The meeting with Bree Young yesterday had given him cause for concern. While she'd been optimistic about Cassie's chances of regaining full use of her leg, she'd been cautious and declined to make any definite commitment. Instead, she'd recited the possible complications of the surgery they had scheduled for Tuesday. It was no doubt something she did every day, so easily did the words trip off her tongue, but it sent shudders through Chris. At least Cassie hadn't been privy to their conversation.

Picking up his usual coffee, Chris also bought a copy of the local paper and, seeing a selection of cakes and slices on the counter, purchased a slice of Cassie's favourite carrot cake in the hope it might tempt her appetite.

'Morning, sweetie.' He dropped a kiss on Cassie's forehead and handed her the bag containing the piece of carrot cake. 'Thought you might like this.'

'What is it?' She opened the bag. 'Oh, thanks, Dad. I'll keep it till later when they bring around tea.' She grimaced. 'I'd die for a cup of proper tea. The stuff they serve here is awful.'

Glad to hear her sounding stronger, Chris pulled up his usual seat, and picked up the copy of *The Dry*.

'Do you mind if we don't read today?' Cassie asked. 'I think I might go back to sleep. Sorry, Dad. It must be boring for you to sit here day after day, reading or watching me sleep. You don't need to, you know.'

'Where else would I be?' Chris clasped Cassie's hand, then looked up as a nurse arrived to take her blood pressure, temperature and to check on the intravenous drips which were still attached to a canula on the back of her left hand.

When the nurse had gone again, Cassie lay back and closed her eyes. She looked so young and vulnerable lying there, her red hair splayed out on the pillow, so different from the girl he'd farewelled at the airport six months earlier. That girl had been filled with excitement, about to embark on a great adventure. How could it have ended like this?

But it hadn't ended, he reminded himself. One more bout of surgery and Cassie would be on the mend. He had to believe it. To consider the alternative was unbearable. He couldn't wait till she was out of there and they were both on the plane back home.

For lack of anything else to do, Chris opened his copy of the Granite Springs Advertiser. It was an old edition. The paper was published twice a week and this one had been published the previous Friday. He flicked through it, scanning the usual local news items. There had been a successful fundraising dinner held for the local bushfire brigade; Granite Springs Choristers were to hold an Easter concert and tickets could be purchased at the newspaper office or the library; and the Saint Patrick's Day parade would be raising funds for the local hospice.

He was about to close it when he saw the column by the editor was about the increase in levels of domestic violence leading to the need for a women's refuge in the town. Chris wondered at the necessity for such a facility in his old hometown, but supposed the crime was probably as rife here as anywhere else.

It was a clear, well-reasoned article. The guy certainly knew his stuff. Chris's eyes drifted to the top of the column and stopped at the photo of the writer. It was a trifle blurred, but the face was recognisable. It was the man he'd seen with Annie. She was married to the editor of the local paper.

Cassie was still asleep and, with a bitter taste in his mouth, Chris felt like some fresh air. At the entrance to the hospital, he hesitated, unsure where he intended to go. The inadequacy of his breakfast was beginning to make itself felt. He was hungry. But it was Sunday. The café he'd taken refuge in last time would be closed like most of the other eateries in town. But he wasn't in the mood for the offerings in the hospital café where he'd eaten the first few days he was here.

Going to the car park, he drove away from the hospital and into town, hoping to find somewhere open other than the RSL which, if memory served him correctly, was open seven days. He found himself driving towards the river.

As a teenager the river and its surrounds provided endless possibilities. In summer, it abounded with groups of young people all intent on showing off their prowess, whether it be swimming across to the opposite bank, diving from a rope which used to hang from a tall branch of a nearby tree, or paddling in one of the dinghies that used to appear as soon as the temperature rose beyond a certain point.

The image of Annie as she'd looked back then arose unbidden. They had been good years.

Today the riverbank was deserted apart from an old couple walking along hand-in-hand. They appeared to be heading for a building not too far ahead. It looked new – certainly hadn't been there when Chris lived here – and seemed to house a bakery or café.

Chris parked the car and walked towards the entrance where a board proclaimed the establishment served breakfast until eleven. As it was only ten-thirty, Chris ordered eggs benedict with smoked salmon and a macchiato and settled down at a table by the river. As he sat watching a family of ducks swim past, the only sounds the lapping of the water on the shore and the cackle of a couple of galahs fighting over something in the grass, he wondered why he had ever left this peaceful place for the hustle and bustle of the cities he'd lived in for the past thirty-five years.

Fourteen

Ann was glad she'd invited Peta to lunch today. After last night's dinner with Sam, and the shock of seeing Gus at the restaurant, she needed something to keep her occupied, to prevent her imagination from working overtime. She'd invited Frank too, but Peta said he'd be busy with some paperwork for the café, so it would just be her and Lily.

Ann was pleased. While she liked her cousin's new partner, she valued the opportunity to see Peta on her own, and she always loved having Lily to visit. She'd missed the little girl when Peta and Lily had moved out, even if part of her was relieved to have the house to herself again. Over the years she'd become set in her ways, and the advent of a young child – even a delightful one like Lily – upset her routine.

Rising early, Ann set about preparing the quiche and salad she planned to serve her guests, before changing into a pair of navy pants with a flower-patterned tunic. She examined herself critically in the bedroom mirror. How had she managed to let herself become the type of woman she used to condemn as old-fashioned? Having taken the first step of revamping her hairstyle, she determined not to stop there. She'd ask Peta's advice. The younger woman always dressed well, fashionable without being flashy like Susie.

She patted her new hair and finished applying her makeup before going back to the kitchen.

Damn! Ann checked again, but there was no doubt. She'd forgotten to buy the sour dough bread she'd intended to accompany their lunch.

Last time, Lily had told Ann it was her favourite, and she didn't want to disappoint her.

Checking her watch, she realised she had time to go out to buy some, remembering the bakery by the river was open on Sundays. She'd drive there and perhaps manage to pick up a Sunday paper on the way back. Lily would enjoy the kiddie's supplement.

Popping the quiche and salad into the fridge, she set off.

*

Ann paid for her bread and was about to leave when she noticed a familiar figure sitting at one of the tables by the river. It couldn't be, but it was. Gus Thomas was sitting there admiring the view. From the empty plate on his table, it looked like he'd had breakfast. Ann wondered what was happening with his daughter.

Tempted to leave before he saw her, she remembered her vow. There were still two days before Tuesday when she planned to waylay him at the hospital, but they were both here now. She glanced around to see all the other tables were empty. There was no one to eavesdrop on their conversation. Ann walked over, laid her tissue-wrapped loaf on the table and slid into the chair opposite Gus.

He looked up, a surprised expression in his eyes, and her stomach did a double flip. After a pause, he said, 'Annie?' He looked in the direction from which she'd come, to the inside of the bakery. 'You're on your own this morning?'

'What do you mean?' Anne blushed. He must have caught sight of her with Sam at the restaurant.

'Last night. Your husband… I saw his column in the paper. Editor of the Granite Springs Advertiser, no less.'

Ann almost choked. He thought she and Sam… 'No, I mean yes, I'm on my own and no, Sam's not my husband. I'm not married. We've only just met. Last night was the first time we…' She broke off. Why was she explaining herself to him? 'I came here for bread,' she gestured to the loaf sitting between them, 'then I saw you. I owe you an apology.'

'You do?' His lips curled into the smile she knew so well. Was he laughing at her?'

'Last time. At the hospital, I was less than gracious.' She bit the inside of her cheek. This wasn't going well. She hadn't had time to prepare. She should have waited till Tuesday as she planned.

'You've always been gracious, Annie. One of your many attributes.' He smiled.

Ann's heart began to beat faster. How could he have such an effect on her after all this time? 'How is your daughter?' she asked.

'Cassie.' Gus's face became more serious. 'They're operating again on Tuesday. Then we should know if they can save her leg.'

Ann saw a bead of moisture appear in the corner of his eyes, as it had at the mention of his daughter's leg last time they met. 'I'm sorry. I hope it goes well.' She took a deep breath. 'Is Cassie your only child?'

Gus's lips tightened.

'The only one. I wanted more but Gail...' his lips tightened again '...she refused point blank, said it would interfere with her blasted career. I sometimes felt she even resented Cassie. I always dreamt of having a big family.' He sighed. 'Gail took that dream from me.'

Ann felt a tension in her chest, she could barely breathe. What would Gus think if he knew what she'd almost done, and how she'd lost their child?' She swallowed. 'Will her mother be coming over?' she asked to hide her confusion. Last time she asked this, she received a cursory reply. This time he was more forthcoming.

'No. My ex-wife seems to forget she has a daughter. Her career means more to her than Cassie does.'

Ann noted the word 'ex' and felt her heart give a leap. 'You're divorced?'

'For five years now. We lived separate lives for longer, but you don't want to hear about my marital difficulties. My life revolves around work and Cassie. If she has to lose her leg, it'll destroy her. I don't know what I'll do.' Gus shook his head.

'The surgeons here are very good,' Ann offered, though she knew it was poor comfort. Good as they were, they could only do their best. Cassie's recovery was in the lap of the gods.

'Thanks.' Gus recovered his equilibrium. 'What about you? What kept you here in Granite Springs? You stayed because of your mother, but surely...?'

'Mum died several years ago. She lasted longer than anyone would have predicted and spent her final years in Eden Gardens.' Ann's eyes clouded remembering how difficult her mother had become in her final years as the dementia escalated. 'By that time, I had no desire to leave. I have a good job. My whole life is here.' *What there is of it*, she thought. Her life would no doubt sound very boring to Gus who had travelled across the world and now owned an internationally renowned business.

'I'm sorry. I know how attached you were to your family. Your sister? Susie?'

'She got away.' Ann tried to keep her voice even to hide the bitterness. 'She and Adrian moved to England soon after you left. They only returned last year, claiming they missed the heat. She's changed. You'd barely recognise her. You never had the urge to come back?' She knew the answer, but couldn't resist asking.

Gus paused for a few moments before replying. 'There was nothing for me here. If I could have come back when Mum and Dad died, but it was difficult, then…' he waved his hands in the air. 'I'm sorry, Annie. I've never forgotten you.' He gave a lopsided grin.

Ann looked down at her hands which were clasped on the table. She laced and unlaced her fingers, shocked when Gus put his hands on them. The feel of his hands on hers after all those years brought everything back. She felt dizzy. What did he mean?

'Annie, it was such a surprise to see you again. A good one. You have to believe that. I'd like to see you again while I'm here. What do you say?'

Ann risked looking up to meet his eyes. They were warm, questioning. She was tempted. What harm could it do, and there were still so many unanswered questions. But, when his daughter was well enough, he'd be off again, back to Canada where he belonged. And she'd be left here in Granite Springs again.

'I…'

'Don't give me your answer now. I need to get back to the hospital and I'm sure you have things to take care of, too.' He gestured to the bread.

Ann had all but forgotten the reason she was there. Peta and Lily would be arriving shortly, and she was sitting there trying to decide whether to risk being hurt again by this man. 'Yes, I…' She was having difficulty in finding the words she wanted to say, the words which would tell him she had no intention of rekindling a relationship that could have no future.

'Will you be at the hospital again on Tuesday? Perhaps we can have coffee there again?'

Still tongue-tied, Ann nodded.

'Here's my number.' Gus handed her a card, the initials CAT embossed in red and a string of numbers. 'You can use the mobile one if you want to reach me.' He stood up and leant on the table. 'I mean it, Annie. Meeting you again is the best thing that's happened to me in years. Please be there on Tuesday. We have a lot to talk about.'

Ann watched him leave, his confident, swinging gait proclaiming the man he'd become. Gus was no longer the ambitious young man who'd left Granite Springs in search of a better life. He'd found that better life, made a bright future for himself, while she'd remained here content to live one filled with regrets in the shadow of what might have been.

*

When Peta and Lily arrived, Ann was still torn as to whether she'd really meet with Gus again on Tuesday. It was her day at the hospital, but she'd been volunteering there for so long it would be simple to ask Wendy if she could take on another task, one which would keep her well out of Chris's orbit. Did she want to do that? She had planned to waylay him on Tuesday, but that was before seeing him today.

Tuesday was the day he'd said Cassie was to have her surgery. Gus was an old friend, one who might be in need of support when his daughter was undergoing such an important operation. Was she being selfish to put her own feelings first, to ignore what he would undoubtedly be feeling, to ignore his need for reassurance?

'Has something happened? You're looking worried,' Peta said as she greeted her with a hug and kiss on the cheek.

'I'm fine.' Ann tried unsuccessfully to smile as tears pricked her eyes at the concerned expression on her cousin's face. 'Really.' She turned her attention to Lily. 'If you go through to the living room, Lily, you'll find something there for you.' Ann delighted in finding gifts for the little girl, the latest being a jigsaw featuring a basket of cats.

'You shouldn't.' Peta was distracted as Ann had hoped. 'You're far too generous to her.'

'Not at all. She deserves to be spoiled a little after what she went through.'

'Oh, thank you, Auntie Ann. Can I start it now?' Lily ran in to give Ann a hug.

'We're going to eat soon, Lily, so maybe wait till after lunch? Why don't you help me set the table? You know where the cutlery is.'

'Okay.' Lily went off happily.

Lunch was a cheerful affair. Ann managed to forget her worries and share Peta's pleasure as she described her latest project. Her interior design business had grown since her first commission with Danny Slater. He was a local realter who'd contracted with her to work on his display homes in a new development on the outskirts of town. Her latest project was with Danny again.

'It's really exciting, Ann,' Peta said. 'A new commercial development, a technology hub, out near the university. It'll really bring Granite Springs into the twenty-first century. Even Frank is enthusiastic about the extra business it'll bring.'

Ann wasn't so sure. She liked Granite Springs the way it was. Life had changed rapidly enough for her already. The town would soon be unrecognisable as the place she'd grown up in. But it seemed there was no way to stop progress.

The mention of a technology hub made her think of Gus again. Perhaps if there had been one in Granite Springs thirty-five years ago, Gus wouldn't have needed to go all the way to the US to find the job he wanted. If he'd stayed here, they'd have married, and... She sighed, remembering what her grandmother used to say, *If ifs and ands were pots and pans, there would be no work for tinkers' hands.*

*

'Now,' Peta said, when she and Ann were enjoying coffee, Lily having disappeared to work on her jigsaw. 'I can still see that look in your eyes, the one you had when we arrived. I'm sure it's not the thought of Danny Slater's IT hub that's bothering you. You can tell me. I'm unshockable. But it can't be so bad. I presume you haven't committed a crime,' she joked.

Ann winced. She thought she'd managed to hide her feelings. She sighed. Maybe it was time to tell Peta her story. 'It all started a long time ago,' she began.

Peta didn't say a word as Ann recounted her story, trying to state it like it was with no embellishments and no hint of self-pity.

'You poor thing,' she said when Ann finished. 'How dreadful to lose your baby like that, and your Gus to be so far away. It must have been a shock to see him again. No wonder you looked a bit spaced out when we arrived.'

Spaced out was a good description of how Ann still felt. She picked up her coffee and took a gulp. It had been difficult to tell Peta. It was like reliving the past, a past she'd never managed to let go.

'I did wonder,' Peta continued. 'When we came to stay with you last year. You'd changed so much from the lively teenager I remembered. I got the feeling something had happened to make you…' she pursed her lips, '…bitter is too strong a word, but you seemed to have developed a hard shell. I think Lily helped you to unbend a little – where we were concerned, anyway.' She chuckled. 'It's difficult to maintain any sort of distance with her.'

'She's lovely. And she was crying out for affection. I think having her here did help me see everything differently,' Ann said thoughtfully.

'So, I guess the big question is, what do you do now?'

'Sorry?'

'Gus, Chris – whatever his name is. Do you intend to meet him on Tuesday, or will you make some excuse? I could understand if you did. Once bitten, twice shy. But it was you who sent him away last time.' Peta cocked her head to one side.

Ann knew Peta was right. It had hurt so much to see him go. Had she thought he'd change his mind and stay – for her? For the first time, Ann tried to analyse exactly how she'd felt when Gus left town without trying to contact her again. Suddenly it came to her. She'd felt let down. Even though she'd chosen to put her family before him, she had expected him to acknowledge her situation, to at least contact her, say goodbye. But there had been nothing. No call. No letter. Nothing for thirty-five years. Until they met at Granite Springs Base Hospital.

'I don't know what I'm going to do, Peta.' Ann gave a heartfelt sigh, fearful that whichever decision she made, it would be the wrong one.

Fifteen

By Tuesday morning, Ann still hadn't made a decision. She wanted to see Gus again. She remembered the sensation of his hand on hers, the feelings it evoked, how her heart leapt and her gut twisted just as it had all those years ago. But they weren't teenagers anymore, far from it. They were older and wiser, at least she hoped she was wiser. Some days she wasn't sure; some days she still felt like the awkward young girl who discovered she was pregnant and didn't know what to do.

She gave herself a shake as she dressed in the new jeans Peta had suggested she buy. After baring her soul to her cousin, Ann had remembered to ask Peta's advice about updating her wardrobe. These were her first purchase along with a grey cowl-necked sweater, not unlike one Peta wore herself. Despite objecting she didn't have time to shop, Ann had made a trip into town in her lunch break to visit the town's newest department store.

She really did look quite nice, Ann thought, twisting this way and that in front of the mirror, while regretting the impulse that had made her agree to meet Sam at the parade. Unwilling to wait for her to contact him, he'd called her at the university the day before and refused to take no for an answer, citing the need for him to be seen to participate in the town's celebrations and begging her to provide him with her company. She'd relented knowing she could fit it in before her stint at the hospital.

While she knew it was a specious argument – a man like him could surely have anyone he wanted accompany him to the Saint Patrick's Day parade – Ann had allowed herself to be persuaded.

With ten minutes to spare, she hurried out and walked briskly towards Main Street which was already crowded with eager onlookers. Although the schools were still in session, many had decided to provide decorated floats, and there were several groups of schoolchildren being shepherded along by their teachers.

Ann had arranged to meet Sam at the entrance to The Advertiser and it took her longer than she anticipated to weave her way through the excited locals. She finally reached the old sandstone building to see Sam glancing worriedly at his watch.

'Hello,' she said, breathlessly, seeing a relieved look on his face. 'Sorry I'm late.'

'No worries. I was beginning to wonder if you'd had second thoughts.'

His words were so accurate, Ann felt herself blushing, but before she could reply he spoke again, 'I'm glad you're here now. Let's find a good spot. This thing looks to be bigger than I anticipated.'

'Granite Springs likes to put on a show,' Ann said. This was the first time she'd attended the parade in years. It had been an important part of her growing up, especially when the day fell on a weekend – her parents didn't believe in her taking time off school, and the schools hadn't been so involved back then. As teenagers, she and Gus had always managed to sneak away, often talking their way into being allowed onto one of the floats where they'd had a bird's eye view of the town. It was strange to be watching it with Sam.

They found a spot not far from the office and watched the procession passing by. Any memories Ann had of previous occasions were drowned out by the cheering as a float with a troupe of Irish dancers passed them, and someone dressed as a giant leprechaun rattled a can to raise money for a local charity. The Irish population of Granite Springs were out in force today. Ann remembered having learned in school how many of the town's early settlers were Irish convicts who'd been awarded their ticket of leave. While many of their descendants had since moved away, there were still enough of them left to ensure this celebration continued.

She couldn't help but laugh as a tiny leprechaun on huge stilts came by juggling gold nuggets and another float with Irish dancers, all dressed in green.

'This is fun,' Sam said, as the final float disappeared down the street. 'I hope our photographer got some good shots. We're bringing out a special edition tomorrow. It'll be more of a broadsheet. It should go down well.'

The crowds were beginning to disperse, and Ann was wondering how she could tactfully leave, when Sam took hold of her hand. It was a friendly clasp and had none of the effect the touch of Gus's had in the bakery, but it surprised her.

'I hear the RSL is serving Guinness today, in honour of the Saint. What say I treat you to one?'

'At eleven o'clock in the morning?'

'It's almost lunchtime. Come on, be a devil.'

Despite her misgivings, Ann found herself being led along the street to where groups of people, many dressed in green outfits, were already streaming into the club.

Seated in an inconspicuous spot with a glass of Guinness and the day's speciality, a plate of corned beef and cabbage, Ann discovered she was enjoying herself. As she'd noted before, Sam was good company, seeming to have a never-ending collection of stories about his exploits as a journalist. But she noticed he rarely touched on anything personal.

As a private person herself, she appreciated his reticence, though she did wonder what had brought him to Granite Springs.

'I really must go now.' Ann had to raise her voice to make herself heard above the raucous singing – not everyone was as moderate drinkers as she and Sam. 'I have to be at the hospital. I volunteer there and I have some library books to drop off.'

And I have a decision to make.

The enjoyment of the morning faded at the realisation she needed to decide whether to meet with Gus while she was at the hospital today. Why did life have to be so complicated? She'd made a life for herself, one she was content with. Then Gus had appeared out of the blue and the barrier she'd erected around herself, around her feelings, had cracked open, forcing her to admit to the possibility of pain again.

In her heart of hearts, Ann knew she would meet him, if only to avoid bumping into him unexpectedly. Fran had been right. Granite Springs was too small for her to have any hope of avoiding him.

'I should be getting back, too.' Sam rose, and the pair pushed their way through the mass of green-clad bodies to the exit, where Sam hesitated. 'Thanks for coming along. It was good to have someone to enjoy the parade with – and lunch.'

Before Ann could reply, she was almost blinded by a flash and a voice said, 'That'll look good in tomorrow's column, boss.'

Ann blinked. Standing in front of them, a wide grin on his face, was young Tim Clark, the Granite Springs Advertiser's photographer. It took a moment to sink in, then she realised what had happened. He'd taken a photo of her with Sam, one he intended to publish in the next day's special edition of the paper. 'No!' she said, holding up a hand as if she could ward off the inevitable. She, who scorned publicity, who had managed to keep herself out of the limelight all her life, was now to be paraded in the local paper standing inside the RSL with its editor. Why had she agreed to Sam's pressure? How could she have been so stupid?

'Don't worry about it,' Sam said, seeing her distress, 'I'll make sure it's not published, if that's what you're concerned about.'

'Thanks, and thanks for lunch,' Ann said before hurrying off. She was glad to leave the crowded Main Street behind to return home to pick up her car. Once behind the wheel, she took a deep breath and tried to work out why she'd been so upset. It was only a photo. But the niggling suspicion, the worry of what people might think, the danger of becoming the target of gossip, made her stomach clench.

By the time she reached the hospital, Ann had bowed to the inevitable. She'd been arguing with herself ever since she left the RSL. Her final decision was based on the fact she still cared for Gus. But, she told herself, she'd do the same for anyone. His daughter was undergoing surgery. He needed support. He didn't have anyone else. She would only do what any decent, caring person would do in the same circumstances. She took out the card he'd given her.

*

The afternoon passed slowly. Ann was allocated her usual task of greeting visitors and new patients and assisting them find their way around the hospital. Whereas she normally enjoyed this role, today it made her want to scream. All she could think of was the card burning a hole in her pocket.

She'd tried to call Gus when she was still in the car, but the call had gone to voicemail. Now her imagination was working overtime. She had a tea break coming up and planned to try calling again. Meanwhile, time was moving slowly as she made the effort to be her usual pleasant self, greeting everyone with a forced smile.

This time, her call went through.

There was a desperate note in Gus's voice when he answered. 'Hello? Chris Thomas.'

'Gus, it's Ann.'

He expelled breath loudly.

'Annie! Sorry, Cassie's been in surgery for what seems like forever. I hoped you were the call from recovery to tell me she was ready to come back to the ward.'

'Oh!' Ann felt guilty. She should have realised. The poor man must be at his wits' end waiting for news. But she was glad she'd called him. It was the right thing to do. And she was good at doing the right thing, had been all her life, except that one time when she almost didn't. She winced as the memory of her dead child resurfaced.

'*I'm* sorry. I chose a bad time. I should go and let you keep the line free.' She was about to end the call when he spoke again.

'No, don't go. I'm glad to hear your voice. Does it mean you'll see me again?'

'I guess it does.' Ann was aware of a lightening of her mood. Now she was talking to Gus, she wondered why she'd been so reluctant to contact him again. 'But I don't want to take up your time now. Call me when you've seen Cassie back in the ward. I'll be here.'

'Thanks, Annie. I'll do that.'

She hung up and slid her phone into her pocket. She'd be there for him, as she knew he'd have been there for her if things had been different, if he'd still been in Granite Springs. She shook her head. There was no sense in imagining things as they might have been. It was what it was. Gus had gone. She had stayed. And she'd made a life for herself here in Granite Springs – a life she'd been content with until Gus blew back into it. Now she had no idea how she felt.

Sixteen

Chris looked at his phone, willing it to ring again. He drank innumerable cups of coffee, walked up and down the long corridor, sat down, stood up again. But he was still waiting for news. Surely Cassie's surgery was over by now? His heart sank every time he saw one of the medical staff walk by in their blue scrubs. What if something had happened to Cassie in the operating theatre? It was so easy to dismiss the list of possible complications which might arise during surgery, but there was a reason the surgeon read them out. Some patients died.

His breath was ragged as he contemplated a future without his Cassie. It wasn't possible. He fetched yet another cup of water from the dispenser and gulped it down. He needed to focus on something positive.

Annie! She had called. She had agreed to meet him again. That should be cause for celebration. And it would be, just as soon as he knew Cassie was going to be okay. He slumped in the chair, dropped his hands between his knees and closed his eyes, offering up a prayer to a God he hadn't spoken to in years. He'd drawn the line at going into the hospital chapel, though he'd been tempted. What was it about the thought of death and dying that made people turn to religion? He hadn't ever considered himself someone who would do that, but what did he know? What did anyone know till they were faced with it?

His phone rang. 'Chris Thomas.'

'Mr Thomas, this is Andrea from Recovery. Cassie is out of surgery and in Recovery. She'll be back in the ward in around half an hour.'

'Thanks.' Chris felt like jumping up and punching the air but settled for giving a satisfied smile as he put his phone back into his pocket. Of course, Cassie had come through surgery okay. He'd been foolish to think otherwise, but for a few moments – quite a few – he'd been so damn terrified.

Now he knew all was well – though, he reminded himself, he still didn't know if they'd been able to save her leg – Chris felt his anxiety drain away. He was hungry. He'd been so worried, he hadn't eaten since breakfast, which had been coffee and toast hurriedly consumed before he came to the hospital. With half an hour before he could see Cassie, he headed to the hospital café where he picked up a tandoori chicken pita wrap and a bottle of ginger beer. He carried them back to the ward, figuring he'd drunk enough coffee to keep him awake for a week.

*

Chris warily pushed open the door of Cassie's room to see her sitting propped up on a bank of pillows. She was pale but alert.

'Hi, Dad.'

'Sweetheart!' Chris went to her side and gave her a hug and kiss on the cheek. 'I can't tell you how happy I am to see you.'

'Were you worried about me?' She gave a weak chuckle. 'Didn't you trust the surgeons?'

'Yes, but you're precious to me.' He swallowed, trying to hide his emotion. 'Has Bree spoken to you?'

'Not Bree, but one of her team came to Recovery and told me the operation had been a success, so I guess that means...' She gave a wry look at the cage still encasing her leg.

Chris felt as if a huge weight had been lifted, but knew he wouldn't be able to completely relax until he'd spoken to Bree Young himself and had her assurance Cassie's leg was on the mend.

*

Ann was sitting in the café when her phone rang. Her heart leapt when it lit up with Gus's number. It was an hour since her volunteering stint finished for the day, and she'd been trying to make one pot of tea last and fill in time reading a magazine someone had left lying on the table.

'Gus,' she said, 'How is she?'

'She seems fine. She's awake and about to have something to eat. I'd like to hang on here till I can speak to her surgeon, if that's okay with you. I'll understand if you want to get away.'

Ann could hear the uncertainty in his voice. 'No, it's fine. I'm in the café. I'll wait for you.' She'd stayed this long, what was another hour or so?'

'Thanks. I appreciate it. After I've seen Bree, I'll need someone to talk to. I hope…' His voice broke.

'I hope so, too. I expect Cassie will be fine.' Ann crossed her fingers.

It was over an hour later, and Ann was wishing she could get something to eat, when Gus finally appeared at the entrance to the café. He looked dishevelled, as if he was in need of a shower and a good sleep. The poor man must have been there all day. Ann wondered if he'd eaten at all.

'Annie, thanks for waiting.' He dragged a hand through his hair and blinked, his eyes red-rimmed with tiredness and worry.

Ann rose, stifling the urge to hug him as she would have in years gone by. Today, she kept her arms firmly by her sides. 'Cassie?'

'Bree says the operation was a success. She should make a full recovery.'

'I'm so glad.'

'But it's not over yet. It's going to be some time before she can be discharged, then there will be a course of rehabilitation which they want to do here in Granite Springs. I don't know how…' He sighed. 'I had planned to take her home.'

His reference to home forcibly reminded Ann Granite Springs was no longer Gus's home. His home – and Cassie's – was on the other side of the world. Of course, he wanted to take his daughter back there as soon as he could.

'When did you last eat?' she asked, stifling the disappointment that welled up, the nauseous feeling at the thought of him leaving again.

Gus gazed into space. 'I'm not sure. I did have something when

Cassie was in recovery. It must have been…' He dragged a hand through his hair again and glanced towards the now closed servery.

Ann thought quickly. There were lots of eateries in town, but Gus didn't look in any fit state to walk into a restaurant. Despite the good news about his daughter, he was still traumatised from what he'd been through. 'Come back with me. I have some chicken casserole left over from last night. You look as if a strong drink wouldn't go astray either.'

Gus staggered and grabbed hold of the back of a chair to steady himself. 'That's kind of you. Thanks. I think it's exactly what I do need. You always did manage to read me.' He gave a wry smile, making Ann's breath catch at the truth of his words. People used to say they were like two sides of the one coin, a couple whose thoughts were so alike, they barely needed to speak.

'Right.' Ann tried to sound efficient, to forget the emotion which threatened to rekindle the past. 'You have a car?'

Gus nodded.

'I'll meet you there. You know the address. I still live in the old house.' Did she detect a slight raising of Gus's eyebrows?

Driving home, her eye on Gus's car in the rearview mirror, thoughts whirled through Ann's mind. Home – she was taking him into her home. And feeding him. And promising him a strong drink. What was she thinking? Ann didn't know what she was thinking, only that whatever it was had her face warming up and her heart racing.

It wasn't till she'd driven into her garage and opened the front door that they met again.

Ann led Gus into the living room, suddenly seeing it through his eyes. She'd always made sure it was clean and tidy, but nothing had changed since her mum died. The furniture was still the same, the curtains, the pictures on the wall, even the ornaments hadn't changed since Gus stood there more than thirty years earlier.

She wondered fleetingly what Peta had thought when she arrived here the previous year. She was an interior designer. Ann had arranged for her to design the interior of Susie's new home when her sister returned from overseas. She must have been itching to get her hands on this one. Ann made up her mind to ask her for some ideas.

'Take a seat. I'll heat up the casserole and pour you a drink. Scotch? Wine? I don't have any beer.' Ann suddenly felt awkward, seeing Gus in her home.

'Whisky would be good. You were right. I do need something to calm me. I hadn't realised how tense I was. It was a long wait, and I didn't sleep much last night.'

'Right.' Ann went into the kitchen. She was taking the whisky bottle she kept for medicinal purposes out of the pantry when she felt a presence behind her. Gus had followed her in.

*

Their meal over, they moved into the living room with the remains of a bottle of wine, Gus having refused coffee on the grounds he'd already drunk enough at the hospital. Conversation hadn't flagged over dinner as Ann asked about Gus's business and his life in Canada. But now, sitting side by side on the sofa with glasses of wine, there didn't seem to be much more to say.

'I'm so glad your daughter will recover.' Ann fiddled with the stem of her glass. 'Will you stay in Granite Springs while she undergoes her rehabilitation?' She tried not to show how anxious she was to hear his response, though what did it matter? No matter how long he stayed, he'd be leaving eventually. She steeled herself for his reply.

'I can't leave her, but I need to get back.' Gus put down his glass and shook his head. 'I don't know what I'm going to do, Annie. She's the light of my life. I couldn't have borne to lose her, to have her permanently incapacitated. As I told you, Gail refused to have any more children. I wanted a tribe, but it wasn't to be.' He sighed. 'I wish Cassie was ours, yours and mine.' He smiled at her, the smile she remembered, the smile she'd fallen in love with, the smile that still had the power to turn her knees to water.

Ann's stomach clenched. She wished it, too, wanted to tell him she'd been pregnant, tell him about the child she'd lost – *their* child – but something stopped her. She was wracked again with the guilt she'd carried for all those years, for the action she'd almost taken, for the way she'd been punished. How could she tell Gus what Susie had almost persuaded her to do?

'Oh, Gus! I'm sorry. But I'm sure Cassie will be all right.' Her eyes filled with tears, whether for Cassie or for their own unborn child, Ann wasn't sure.

Suddenly, she was in his arms, the tears running unchecked down her cheeks. When she looked up, she saw tears in Gus's eyes, too.

'Sorry.' Ann pulled away, disturbed by the effect of closeness. After thirty-five years, she thought she was immune to such feelings. 'I'm sorry,' she repeated, not exactly sure what she was sorry for. For breaking down? For refusing to go with him? For almost aborting their child? That was something for which she'd never have been able to forgive herself.

'Cassie needs you to be strong,' she said.

'You're right.' Gus heaved a sigh. 'Thanks for dinner. This evening… it's been…' He smiled faintly, the slightly crooked smile she remembered.

Ann wanted to feel his arms around her again but couldn't bear the thought of what he'd think if he knew. She rose and picked up their empty glasses, hoping he'd take the hint and leave. She just wanted to be alone.

'I should leave. It's getting late.'

At the door, Gus turned toward Ann. 'Thanks for tonight. I needed the company – your company. I need to see you again. I'd like you to meet Cassie. I know you've probably come across her at the university. But I'd like you to meet her as my daughter. Will you do that for me?'

Ann hesitated, then agreed. It was a small thing for him to ask. 'I can meet you at the hospital again.'

'Tomorrow?'

'I can't make it till after work. After six?'

'Great. Thanks.' Gus turned and strode off to where his car was parked at the kerb.

Ann closed the door and stood motionless. The evening hadn't gone at all how she expected. It had rekindled emotions she'd kept stifled for years, forced her to admit she still had feelings for Gus Thomas.

Seventeen

Chris was beginning to feel as if he belonged here at the hospital. He had developed a routine. He picked up his coffee, made his way to Cassie's ward and settled down for the morning. While she was eating lunch, he went down to the cafeteria where he ordered a wrap – some days tuna, others chicken. Then it was back to spend the afternoon with Cassie and to continuing reading *The Dry*. He was enjoying this author's writing and her descriptions of the Australian bush.

He feared his business was being sadly neglected, but each evening before going to sleep, he skyped his second in command. Stan Gray had been with him almost from the start and he trusted him with his life. From his daily reports, Chris knew everything was ticking along like clockwork. But he missed the buzz of the office, the daily challenges. He was in danger of becoming bored.

'What's up, Dad?' Cassie peered at him. She was sitting up this morning, had done something with her hair and appeared much brighter. 'Are you getting as bored with this place as I am?'

'No, not at all,' he lied, surprised how perceptive she was. 'I just want you to get well again so we can go home.'

'Home? To Canada? No, Dad. You can go back, but I want to stay here. Isn't that what the doc recommended? I have plans.'

'Plans?'

'Plans. Miles will be back at the end of the month. It'll soon be Easter. There's a race meeting in Granite Springs, picnic races. It sounds so much fun.'

'But...' Chris couldn't imagine how Cassie could attend a race meeting in her state. But he hadn't counted on her determination.

'I spoke with one of the surgical team. He said I can be discharged soon. They'll provide me with a wheelchair, then crutches. I'll be able to get around. I might even manage to get back to classes. I really miss the university.'

Much as Chris missed the buzz of the office. But he couldn't leave till Cassie was completely recovered. What sort of father would he be if he left while she was still undergoing treatment? He decided to change the subject.

'I bumped into an old school friend the other day.' *Another lie.* 'I'd like you to meet her.'

'Her? An old girlfriend? One of the girls you left behind when you set off to make a name for yourself?'

Chris reddened. Trust Cassie to get to the heart of things, to see through his subterfuge. 'Perhaps. But it was a long time ago. You've always wanted to know about my life here, growing up in Granite Springs. Ann...' he caught himself just in time from calling her Annie, '...Ann Baird was part of it.'

'Why haven't I heard you mention her before?'

'I don't know.' *Another lie.* Chris had never mentioned Annie's name to anyone. She had been his secret, the one he only took out when he was alone, when he felt dispirited, when he wanted to relive happier times. 'Anyway, she's agreed to drop in when she finishes work today. She works out at the university.'

'What's she like?' Cassie asked. 'Is she like Mum?'

'No.' Chris had a mental picture of Gail at the airport to farewell Cassie. Her hair had been cropped short and coloured to an unnatural hue. She'd been dressed in what he supposed she'd call top fashion but looked to him like mutton dressed as lamb. She was nothing like Annie who dressed conservatively.

'Wait a minute!' There was a gleam in Cassie's eyes. 'Ann Baird... and she works at the university? Not the dragon who runs the Education office? Oh, Dad!' She began to laugh. 'You and her!'

'She was much more polite about you.'

'You know we've met? So, what's with this introduce stuff? Was she really your girlfriend back then? Did you leave town to get away from her? What a story!'

'No!' Chris should have known Cassie would put two and two together and make five – or even six. 'It wasn't like that.' He'd hoped to gloss over the past, but knew he had to provide Cassie with a better explanation before Annie arrived.

'What was it like, then? Has she been pining for you all this time? It's well-known Miss Baird has never married.'

How did Cassie know? But he supposed the students managed to know everything about the staff they dealt with on a daily basis.

'I doubt it.' He pulled on one ear. 'Yes, we were a couple, all through our final years at school and through my university degree. We were planning to marry.'

Cassie's eyes widened.

'Then I was offered the job in Silicon Valley. It was an exciting opportunity, a chance for us to start a new life there. But it came at a difficult time for Annie.' He looked down at his hands which had clenched in his lap.

'How so? I'd have gone like a shot.'

'Her father had died, and her mother wasn't handling it well. Annie felt she couldn't leave her.' It sounded so stark to put it like that.

'So, you went without her?'

'I'm not proud of myself. But I was young, ambitious and...' Suddenly, Chris saw his behaviour in a different light. Had he been too cavalier? Should he have tried harder with Annie? 'Yes, I went ahead on my own.'

'And you didn't see each other till now?'

Chris shook his head.

'How romantic!'

Chris raised his eyes, startled at Cassie's reaction. *Romantic? Was their reunion romantic?*

'It's like a movie,' Cassie continued. 'The two star-crossed lovers meet again after so many years and fall into each other's arms vowing eternal love.' She giggled.

'Hardly.' But was his and Annie's reunion really so very different. They *had* fallen into each other's arms, even he wasn't sure how it had happened. But he reminded himself, she'd pulled away, seemed determined to keep him at a distance.

'I can't wait.' Cassie's eyes twinkled with glee. 'Does Mum know?'

'Know what?'

'You've met up with an old flame – isn't that what they called them in your day?'

'It's nothing to do with your mum. She washed her hands of me years ago.' But Chris knew what Cassie meant. Although Gail wanted nothing to do with Chris, and paid little attention to Cassie, she still enjoyed the kudos of being the wife – albeit ex-wife – of the renowned Dt Christopher Thomas of CAT fame. She'd hate to give that up.

'Anyway, there's nothing to know. I hadn't seen Annie for over thirty years until we bumped into each other. It was when she was delivering the flowers Mum sent you.' Chris recalled his surprise, how time had stood still.

'She was here?' Cassie's voice rose.

'She volunteers at the hospital.'

'Definitely not like Mum.' Cassie chuckled at the idea of her mother doing anything that didn't further her career.

'Would you like me to read to you?' Chris wanted to bring this conversation to an end.

'Not today. I think I'll listen to some music.' Cassie fitted her earbuds. 'Why don't you go and see if you can find out when they're going to let me out of here?'

Feeling dismissed, Chris wandered out to enquire at the nurses' station who he needed to talk with.

*

The news was good. The member of the discharge planning team he'd been able to talk with had been optimistic Cassie would be discharged in a few days – as soon as the consultant was happy with her progress and they had developed a plan for her. But it left Chris with a problem. His motel might be comfortable, but wasn't suitable for someone like Cassie, who'd most likely be confined to a wheelchair initially, then be using crutches for a lengthy period. And there was his company back in Canada to consider.

With no real plan, he wandered out of the hospital and drove into town, intending to take time to think over a decent cup of coffee.

He was about to turn into the café when he noticed a real estate agency across the road and, curious what rentals might be available, he went over to take a look at the homes in the window.

Granite Springs Realty appeared to be a thriving business. To Chris's disappointment, most were for sale, with only a couple for rent. About to turn away, a sign at the edge of the window caught his eye. *Granite Springs Technology Park – now leasing.* Chris leant down to read the fine print. It appeared the park was a new development close to the university. It comprised a series of office and warehouse spaces and was touted as bringing Granite Springs into the twenty-first century. That made him chuckle. Everywhere else had been there for some time. But it was food for thought. Immediately Chris's mind started working overtime.

When he was seated in The Bean Sprout Café with a cup of coffee, he took out his phone, eager to find out more about this technology park. Entering Granite Springs Technology Park into Google brought up a website and several newspaper articles. Chris decided to read the newspaper articles first.

It appeared a young local developer called Danny Slater was behind the park and several other new developments on the outskirts of the town. From what Chris read, the young man was a mover and shaker, managing to obtain planning permission more rapidly than anyone expected. He was reported as likely to follow his father into local government.

Slater...the name rang a bell, but Chris knew there hadn't been anyone called Slater in his year at school. If this one was a native son, he must have been older.

He focussed on the articles again, then opened the website. It was professionally done, stated the office design was to be by *Forrest Interiors* who had already designed the interiors of display homes in a recent development as well as *The Springs*.

Chris's interest was sparked. The designer must be local. Granite Springs was certainly moving ahead if there was enough work for an interior designer. But it was the office space itself that caught Chris's attention. The openness of it appealed to him. It was light years away from the high-rise office block which housed CAT back home, but there was something about it... He wondered.

Finishing his coffee, Chris headed across the street and pushed open the door of Granite Springs Realty, before he could change his mind.

*

'Annie!' Chris smiled. 'This is Ann Baird,' Chris said to Cassie when Annie appeared in the doorway. She looked wonderful if somewhat forbidding, dressed in a smart navy suit with a white blouse. He guessed this was her work outfit. She certainly looked the consummate professional.

'Annie, this is my daughter, Cassie,' he said proudly.

'Hi, Cassie. We haven't met properly before now, but I remember seeing you at uni – in the Education office. I didn't know then you were the daughter of an old friend of mine.' She threw a smiling glance in Chris's direction. 'I'm so sorry this happened to you, to see you like this. But the staff are really good here. I'm sure they'll soon fix you up. I hope you're not in too much pain and will be able to go home soon.' There was a slight break in her voice. 'I brought you these.' She handed Cassie a box of chocolates.

'Ooh, thanks. My favourites,' Cassie said, eyeing the Ferrero Rocher in their distinctive crushed gold wrappings. 'Should I call you Ann, or Annie, or Ms Baird?' She chuckled. 'This is seriously weird.'

Ann's eyes met Chris's over Cassie's head, but he couldn't read their message.

'Ann will do,' she said. 'Annie is… was… a long time ago.'

'Okay.' Cassie seemed unperturbed, but Chris sensed tension emanating from Annie.

'Take a seat,' he said, gesturing to a second chair.

Ann went to the chair and perched on its edge as if ready to flee.

What could he say to help her relax? 'I was telling Cassie I visited a realtor today to find out about a Technology Park being developed up by the university. Did you know about it?'

'Yes. My cousin is designing the office interiors.'

'Your cousin? Your cousin is *Forrest Interiors*? I love what he's done with *The Springs*.'

Ann chuckled. 'Yes, *she's* very clever. Peta has only been in Granite Springs a short time, but she's managed to make her mark.'

Chris reddened. 'Sorry, I assumed...'

'Caught out, Dad.' Cassie giggled. 'But the Technology Park. You were going to tell me about it.'

'Yes. It occurred to me, that if I was going to be here for any length of time, I'd need to get some work done. I actually was planning to look for a house to rent, one which would cater for you when you're discharged.'

'No, Dad!' Cassie interrupted.

'No?'

'I can go back to the house I share with Deb, Jack and Miles in Small Street.' She blushed, perhaps realising this was the first Chris had heard of her sharing a house with Miles. Regardless, she ploughed on. 'I don't need to be mollycoddled. I'm not a child. I can look after myself. There's no need for you to stay.'

Embarrassed, Chris threw an apologetic glance at Annie. She didn't need to hear this argument. 'Sorry, but I've already made the decision, honey. I'm not leaving till I know you're back on two feet. I don't think a student house is the appropriate place for you to recuperate.'

'Why not? Deb's studying physio. She's the perfect housemate, and Jack and Miles are both strong enough to cart me around if necessary.' She giggled again, clearly enjoying the idea.

'Well, I don't know.' Chris furrowed his brow. He hadn't expected this.

'I think Cassie has a point,' Ann said.

Chris looked at her in surprise. What did she know about it?

'I've been working with young people like Cassie for many years now. I know how resilient they can be. I suspect she might recover better in familiar surroundings with her friends around her. Sorry, Gus.'

'Well, that's put me in my place.' Chris gave a wry grin.

'What did you call my dad?' Cassie's eyes widened.

'Gus. It's what...'

'I was always called Gus when I was growing up, Cassie. You know my full name. Gus is short for Angus. It was when I went to the States people started called me Chris and it stuck.'

'I can't imagine you being called Gus.' Cassie grinned. 'Gus and Annie – now Chris and Ann. It's as if you were both different people with different names. How weird.'

'It was a long time ago,' Ann said. 'Another lifetime.'

There was silence.

'Did you find a place to rent?' she asked Chris.

'Unfortunately, not. Looks like I'll be paying through the nose at the motel for the foreseeable future. Danny Slater didn't have anything remotely suitable. But I did make arrangements for some office space as soon as it's available.'

'I wonder,' Ann said.

Chris raised an eyebrow.

'It's just a thought. But Peta – my cousin – has recently moved in with her new partner, and I think the flat she was living in is still vacant. It's furnished. It's above The Bean Sprout Café.'

'The café in Main Street? That would be perfect. If you're sure you don't want to live with your old dad?' he asked Cassie.

Cassie shook her head. 'No way.'

'Who should I contact?' he asked Ann.

'I'll call Peta tonight. Her new partner is Frank who owns the café. I can let you know. Now, I need to get home. Lovely to meet you, Cassie. I hope you'll be well again soon.'

Chris followed her out, stopping outside the door. 'Thanks for coming. Though I'm not sure I'm so happy about you taking Cassie's side of the argument. I hope, now I'm going to be around for a bit, we can see more of each other.'

'Perhaps. I'll call you about the flat.' She slipped away before Chris could respond or say a proper goodbye.

Back in the room, Cassie was grinning. 'I was wrong, she said, 'Ms Baird – who you call Annie – isn't such a dragon after all. She's really quite nice, Dad. I approve.'

Chris was speechless.

Eighteen

Ann hurried out of the hospital, stopping only when she arrived at to her car. She wrenched open the door and sat there, her mind in a whirl. Gus was intending to stay around Granite Springs. He was even planning to set up an office here. And he wanted to see more of her.

She couldn't bring herself to fit her key into the ignition. Then she took a deep breath and tried to talk sense into herself. It didn't change anything. Even if Gus did stay until Cassie was mobile again, it didn't mean anything other than he was concerned for his daughter. It had been nice of him to want her to meet Cassie properly, but that was all.

Who was she kidding?

Deep down, Anne knew Gus wanted to try to rekindle their relationship. She knew it was what she wanted too. But she was afraid. She'd given her heart to him once, and it had taken her years to recover when it was broken. She was surely too old to risk it again. And how could she become involved with him without telling him about her pregnancy? But what if she did and it ruined things between them? She'd done that once already.

Ann took another deep breath wishing she hadn't mentioned Frank's flat. Now she needed to do something about it.

It was still light so, instead of driving straight home, Ann headed in the direction which would take her past the house Peta was living in with Frank Beattie.

'Auntie Ann!' Peta's granddaughter, Lily, opened the door to Ann and hugged her. 'Grandma didn't say you were coming tonight.'

'She doesn't know. Is she...?'

Lily didn't wait till she finished speaking. 'Grandma, it's Auntie Ann,' Lily yelled, turning to run back through the hallway, her footsteps echoing on the polished floor.

Smiling, Ann closed the door behind her. What a transformation! It was difficult to realise this this lively nine-year-old was the same girl as the shy withdrawn child who'd arrived in Granite Springs only a year ago.

'Ann!' Peta appeared and gave Ann a kiss on the cheek. 'What a lovely surprise. It's not like you to drop in. Is everything all right?' She frowned, making Ann aware how out-of-character it was for her to turn up unexpectedly. She was normally too organised to do that, preferring to plan her visits. The meeting with Gus must have affected her more than she realised.

'Ann. Good to see you.' Frank gave Ann a peck on the cheek as the two women reached the kitchen where he had been stirring something on the stove. 'You'll stay to dinner?'

'Oh, I didn't...'

'Please, Auntie Ann.' Lily hopped up and down at her side. 'I want to show you the new trick I taught Archie.'

'That cat!' Peta said.

Archie was an old cat which she and Lily had rescued when his elderly owner could no longer take care of him. They'd been living in the flat above the café at the time, and Peta had been doubtful about the wisdom of having a cat there. But, with Frank's encouragement, Lily had prevailed.

Hearing his name, the ginger cat sidled up to rub himself against Ann's legs. She looked down at him uncertainly. She was never sure about cats. But he didn't linger, padding off to settle in a basket in the corner.

'That's his new favourite place,' Lily said. 'He loves it here in Uncle Frank's house and there's a garden for him to play in when I'm at school.'

'That's nice.'

'You will stay to dinner?' Peta asked. 'Then you can tell us why you dropped in.'

'I can tell you now.' Ann took a seat at the kitchen table, which was already set for three.

Without waiting for Ann's answer, Peta added another setting. 'It's about your flat, Frank.'

Frank stopped what he was doing and wiped his hands on the black apron he was wearing. It was the one he usually wore in the café. 'The sauce will be fine for a few moments.' He came over to join Ann and Peta at the table. 'What about the flat?'

Now she'd begun, Ann wasn't sure how to continue. But she had promised Gus. 'It's like this. An old friend of mine arrived in town – his daughter was in an accident.'

'The Canadian student,' Peta prompted, nudging Frank with her elbow. 'You remember. She was on a motorbike.'

Frank appeared puzzled. 'How did you get involved?' he asked Ann.

'It's a long story. But the gist of it is, he's looking for somewhere to stay. He's at *The Springs* at the moment but doesn't want to stay in a motel for however long it takes Cassie to become mobile again.'

'But the flat would be no good for her. There are all those stairs,' Peta said, getting up and fetching a bottle of wine from the fridge and two glasses from a cupboard. Then she handed Frank a can of beer.

'It's just for Gus. Cassie refuses to go anywhere but the student share house she's been living in.'

'But…' Peta began.

'You've forgotten what young people are like,' Frank said, popping open the beer and taking a sip. 'Thanks, honey. I imagine Lucy will be just the same in a few years' time if not sooner,' he said, referring to his niece who lived with his former partner. 'She's living in a student hall at university in Canberra this year but is already making noises about being more independent.'

'I didn't have that problem with Joy. She stayed home till she married.' Peta's eyes clouded over at the memory of her daughter who'd died at the hands of her husband a year earlier.

'Anyway, you were asking about the flat. It's vacant, if that's what you wanted to know. I'd be happy to rent it out to this fellow. What did you say his name was?'

'Gus… Chris… Chris Thomas. He's a big name in the IT industry in Canada. And he's been talking to Danny Slater about office space in the new Technology Park.'

There, she'd managed to get through an explanation without giving too much away.

But her cousin wasn't easily fooled. 'He must be intending to stay around for quite a time if he's making all these plans.' She gave Ann a speculative look.

Damn! Ann now regretted telling Peta about her past. Now, she was no doubt putting two and two together and coming up with a result that was far from the truth.

Seeming to sense her discomfort, Frank jumped up. 'Dinner should be almost ready. I just have to pop the pasta into boiling water. Why don't you two take your wine through to the other room while I finish up here?'

'Good idea.' Peta picked up her glass, and Ann followed her through the house to settle in a comfortable armchair in a room which looked out onto the garden.

'You seem to have settled in here very well,' she said to Peta. 'And Lily looks happy.'

'Yes. Frank's been wonderful. I could never have imagined finding someone like him.' She smiled contentedly. 'But what about you? If this Chris is planning to be in Granite Springs for some time...?' She tilted her head to one side.

'He's not staying here for me.' Ann reddened, remembering his parting words.

'Are you sure meeting you again hasn't influenced his decision?'

'No!' But had it? Would he have been so eager to make such long-term plans if they hadn't met again? 'I don't think so,' she said weakly. 'He's very fond of his daughter.'

'Who, you say, is fiercely independent. What about the mother?'

'They're divorced and she seems to be caught up in some high-powered job.'

'So, you and he have talked about personal stuff.' There was a smug note in Peta's voice. 'Who was it who encouraged me to accept Frank's invitations, told me what a good man he was?'

'Did I?' Ann couldn't recall. But if she had, she'd certainly never have expected her advice to come back to bite her.

'You *are* going to see him again.'

'I'm not sure.' Ann sipped her wine, then stroked the rim of the glass with one finger. 'It's all too difficult, Peta. I'm not a teenager anymore. I've spent the past thirty-five years trying to forget how I felt when Gus left. I can't go through that again at my age. And he will leave again. His life isn't here.'

'But he's here now. It's an opportunity to…'

'To do what exactly? I don't think I want to find out.'

'Oh, hell, Ann. You only live once. This might be your last chance. Why don't you live dangerously for a change?'

There was a stunned silence.

'Sorry!' Peta apologised. 'I shouldn't have said that. I don't know where those words came from. It's your life and you must make up your own mind.' She paused. 'But I'd hate to see you miss out on happiness because you were too afraid to take a chance.' She bit her lip.

Ann didn't know what to say. She'd never seen Peta like this. She took a gulp of her wine, almost choking. Was Peta right? Was her habit of always taking the safe option, of avoiding anything that might hurt her, really a way of copping out, of avoiding life? Was this the woman her younger staff saw when they mocked her? She knew she was set in her ways, but was she living in a bubble of her own making?

'Dinner's ready.' Frank's cheerful face appeared in the doorway. 'Why are you both looking so serious?' he asked.

'No reason.' Ann shook her head.

During dinner, Lily kept them amused with tales of her two friends who were twins called Lottie and Livvy. The terrible trio, Frank called them, much to Lily's amusement.

Over coffee, when Lily had excused herself from the table, Peta asked Ann, 'What happened with the editor you were having dinner with? Frank said he saw you both at the Saint Patrick's Day parade last week. For someone who says she has no time for men in her life, you're certainly getting around.'

Ann blushed. 'Sam Walker is new to the town. He wanted company for the parade and wouldn't take no for an answer. There's nothing there to gossip about.' Though Ann did wonder how many others had seen them together as Frank had. Fortunately, the photo hadn't appeared in the paper. Sam proved to be a man of his word. But, having managed to stay under the radar for more than thirty years, it seemed the fates were conspiring to force her into the limelight.

Nineteen

It was surprisingly warm when Chris awakened on the day Cassie was to be discharged from hospital. Granite Springs was experiencing what, in Canada, would be called an Indian Summer. He went into the living room and peered out the window overlooking Main Street. He'd been living here, above the café, for almost a week now. It had been a good move and surprisingly easy to organise. He liked his landlord, Frank Beattie, and had met Ann's cousin and complimented her on her design at *The Springs*.

It was good to have a place of his own where he could spread out and cook for himself. He'd grown tired of the food in the hospital café and was glad to be able to come home and cook himself a meal. It was healthier too. He patted his still flat stomach. Maybe he should think of getting more exercise.

Annie had been as good as her word in talking with Frank and had called him next day. A visit to the café, followed by a quick tour of the flat and his mind was made up. It would provide him with a base for however long he needed it.

He hadn't heard from Annie since. He frowned, remembering her hesitation when he suggested seeing her again. He'd repeated it on the phone, inviting her for a meal, but she'd been evasive and said she'd let him know.

Now he wondered if she was ever going to agree to meet with him. Seeing Annie again had been a breath of fresh air, a reminder of a life without care. He could understand her reticence – almost. But what had she to lose? From what he'd seen, she'd made herself a good life here, but a lonely one. When he met her cousin, Peta had hinted she thought Annie was lonely.

Chris sighed. He couldn't do anything about it today, but he made up his mind to call her soon, and, if necessary, to insist they meet.

After a breakfast of eggs benedict washed down with coffee downstairs in the café – another advantage of this place was the amazing menu in The Bean Sprout, all cooked on the premises – Chris set off for the hospital. He was glad this would be his last trip there.

At the door of Cassie's room, Chris stopped in his tracks. It seemed to be filled with people.

'Dad! You can come in,' Cassie's lively voice greeted him. 'This is Miles. He just got back last night. Isn't it wonderful?'

'Dr Thomas.' A tall, skinny young man with a wispy beard, his blond hair tied back in an untidy bun, a wide grin on his face, held out his hand. 'Cassie's told me all about you.'

Mesmerised, Chris shook his hand.

'And these two are Deb and Jack.'

Chris turned to see another young man, this one with short dark hair, and a young woman, her cropped black hair sporting a bright pink streak. A large tattoo featuring what looked like drama masks was noticeable on one arm. This was the physio student who was going to take care of Cassie?

'Hi, Dr Thomas,' they chorused.

'We came to see if Cassie needed any help,' Deb said, 'and to bring her these.' She gestured to the two large red balloons similar to the one which had arrived with flowers after the accident.

Chris wondered what had happened to that one. He'd seen no sign of it in Cassie's room, or anywhere else on the ward.

'Aren't they great, Dad?'

Bemused, Chris nodded, unsure whether she was referring to the balloons or her friends.

'We'll get out of your hair, now. See you at the house, Cassie,' Deb said as she and Jack left.

Miles took longer, stopping to give Cassie a hug and throw a wary glace at Chris before following his friends.

When he was alone with Cassie again, Chris looked at his daughter.

She was flushed, her eyes bright. He hoped her visitors hadn't caused a setback. No, he was being stupid. The injury was to her leg. She was merely excited.

'What did you think of Miles, Dad? Isn't he the best?'

Chris cleared his throat. He had no impression of the boy at all, apart from his appearance. 'He seems very nice.'

'Isn't it great he got back in time for me to be discharged? And we're all going to the picnic races on Saturday. They can take turns to wheel me around.' She giggled.

One thing Chris was sure of was that the arrival of her friends had certainly cheered Cassie up. He wondered why they hadn't visited before.

'It's perfect timing,' Cassie said, answering his unspoken question, 'Jack and Deb have been out of town. He's an IT student and they had a field trip to Sydney, and Deb had a prac placement in Canberra. And, before you say anything, I knew they'd be back in time.'

'Right.'

Cassie had forestalled him again. She was good at that.

'Have you heard from Mum?' he asked.

Her ebullience withered. 'No. Not since those ghastly flowers. One of the nurses showed them to me and I told her to take them away – and the balloon. I didn't feel like it then. It's different today. I'm celebrating. The gang understands. Have you spoken to her?'

'Not lately. I have been calling to give her updates on your progress, but not since we had a discharge date.'

'I bet she wasn't interested.' There was the hint of moisture in the corner of Cassie's eye. She shook her head as if to shake away her disappointment.

Poor Cassie. She rarely mentioned her mother to Chris, but he suspected she missed her. He cursed the woman he'd been married to. How much would it take for her to express an interest in her own daughter? Gail was lucky to have her.

'She's busy,' he said weakly.

'I know.'

'The next edition,' they said in unison, bringing a smile to Cassie's face.

There was a gentle knock on the door and Marilyn appeared with a sheaf of paperwork. 'Can I come in?'

'Hi, Marilyn, good to see you,' Chris said.

'Can I get dressed and go now?' Cassie asked, her eyes brimming with excitement.

'Soon. I'm just waiting for the final documents to arrive then you're good to go. You can get dressed now. Would you like some help?'

'No, I think I can manage. Dad's here if I come unstuck. Right, Dad?'

'Right.' But her words made Chris wonder who'd be helping her once she was back in her accommodation. She'd said Deb would be there to help. But would it be her or Miles who'd be her first port of call? He chewed on the inside of his cheek at the realisation his daughter wasn't his little girl any longer. She was a grown woman with every right to her own life. But the thought she might be – probably was – sleeping with the long-haired youth he'd recently met, took a bit of getting used to.

Finally, they were ready. All the documentation had arrived, along with a wheelchair and a pair of crutches.

'I've been practicing with them, Dad,' Cassie assured him when he looked surprised, 'but they're a bit hard to manage at the moment. That's why I need the wheelchair, too. The hospital physio said it'll get easier with the rehab sessions. She's given me a timetable, the first one is next Tuesday. It'll be the wheelchair for me till then.'

'Okay, let's go.'

With Chris pushing the wheelchair, the crutches lying on Cassie's lap, they made their way down in the lift and out to the car park.

'It's so great to feel the fresh air on my face.' Cassie closed her eyes and tipped her face up to the sun. 'Gosh, it's warm. Isn't it supposed to be autumn?'

'It is, but Granite Springs often surprises us.' Chris could remember days like this in his youth, in years when Easter came early, and it still felt almost like summer. 'Now let's get you into the car.'

It was a difficult manoeuvre, but between them, they managed it, and Chris stowed the chair and crutches away in the boot. Soon they were on their way.

*

The house in which Cassie and her friends were living wasn't at all what Chris expected. He'd lived in university halls in his own student days, eager to be home every weekend to see Annie. But he'd had many friends who shared houses and was familiar with the dilapidated construction and clutter which seemed typical of them.

Cassie's temporary home was quite the opposite. Following her directions, he drove out towards the university to stop outside a low set bungalow which couldn't be more than ten years old.

Cassie chuckled at his surprise. 'What did you expect? Some rundown shack? It actually belongs to Deb's aunt. She used to live here but moved away just as Deb started uni. It's really perfect, a lot better than most of the guys have to put up with. I was lucky to see their ad soon after I arrived. The campus accommodation sucks.'

Inside was another surprise. Unless they'd had a special clean-up in anticipation of his arrival, Cassie's housemates were among the tidiest group of young people Chris had come across.

There were cheers when he wheeled her inside and into the open kitchen, helped by all three of her housemates.

'You'll join us for lunch, sir?' Miles asked, surprising Chris again with his manners.

'Thanks. Call me Chris,' he said, embarrassed. He must seem an old fogey to these kids. To be called *sir* made him feel ancient.

He was curious to learn more about this group of people who were Cassie's friends and about whom she said very little in her emails and calls. He remembered being vaguely concerned when she told him she'd moved off campus, but she'd reassured him it was all above board, and she was happier in her new accommodation.

Lunch was a very cheerful affair, the cheese flan and salad a far cry from his own student days, though Deb did mention it was courtesy of a bakery by the river, no doubt the one where he'd enjoyed breakfast that Sunday. For the most part, the conversation related to campus politics, which held no interest for Chris, but he did learn Cassie's three housemates were in their final years of study, which made them a year older than her.

Lunch was almost over when the subject of the Technology Park came up. It appeared there was some disagreement in town about the benefit of what many called an eyesore. The group's opinion was divided, Jack being in favour, seeing it as a huge step forward, and Deb and Miles thinking it was an unnecessary development.

'What about you, Dr Thomas – sorry, Chris?' Jack asked. 'Surely with your background you'd see this sort of park as the future?'

'Dad's taking space in it.' Cassie didn't wait for Chris to respond. 'And it looks as if I'm the only one here who doesn't have an opinion. I can't see it matters.'

To Chris's amusement, there was vigorous disagreement from both Jack and Miles, while Deb just smiled at their fervour. It reminded him what life was like as a student. Every issue seemed so important. It was only as you got older, you were able to sort out the wheat from the chaff and decide which ones merited your time and effort.

When the debate slackened, Jack asked, 'Are you intending to set up a subsidiary here, Chris? I'd be very interested.'

'Dad didn't come here to give you a job,' Cassie remonstrated.

'No, I just need somewhere to work while I'm here. It seemed a good option.' But Jack's question had merit. It gave Chris food for thought. To date he hadn't expanded the CAT offices outside of Canada. Although he had been considering other sites, Australia had never been in his sights – too many memories. But now he was here, now he'd met Annie again, it was a different story. 'But you never know, Jack,' he said. 'It's always a possibility.'

The discussion turned to Easter and the picnic races to be held on Saturday. The group were going, along with other friends, and planned to take part in the traditional picnic in the car park.

'You'll come, too, won't you, Dad?' Cassie asked. 'I've never been to a race meeting and this one sounds such fun. Did you go when you lived here?'

'Yes.' So many times. The races were a Granite Springs institution. He wondered if Annie continued to attend the picnics after he left. There was no reason for her to stop. 'But I'm not sure you want an old fogey like me with you.'

'Of course we do,' Miles said with a smile, forcing Chris to agree.

'I think I'd like to lie down now,' Cassie said, pushing her chair away from the table.

'I'll help.' Chris started to rise.

'I've got it.' Miles moved towards Cassie's chair and, slipping his arms around her slim figure, picked her up to carry her gently out of the kitchen, her arms around his neck.

Chris watched their progress with a sense of loss. He could see how much Miles cared for her – an affection which Cassie reciprocated. It made him feel envious – not of Miles' feelings for his daughter, but for what he and Annie had lost.

Twenty

Chris had forgotten the excitement engendered by the annual picnics, though these Easter ones were an innovation. He soon found himself caught up in the memory of coming to the races, first with his parents, then with his mates, and in later years with Annie.

At first it was fun to see the event through the eyes of the younger generation. But, as some members of the group became more boisterous, he wandered off, preferring to be alone with his memories.

He was deciding whether to risk placing a bet when he saw a familiar figure walking towards him.

Annie raised her eyes at the same time as he noticed her. She looked as if she was about to veer off in another direction. Chris quickened his pace.

'Hello, Annie. Brings back old times?'

She appeared flustered. 'I haven't been to the picnics for years. I've been to have a look at the horses.'

'Which ones do you recommend?' Chris remembered Annie had always had a good eye for horseflesh. Despite being what they called *a townie*, she could pick out a winner nine times out of ten.

'Oh,' she laughed, 'I haven't picked a winner in years. But...' her expression became serious, '...I did like the look of Swanky Lady and Silveroo.'

'Good enough for me. I was about to place a bet, then head for the stand. Join me?'

Ann looked around as if seeking somewhere to go, someone to save her from agreeing, then gave in. 'Okay.'

Seated in the stand, their thighs touching, surrounded by noisy racegoers, it was just like old times. 'Remember?' Chris nudged Ann.

She nodded, somewhat reluctantly, he thought.

'They were good times.'

She nodded again.

'Look, Annie…' Chris knew this wasn't the time or place for this discussion, but he'd put it off long enough. '…I'm not sure why you're being so offhand with me. Sure, I was the one to leave, but I wanted you with me. I waited for a letter, for you to say you'd changed your mind, that your mother was fine, you'd made a mistake. Any of those.' He was interrupted by a couple squeezing past. Undeterred, he continued. 'I'm sorry I didn't write.' He drew a hand through his hair. 'I guess my pride got in the way. But I waited. It wasn't till I gave up hope that I moved to Canada and I accepted I needed to make a life for myself. And in Canada I met Gail. End of story.'

He glanced at Annie out of the corner of his eye to see her gazing down at her hands. Summoning up all his courage, Chris took her hands in his. 'Annie, won't you give me another chance?' He held his breath.

She looked up, the glimmer of a smile on her face.

*

Ann couldn't help being moved by Gus's words. He'd suffered too. Him and his blasted pride! What if things had been different, if he had written? Would anything have changed?

She looked into his eyes, the crowds surrounding them disappearing. 'I was hurt, too. I wanted to join you, to start our new life together, but… I couldn't leave. You do see that, don't you?'

'I do now, but I was young and in love. At the time, all I could see was your refusal to come with me, your decision to put your family before our future. So, yes, I was angry, so angry I left without saying goodbye. I'm sorry.'

A lock of his hair had fallen over his forehead. Ann itched to touch it, to feel the texture of his hair in her fingers again. She stifled the thought, the memory of how it used to feel, how he used to feel.

'I'm sorry too.' Ann wasn't sure what she meant. Was she sorry for his anger, for her decision? If she had to do it over again her choice would be the same, even though she knew the heartache it would bring, the empty years, the loss of her child – *their* child. The familiar pang hit her, almost making her gasp.

'So, a new start?'

Ann realised Gus was still holding her hands, his warm grasp bringing flashes of the past: of walks by the river, holding hands, of youthful lovemaking, deep kisses and…

The noise around them changed, forcing both to look up. The race had finished, and people were moving, chattering loudly, eager to collect their winnings or drown their sorrows.

'I wonder who won.' Ann tried to sound calm, while emotion threatened to overwhelm her.

'Who cares? I asked you a question. Annie?'

Those happier memories were replaced by what Ann had always saw as the aftermath; her arid life; the lonely evenings; the ache she felt seeing other happy couples. Could she become part of that, if even for a short time? Could she bear to enjoy the happiness Gus offered, then have it taken away again? Could she bear to take the risk? And should she tell him about her miscarriage and risk losing him again?

She thought of Fran, of Peta, of the advice they'd offered. They were right about one thing. She wasn't getting any younger. Maybe it was time to throw caution to the winds. 'I'm willing to give it a try if you are,' she said, only to feel his hands release hers. Then his arms were around her and their lips met.

It was as if time stood still. How could she have forgotten the softness of Gus's lips on hers, the way her body responded to his to touch, the twist in her gut, the ache of wanting more?

'We should celebrate,' Gus said, when they finally separated. 'I believe I heard something about a champagne bar. What do you think?' His boyish eagerness was so reminiscent of the younger Gus, Ann couldn't help but laugh. It was as if they'd gone back in time, as if they were both seventeen and carefree again.

In the champagne bar, they were jostled by other racegoers as they tried to find a space, eventually settling for a corner by a full-length window. Gus put his arm around Ann's shoulder to prevent her being crushed. It made her feel protected, safe, something she hadn't felt for years, hadn't known she was missing.

They smiled at each other over their second glasses of sparkling wine.

'Won't your party be wondering where you are?' Ann asked, when she'd taken a first sip.

'Cassie and her crew? They've probably forgotten all about me. It was a mad idea to come with them, but Cassie was insistent. And I'm glad I did.' He bent down to drop a kiss on her forehead. 'Did you come with Susie?'

'No way.' Ann chortled at the idea of her sister including her. 'I don't fit in with her friends. I never have, but it's worse since she and Adrian came back from England. She's decided to mix with the country set. The only times I'm invited is when she's trying to matchmake. That's where I met Sam Walker – at one of Susie's dinner parties.'

'Sam Walker. The editor.' Gus dropped his arm.

Ann shivered as her warm protective shield disappeared. Why did she have to mention Sam?

'Seeing a lot of him, are you?' Gus's voice was stiff. It was as if their earlier embrace had never happened.

'No.' But why should she have to explain herself? She'd managed to deflect Sam's calls and texts since St Patrick's Day, hoping he'd get the message when she said she was busy. 'We've only met a couple of times. There's no need to…' Her voice trailed off. Why did she assume Gus was jealous? He was the one who had married. And she was willing to bet he hadn't led a squeaky-clean life since his divorce.

'Sorry.' Gus took a gulp of wine, then drew a hand through his hair. 'Now I've met you again, Annie, I can't bear to think of you with anyone else. I know I have no right. It's been over thirty years. But, holding you, kissing you, it's as if it was yesterday.'

'For me, too.' Ann reached up to push back the lock of hair that always fell onto his forehead. It was such an intimate thing to do, almost more intimate than their kiss. It felt good.

The crowd moved, pushing them closer together. They were in danger of spilling their drinks, and the noise of voices was growing unbearable. Ann thought she could hear Susie's voice in the clamour.

'Let's get out of here.' Gus drained his glass and held out his hand for Ann's.

Ann quickly emptied hers and gave it to him.

Taking her hand, Gus pulled her through the crush, depositing their empty glasses on a table on the way. 'Phew!' he sighed as they reached the outside of the building. 'How did you get here?'

'I came with Peta and Frank and another couple.'

'So you don't have a car?'

Ann shook her head, fumbling in her bag for her phone. 'I can call them, find out where they are.' She peered around, unable to see anyone she recognised.

'Text them. Tell them you're making your own way back. My car's over there.' He pointed to the car park which was beginning to empty.

It seemed the races were over, despite the champagne bar still being full of merry drinkers. Ann thought the group she came with would probably be there till late in the evening. She hesitated for only a moment before texting Peta.

Don't wait for me. Found a ride home. Talk soon. Ann

As she closed her phone, Ann realised this was the first spontaneous action she'd taken in years. Gus had influenced her to make the change Fran and Peta had been urging her to make. She hoped she wouldn't regret it.

Twenty-one

Ann gazed around the flat. It had changed since Peta and Lily lived here. Papers were strewn around, there was a laptop open on the coffee table, which also held several empty mugs.

'Sorry.' Gus hurried to pick up the mugs and stack the papers into some sort of order. 'I wasn't expecting to bring home a guest.' He stood in the middle of the room looking lost.

Ann took pity on him. 'Give me those.' She took the mugs and carried them into the kitchen which to her relief was spotless. Gus wasn't a complete slob, then. When he'd asked, 'Your place or mine?' in the car, she'd hesitated too long, and they'd ended up here. She had to admit she was curious to see how he lived.

Gus followed her into the kitchen. 'Another glass of wine?'

'I don't think so. I'm not accustomed to drinking in the middle of the day.' Did she sound too virtuous, too sanctimonious? Ann's head was beginning to spin. She needed to lie down. But she wasn't at home. She tottered, putting one hand on the back of a chair to maintain her balance, the other to her forehead.

'Whoops!' Gus was at her side in an instant. 'Looks to me as if the champagne has gone to your head. Let me make you a cup of coffee.'

'No thanks, I'm feeling a bit woozy. Perhaps…' she slumped against him.

'Why don't you have a rest while I catch up on some work. We can have a bite to eat later.'

Reluctantly, Ann agreed and allowed herself to be led into the bedroom. Unlike when Peta lived here, the room now definitely displayed a male influence. There was a copy of an Ian Rankin novel on the bedside table along with a pair of dark-rimmed spectacles and a handful of change, and a freshly ironed shirt was hanging on the back of the door. When she lay down, and Gus left, gently closing the door behind him, she could distinguish the scent of his aftershave mixed with a sharp soapy aroma on the pillow. It hadn't changed. The Old Spice fragrance took her back to her past. Her phone pinged and, taking it from her pocket, Ann read the text from Peta.

Fran saw you with a man. Chris? Go for it! Px

Ann grimaced, then smiled and closed her eyes.

*

It was dark when Ann opened her eyes again. Startled, it took her a few moments to remember where she was. She was about to rise when she realised she wasn't alone. Gus was lying beside her. He was awake and holding an iPad. He had earbuds in his ears. When she stirred, he put down the device and pulled out the earbuds.

'You're awake,' he said, grinning at her.

'So it seems.' How long had he been there? Had he been watching her sleep?

'Oh, Annie! I've missed you.' Placing the iPad on the bedside table, Gus pulled her into his warm arms.

Although still half-asleep, Ann felt as if she belonged there. The emotions she'd experienced at the racetrack returned, only this time, there was no crowd of racegoers to protect her. She sank into his embrace, all the inhibitions of the last thirty years disappearing as she gave herself up to the passion which flared between them.

What seemed like hours later, the pair disentangled their limbs to lie side-by-side on the queen-sized bed. Ann had no idea how they managed to shed their clothes, to be lying here naked, having rekindled the passion of their younger years, a passion she thought she'd never experience again.

'Wow, Annie! You've still got it!' Gus propped himself up on one elbow and gazed down into her eyes.

'You, too. It was as if…'

'…we were in our twenties again,' he finished. 'As if the years between never happened, as if we were at the beginning of our life together. Only a few days ago, I was afraid I'd lost all this. Can you believe I actually felt envious of Cassie and her Miles, of what they had together – after I recovered from the fact he was sleeping with my daughter.' He chuckled and stroked a strand of hair from Ann's forehead. 'And all the time, you were here, waiting.'

Not exactly, Ann thought, but didn't correct him. 'What time is it?' she struggled to move, hampered by Gus's body which she was tempted to snuggle into again.

'Does it matter?'

Ann had no reply. When they were in their teens and twenties, every second she and Gus spent together was a bonus to be treasured. But for the past thirty-five years, Ann had lived her life by the clock. There was a time to rise, to go to work, to go to bed, carefully arranged mealtimes and meetings with friends and family meticulously organised. She'd forgotten that other world where time had no meaning. She fell back against the pillows again.

'Hungry?' Gus leant his chin on her head.

Ann could feel his lips in her hair. She could smell his unique aroma, the aftershave and soapy fragrance much stronger than it had been on the pillow. She shuddered as a wave of desire engulfed her.

Was she really here? Was Ann Baird really in bed with Gus Thomas? Was she heading for another heartbreak? For a wild moment she didn't care, as long as she could feel his body close to hers again.

Then, Ann's innate common sense took over as she remembered Gus's question and realised she was hungry. 'Yes,' she murmured, reaching up to tangle her fingers in his hair. It felt just as she remembered – thick and springy.

With a quick kiss on her hair, Gus leapt up, surprising Ann. 'I can make a mean omelette, and I think there's the makings of a salad in the fridge. I've had to cater for myself for the past few years and haven't done too badly. So Cassie tells me.' He grinned, pulling on the pants which were lying on the floor.

Ann saw her own garments lying there too. She had a vague memory of throwing them off. Had she really behaved so wantonly? 'Sounds good,' she said, weakly, pulling up the sheet to cover her nakedness. Now they were awake, and Gus was dressing, she felt at a disadvantage.

'You don't need to do that.' Gus came over to kiss her. 'You're still as beautiful as I remember. My beautiful Annie.' He kissed her again, making her limbs turn to water. Then he left the bedroom, leaving Ann to remember how it had felt to make love with Gus, something she thought she'd never experience again.

The aroma of fried onions forced Ann to rise and dress. Wearing her pants and shirt, she picked up her jacket and wandered into the kitchen to see Gus at the stove, his open shirt hanging outside his pants, his hair still dishevelled from their love making. He looked more like the young Gus she remembered than the well-heeled fifty-something owner of an internationally renowned company.

Although she wanted to stand behind him and clasp her arms around his waist as she'd have done all those years ago, Ann carefully hung her jacket over the back of a chair. 'Can I do anything to help?' she asked.

'You'll find salad stuff in the fridge. Maybe you could cut up some lettuce and tomatoes and anything else that's there?'

Ann opened the fridge to discover it was well-stocked. Another surprise. Gus was full of surprises.

It was close to nine o'clock when they finished eating the delicious omelette. Ann refused the wine Gus offered, deciding she'd had sufficient alcohol for one day.

'I should go home,' she said, as Gus began to load the dishwasher.

Gus stopped what he was doing and looked up. 'Stay!'

It was so comfortable here, like playing house, but Ann resisted the idea even though the thought of waking up with Gus next morning did have a lot of appeal. She knew she couldn't stay overnight. Tomorrow was Easter Sunday and she'd promised to go to a barbecue at Fran and Owen's. Peta and Frank would be there, too, along with Marie and Drew and their two teenagers. She needed time alone to prepare herself.

'No, I need to get back, tomorrow…'

'I thought we might go on a picnic – like we used to.'

Ann was torn. She had loved their picnics; time spent by the river or in the bush; time away from everyone else; time when they could relax and pretend they were the only people in the world. But she'd made a commitment. And Fran and Peta would already be wondering about her and Gus after her abrupt exit from the races. 'It does sound lovely,' she said, 'but I've agreed to attend a friend's barbecue. I can't change my mind now. Fran and Owen are expecting me. What would they think?'

'The same old Annie, always worried about what others might think. For a time, I wondered if you'd only stayed to look after your mother to still the gossips.'

'What! You didn't?'

'Only fleetingly. Then common sense prevailed. I knew how your mum was. It was bad luck, but I guess deep down I respected your decision.' He drew a hand through his hair. 'I don't know if I could have been so selfless, if it had been my mum. Well, if you're determined to leave, I'll drive you home.'

'I can walk.'

'No. I don't want you walking the streets of Granite Springs alone in the dark.'

'I'd be…' Ann started to say, then stopped, noticing the determined expression in Gus's eyes. It was rather nice to have someone worried for her safety, even if she was in no danger. 'Okay, thanks.'

In the event, Ann was glad of the ride home. There were a few revellers in the streets – probably students on their way to or from a party. It felt good to sit in the Subaru Forester Gus had hired, his hand on her thigh, the radio playing old tunes in a low tone. It was almost like old times, though back then, the car had been an old rattler, and the music had been played at full blast.

'Annie!' As soon as the car stopped, Gus turned towards her and took her face in his hands. 'Don't hide away from me again. Let's make this our new start. I don't know how we're going to manage things, but I still feel for you the way I always have. I love you, Annie Baird, and I want you to love me again, too.' He kissed her soundly on the lips., then opened the door and almost pushed her out of the car. 'Seriously, Annie, if you don't go now, I won't be able to let you go at all. I'll call you tomorrow, and make sure you answer this time.'

He drove off, leaving Ann gazing after him, a smile on her face. She looked up at the moon – waning but still visible – at the stars bright in the clear night sky, and hugged the knowledge of their lovemaking to herself.

Twenty-two

The Subaru's tyres squealed as Chris drove off along the deserted street. He hated to leave Annie like this after what they'd shared. He had to respect her decision – just as he had before – though this one wasn't likely to have such dramatic consequences. He hummed along to the music on the radio, feeling pleased with himself and with life in general. No! It was more than that. A whole lot more.

He hadn't intended to fall into bed with Annie. He'd been at a loose end when she went to lie down, unable to settle to anything. Then it had occurred to him to join her in the bedroom, for company – or that's what he told himself, refusing to admit his desire to feel close to her.

He'd opened up ABC iView on his iPad, intending to catch up on some documentaries he'd heard of, and his eyes were starting to close when Annie opened hers. It had all happened so naturally. He didn't regret it for a moment. He hoped Annie didn't either.

As he drove along, he relived the sensation of Annie's skin, of her body next to his, of… He shuddered at the surge of desire threatening to overwhelm him and bit the inside of his cheek. It was true what he told Annie. He was still in love with her. But he hoped he hadn't scared her off. She'd been keen to leave after their meal when he'd hoped to take her back to bed.

The Annie he'd made love with had seemed to morph back into the Annie he'd met in the hospital – an Annie who was her own woman, a far cry from the Annie he'd first fallen in love with. But what had he expected? To come back after over thirty years and find her unchanged, to be able to pick up where they left off? He'd changed, Granite Springs had changed. How could he expect Annie to remain the same?

But, he realised, he had expected exactly that. When he discovered she still lived here, had never married, it was as if he'd been given a second chance. And he didn't intend to screw up this time.

Chris had no idea how things would pan out. He had no master plan. He only knew he didn't intend to leave Annie a second time. Whether she came back to Canada with him, or he remained here in Granite Springs, they'd be together. He hadn't fully considered the possible implications of either outcome. But he was confident he'd work it out in time. That's what he did – work things out. He'd made his fortune doing exactly that in his chosen field. Surely, he could make it work in his personal life, too?

*

Church bells wakened Chris next morning. It was Easter Sunday. He stretched out in bed, the events of the previous evening still fresh in his mind, as was his dream of Annie. It was difficult to believe it hadn't *all* been a dream, that Annie had been right here in his bed. He grinned to himself, wishing he could spend today with her, spend every day with her. Then he gave himself a shake. He knew he had to treat Annie carefully, lest she shy away again.

Chris lay there, luxuriating in the memory of their time together then, as he now did every morning, he picked up his phone to call Cassie. Perhaps he could spend the day with her, maybe go for a drive. There wouldn't be much happening in Granite Springs on Easter Sunday.

'Dad, it's early!' Cassie exclaimed when she finally answered her phone. 'What's up? Where did you get to yesterday?'

Chris checked the time. It was close to nine o'clock. Surely a respectable enough time to call, even on a Sunday. 'You guys seemed to be having a good time by yourselves, so I wandered off. I bumped into an old friend.'

'An old friend as in old girlfriend? Did you team up with Ann Baird?'

He should have known Cassie would guess. 'I did. We put a bet on a couple of horses, had a glass of champagne...' No need for her to know any more. 'I wondered what you were up to today.'

Cassie yawned. 'The guys are organising a barbecue. They're doing all the work, so I can sit in my chair and be a lady of leisure. It'll be good to see some of the old gang again, I've missed them. We're all going on a picnic tomorrow, too. Out to the dam.'

'Oh!'

Cassie must have sensed his disappointment, because she added, 'You're welcome to come along.'

It was good of Cassie to invite him, but Chris remembered how superfluous he'd felt with the group of young people at the races the day before, sure those feelings would be multiplied at the barbecue. 'Thanks, honey, but I'll pass. You feeling okay?'

'Sure. Remember I have my first rehab session on Tuesday. You'll come with me?' There was a tentative note in her voice indicating she still needed his support for some things.

'Wouldn't miss it. Pick you up at nine?'

'Thanks, Dad.'

He hung up, the two days yawning empty before him. Maybe he could fill them with work. He had a key to the office space he'd leased from Danny Slater, but hadn't moved in, having decided to wait till after Easter. But, with no one to spend it with, the holiday weekend was just like any other two days for him.

But the thought of spending the next two days alone didn't sit well. He wanted... he wanted to see Annie again. Before he could talk himself out of it, he picked up his phone again.

Annie chuckled when she heard his voice. 'Good morning to you, too,' was her response to his hesitant greeting.

He breathed a sigh of relief. There was no sign of regret in her voice. He decided to be honest. 'I can't stop thinking of you, Annie,' he said in a rush. 'I know you're busy today, but what about tomorrow? You didn't seem averse to the idea of a picnic. I should have thought of it last night.' He held his breath and waited for her reply.

'That sounds lovely, Gus. I do remember our picnics.'

For a moment he visualised her sitting by the riverbank wearing his shirt over a miniscule bikini and laughing at something he'd said, her eyes brimming with delight. The vision faded.

He sighed. 'Me too, Annie. Pick you up at ten?'

'Sounds good.'

Chris clasped his phone when the call finished. It had been easy. Why had he worried about Annie's reaction? Now he only had to fill in today and work out what he had in his fridge and pantry that would constitute appropriate food for a picnic. Sandwiches seemed like a good option.

Feeling the need to work off excessive energy, Chris decided to go for a run. He'd intended to get into some form of regular exercise after the days spent sitting in Cassie's hospital room, but the opportunity hadn't presented itself till now. He remembered an old running track along the riverbank towards the outskirts of town and, donning a pair of shorts and a tee-shirt, and slipping on his Converse runners, he set off.

*

It felt good to be pounding along the well-worn path, accompanied only by a group of ducks swimming along and the occasional flock of galahs or corellas flying past with their unique cries. How could he have forgotten the raucous call of the Australian birds, so different from their Canadian counterparts? It was as if he was the only person in this part of the world.

Until he stopped for a rest.

He was bending over, hands on his knees, taking deep breaths, when he heard another set of feet coming towards him from the opposite direction.

The man stopped. 'Hello, Chris.' He reached out his hand.

'Nick.'

The men shook hands.

'How's Cassie? I've been meaning to be in touch.' Nick pulled on his beard. 'I heard she's out of hospital.'

'Discharged last Monday and back living in her share house. She still has a way to go, rehab and so on, but she's keen to get back to uni after the holidays.'

'Well, we'll make it as easy for her as we can. Glad to hear she's on the mend. But what about you? You're still here.'

'I intend to stay till she's fully recovered. Though, now she's out of hospital, it seems she has less time for her old dad.'

'Don't I know it. I have one just like her. Parents are useful when they want something, otherwise we can just get in the way. I can understand your feelings. You're spending today with her?'

'She and her housemates are having a barbecue. I was invited, but the thought of another afternoon with a group of twenty-year-olds intent on getting drunk didn't have a lot of appeal. I had enough of that yesterday at the races.'

'You were there? Pity we didn't connect. Look, I know this is pretty last-minute. We're having a couple of friends around for a barbecue today – yes, I know, another barbecue. It sometimes seems as if we Aussies don't know any other way to entertain. Why don't you join us? I guarantee no twenty-year-olds – our kids are doing their own thing – and one more won't make any difference to Kay. It would be good to get to know you better. I've been reading up about the work you've been doing. It fascinates me.'

Chris had been going to refuse until Nick mentioned his work. He'd missed talking about his pet projects and would welcome the opportunity for some intelligent company. 'Thanks. I'd like that.'

'Drop by around twelve. We're very informal. See you then.' Nick ran on the spot for a few moments before heading off.

*

There was only one other car parked outside the Kerr home when Chris drove up. He was relieved. He didn't think he could cope with meeting a large group of strangers. As he stepped out of the car, a silver Honda CR-V backed out of the neighbouring driveway and the passenger waved to him. He blinked, recognising Marie from The Bean Sprout Café.

Nick Kerr answered the door almost before Chris took his hand off the bell. 'Thought I heard a car,' he said with a grin. 'We're out in the back. Come through.'

Chris followed him through the house to the backyard. Kay Kerr and two others were seated around a large wooden table looking out onto a manicured lawn surrounded by flowering shrubs and bushes. A state-of-the-art barbecue sat to one side.

Kay rose to greet him. 'Hi, Chris. Glad to see you. Nick said he bumped into you earlier. I'm glad to hear Cassie is on the mend.' She turned to the two strangers, both appeared to be of the same vintage as Kay. 'This is Chris Thomas. He's from Canada. His daughter is one of our Canadian exchange students. She was in an accident. Chris, these are good friends of ours, Jo and Col Ford.'

The elegant silver-haired woman smiled. 'I heard about the student who took a tumble on her bike. I hope your daughter is making a good recovery.'

'Yes, thanks.' Chris shook her hand, then turned to her grey-haired husband to do the same.

'Good to meet you, Chris,' Col said. 'Your first time in this part of the world?'

'Actually, I was born here.' Chris took the seat Col had pulled out beside him and accepted a beer from Nick.

'Really?' Jo peered at him. 'I don't think I can remember a Chris Thomas, but you'd have been younger than our crowd. Isn't it odd how we remember those above us in school, but not those younger?'

Col was wrinkling his forehead. 'Thomas,' he said, tapping the table with his forefinger. 'Did your folks live out Monkton Way? Farmers?'

'They did. Hugh and Jan Thomas.'

'Got it!' Col slapped the table. 'They were Gordon's clients, but I remember them coming to the office. Sheep property, wasn't it?' He didn't wait for a reply. 'We were a pretty new practice at the time. You didn't come back for the funeral?'

'No, to my regret. Things...' Why should he have to explain himself? Who was Col Ford?

Jo put a hand on her husband's arm. 'Col was a local solicitor until he retired a few years ago. His partner still has the practice. Gordon Slater.'

'Any relation to Danny Slater?'

'His father. Danny's my son, too. I won't try to explain that now.' She chuckled seeing Chris's puzzled expression.

Chris took a gulp of beer. This barbecue was proving more surprising than he'd anticipated, and he'd only just arrived. He did have a vague recollection of receiving communications from his parents' solicitors. That must have been Col Ford's firm – and this Gordon Slater. It had been a long time ago.

'So,' Col said. 'First time back in the old town? You must see some changes.'

'Not too many,' Chris was glad of the change of subject. 'I'd expected more developments. But the Technology Park is a good move. Your son has his finger on the pulse of where the future of a town like Granite Springs lies,' he said to Jo.

'Do you think so?' Jo asked. 'He's come up against a lot of opposition. But that's never stopped Danny.' She sighed and picked up her glass of wine.

'Chris is an expert in IT,' Nick explained. 'He owns a software company in Canada – a world leader in Computer Aided Design, Computer Based Instruction and Artificial Intelligence.'

'You've lost me there.' Col chuckled. 'You must have good staff if you can take time off like this.'

'They're a good crew, and very dedicated. But...' he wondered if he should confide in this group, but given the connection with Danny Slater, they'd no doubt find out anyway, '...I've leased office space from Danny. In the Technology Park,' he added, seeing Jo's puzzled expression. 'I'm thinking of setting up a permanent office here.'

'Here in Granite Springs?' It was Kay who spoke this time. 'Why here? If you wanted an Australian base surely Sydney or Melbourne would be a more attractive prospect?'

All four were looking at him expectantly.

Damn, why had he started this?

He leant forward, elbows on the table. 'Danny's Technology Park is the ideal setting. It's close to the university, which has a good school of Computer Science, producing keen graduates, and Granite Springs is close to Canberra and the politicians which can only be of benefit to a venture like mine.'

And close to Annie Baird, he thought but didn't say aloud. He remembered both Nick and Kay knew Ann well, saw her every day.

'Right. Sounds like a good plan. Well, it must be time to throw a few steaks on. The barbie's been heating up nicely.' Nick went inside the house to return with a platter of large, dripping, marinated steaks which he proceeded to place on the grill.

While the steaks were cooking, Jo asked Chris about his years growing up in Granite Springs, trying unsuccessfully to find some common acquaintances. Chris had lost touch with all his old schoolmates long ago and had never taken much interest in any of his parents' friends.

Once they started eating, Nick quizzed Chris about how he'd got CAT started, showing a surprising knowledge of the CAT programs. Then the focus turned to Jo and Col. Chris learned they lived on an acreage outside of town, one Jo had lived on since she was first married. She and Col had only been married for a few years, and he had recently purchased a herd of alpacas which kept him busy. It appeared Col had no children but Jo, in addition to Danny, had another son and a daughter and twin granddaughters who Col referred to affectionately as 'the two terrors'. Jo was also co-owner of the Riverside Restaurant where Chris had eaten when he first arrived in town.

'I probably know as much about rearing alpacas as you do about my line of work.' Chris chuckled, as he forked up the last piece of steak and drained his second can of beer. They were good company. He was glad he'd come. Even though they must all be around ten years older than he was – with the exception of Nick – he found them easy to talk to and they shared his values when it came to the things that mattered – child-rearing, caring for the environment and the importance of education.

When Chris was leaving, Col clapped him on the shoulder. 'You should drop out to see us sometime. Alpacas are a bit different from sheep, but I think you'd find them interesting. Yarran is a small acreage, only twenty acres – I'd guess you'd call it a hobby farm. But we like it. We have a few like-minded neighbours – Magda with her horses, and Fran and Owen with their goats. We're like one big happy family.' He chuckled. 'Never thought I'd be spending my retirement on an acreage rearing alpacas. It's amazing what the influence of a good woman can do.' He gazed affectionately at Jo who was chatting with Kay.

'Thanks. I'll take it on board.' While Col was jotting down his contact details, Chris mentally agreed with him. Look what *he* was doing. He was planning to open an office in the town, the dust of which he'd shaken off his shoes more than thirty years earlier. And it was all due to meeting Annie again.

It was only as he was driving home, the import of Col's words sank in. The names of his neighbours – Fran and Owen. Weren't they the names of the couple Annie was visiting today? Had she said they lived on an acreage? He couldn't remember, but it figured. The Granite Springs community was still as insular and interconnected as it had been all those years ago.

Twenty-three

Ann was feeling unexpectedly happy as she drove out to Fran's for lunch. She'd refused Peta's offer to pick her up, preferring to make her own way. If she was honest with herself, she knew she wanted to delay the inevitable inquisition from Peta about what had happened after the races.

This was the first time in years she hadn't spent her Easter weekend alone. Gus's return had been cathartic. But things had started to change before that, last year – when Peta and Lily arrived in town. The little girl's presence had helped breach the dam she had built up over the years, had allowed her to feel emotion again. Fran always told her she had a heart of gold but kept it well guarded.

Peta and Frank had already arrived when Ann drove up to the ranch-style house. The surrounding veranda was strewn with a collection of children's toys, and a couple of goats were nosing at the fence around the house paddock. There was also a car Ann didn't recognise parked alongside Frank's ute.

'Welcome!' Fran came out to greet Ann with a hug. 'Pia's here today, with young Tor and her new fellow.' She winked. Owen's daughter, Pia, had arrived in Granite Springs, pregnant, two years earlier. The baby's father wanted nothing to do with the child, and Pia had arrived on her father's doorstep, unsure what to do.

She'd decided to have the baby, who was now a toddler and a delightful little boy. Pia had found work in Granite Springs and, according to Fran, had recently formed a relationship with a new vet in town.

'Come and meet them.' Fran linked arms with Ann and the pair walked towards the house where the others were standing in two groups. In typical Australian fashion, the three men were by the barbecue, while Peta and Pia were by an outdoor table enjoying a glass of wine.

'Auntie Ann!' A blonde whirlwind flew up to throw her arms around Ann. 'Mum said you'd be here. I've been looking after Tor,' Lily said importantly.

At that moment there was a thud and a loud wail.

'Oh!' Ann and Fran turned just in time to see Pia rush to the aid of her son, who had fallen over on the brick veranda. A black cat was scurrying away.

'He was playing with Stormy,' Lily said, her lip drooping. 'I only left them for a moment.'

'It's not your fault, sweetie,' Fran reassured her. 'Tor's likely to get into mischief wherever he goes, He's a bit like his grandfather in that regard.' She laughed.

Ann wondered if she could ever feel so relaxed, so confident in a relationship ever again. While last night with Gus had been good – more than good – and had proved she wasn't the dried-up old maid some of her staff thought her, Ann wondered what future there could be for them.

Once again, she thought of Cassie's full recovery, when Gus would be off back to Canada and she'd be left here with more memories. Was the pleasure of more evenings together worth the pain of a future parting?

Still lost in her thoughts, she accepted a glass of wine from Fran and joined her and Peta at the table. Pia had taken Tor inside, Lily was attempting to attract Stormy out from under a bush, and the men were still engrossed in conversation at the barbecue.

'Where did you get to after the races?' Peta asked. 'We looked everywhere, then I got your text to say you had a ride home.'

'Was Chris Thomas at the races?' Fran asked with a twinkle in her eye. 'I thought I caught sight of you with a man. Was he your ride home?'

Ann blushed and gazed down into her glass. 'We bumped into each other when I was coming back from checking out the horses,' she admitted. 'He was on his own, so I took pity on him.'

'Did you take my advice? Have you been seeing him?' Fran asked, gesturing towards Ann with her glass.

'Yes and no.' Ann didn't want to give too much away.

'We know what it's like, Ann,' Fran said, sharing a glance with Peta, who nodded. 'We've been there. It's not easy to meet someone when you thought life was over – at least that part of life.' She chuckled, making Ann's face turn even redder. 'Oh, you didn't…' She peered at Ann. 'You did, didn't you? You and Dr Thomas. Well!' She sat back in her chair, smiled smugly, and took a drink of wine.

'There's no need to be embarrassed, Ann,' Peta said, putting a hand on Ann's arm. 'It's not easy, when you've been on your own for years. It's hard to trust again. It must be especially hard for you with Gus, since he's your first love. Second time around is different even, I would imagine, if the man is the same. You're both older. You're not the young boy and girl you were. I never thought Frank and I… Yet, now, I couldn't imagine life without him.'

'It was the same for me, Ann,' Fran interjected. 'Owen is the complete opposite of everything I thought I wanted in a man – I didn't think I wanted a man at all – but here we are, and I couldn't be happier.' She looked fondly across to where Owen was gesticulating to the other two men.

'But it's different with Gus,' Ann objected. 'He doesn't live here. As soon as Cassie is well, he'll be off back to Canada,' she said, voicing her thoughts. 'And I'll be left high and dry again – just like before.' Although she knew that wasn't exactly the way it happened, it was how she'd always felt about Gus's departure.

'So, are you seeing him again?' Fran asked.

'Tomorrow.'

'Well, looks as if you've made up your mind.'

But Peta seemed to sense Ann's uncertainty. 'You've forgotten, Fran. You and Owen have been together for a couple of years now. Remember how unsure you told me you were at the start? It's not easy to give up the habits of a lifetime. And Ann has more than most to get over. I knew something had happened to change you,' she said to Ann. 'When Lily and I came last year, you were different.'

'I was a lot older.'

'It wasn't only that. You gradually thawed, but it wasn't till you told me about you and Gus that I understood. You had every reason to react the way you did. I can see a different Ann emerging now and I hope she's going to stay. But that's something only you have control over.'

Ann was beginning to wish she'd given in to her instinct and stayed home. This conversation was making her very uncomfortable. Fran's next question shocked her to the core.

'How was it – with Gus? Was it as good as when you were young?'

Ann almost choked on her wine. She glared at her friend, then seeing only concern in Fran's eyes, said, 'It was good.' She paused, hardly believing she'd said that aloud, then added, 'I never thought I could feel that way again. Oh, hell, what am I going to do?'

'Go for it and damn the consequences,' Fran advised. 'At our age, there's no sense in being sensible. Oh, I know I hesitated about Owen, but if I hadn't given in to what I knew were my innermost feelings, I'd have missed out on so much. Has Chris actually said he's going back to Canada?'

'Not in as many words. But what else would he do? His whole life's there.'

'Frank said he was asking about Danny Slater's Technology Park,' Peta said. 'Maybe he has plans to stay in Granite Springs.'

'I don't think so.'

'Have you given any thought to moving to Canada?' Fran asked.

Canada? What would she do in Canada? The thought of leaving all she was familiar with scared Ann more than the possibility of Gus leaving.

Seeing her distress, Fran tried to reassure her. 'A wise woman once told me that there's always a light at the end of the tunnel, if you're willing to be patient, to accept what is given to you and to be willing to give in return – or something like that,' Fran finished hurriedly as if embarrassed to repeat it.

'Wise words.' Peta nodded. 'None of us knows what's round the corner. I tend to agree with Fran, though I might not put it in those words. What have you to lose, Ann?'

Ann couldn't think of a reply but was grateful for their suggestions. She'd always known any decision about Gus was up to her. These two women were of her vintage. They'd found love again when they least expected it. Was it waiting for her, too? Could she and Gus really have a second chance? But she was very conscious of the secret that lay between them. How could she form a relationship with Gus without telling him?

She was saved from having to reply, by the arrival of another car and, the ensuing kerfuffle of greeting Marie and Drew, along with their two teenagers, Lucy and Jess.

Then the three men joined them, Owen rubbing his hands together and saying, 'Now we're all here, we can get the steaks started. Where are they, honey?' he asked Fran who threw up her hands in mock annoyance.

'They're marinating in the fridge. I'd better go in and give him a hand,' she said with a grin.

Peta squeezed Ann's hand to remind her of her support, making Ann regret her own lack of support for Peta when she first became involved with Frank.

The rest of the afternoon passed pleasantly. Fran had organised an egg hunt for the smaller children and even Lucy and Jess joined in, pretending to be surprised when Lily or Tor discovered a chocolate egg in a spot the older girls had just left.

For once, Ann didn't feel left out. The group enfolded her in a warmth of friendship. It was a pity Gus wasn't here, she thought as they all packed up preparing to leave. He'd have enjoyed meeting her friends and they'd have liked him. Could they really make a future together?

Fran's words rang in her ears. Then she remembered what that weird Magda woman had said to her   something about a journey yet to be completed, a chance to put right something you regret, about not letting an opportunity escape. Ann didn't believe a word of it, but maybe the old woman had been talking about Gus. She shivered.

Twenty-four

Buoyed by her conversation with Peta and Fran the previous afternoon, Ann was excited as she slipped into her new jeans and a soft pink sweater and slung her old brown suede jacket across her shoulders. She couldn't remember when she'd last been on a picnic. It brought back so many memories.

Unsure what Gus would manage to provide in the way of food, she boiled up a few eggs and buttered a bread stick she'd bought before Easter. Then she foraged in the pantry to discover a tin of tuna. She packed them into a backpack which had been lying in a cupboard ever since the day Fran persuaded her to join her on a bush walk. She couldn't remember how long ago it had been. Finally, she added two cans of sparkling apple juice.

Ann was just arranging her favourite multicoloured scarf around her neck when she heard Gus at the door. Taking a deep breath, and trying to subdue the butterflies in her stomach, she went to answer it.

'Annie, you're looking lovely.' Gus gave her a peck on the cheek, sending the butterflies careering around. When had anyone last told her that? She felt his arms go around her briefly. 'Ready to go?'

'I certainly am.' Ann picked up her bag and the backpack, wondering if she needed both. She was out of practice in this sort of thing.

'I thought we'd drive up towards the mountains. It's been a long time, but I have fond memories of trips there with the folks when I was little.'

'Sounds good.' Ann was a little disappointed Gus hadn't chosen to revisit one of their old haunts, but perhaps it was just as well. There were enough memories in Granite Springs itself.

On the drive, Gus recounted the unexpected invitation he'd received the day before, and the subsequent barbecue. 'I met a couple who I think may be neighbours of the friends you visited yesterday. Jo and Col Ford? A nice couple. Older. They live out of town on an acreage. They mentioned a Fran and Owen.'

'Yes, they live on the neighbouring acreage to Fran and Owen. I've met them at Fran's a couple of times, and Jo volunteers at the library. Col helped my cousin with some legal stuff last year. They're good value. It was good of Nick to have you over. He's kind like that – both he and Kay.' *And another couple who met in later life and took a second chance on love*, Ann thought. *They're everywhere.* Why had it never occurred to her before? Because she had her head in the sand – she answered her own question.

'And how was *your* barbecue?' he asked, as they drove along the highway past paddocks dotted with sheep and the occasional horse stud, the Snowy Mountains visible ahead of them in the distance.

'It was good.' If she could forget the unsolicited advice she'd received. But Fran's words had stayed with her. Patience wasn't her strong suit, and she wasn't good at acceptance either. But perhaps she could learn. 'There was the usual steak and salads, lots of conversation, and a fun chocolate egg hunt to finish off the day. My cousin's granddaughter had a wonderful time, and Marie and Drew's two teenagers kept us amused with their tales of Canberra. They both attend university there, like you did.'

There was a pause, Ann remembering the years when their precious time together was packed into weekends before the tearful farewells when Gus drove off back to Canberra.

'It's a good university,' Gus said. 'But I'm sure William Farrer is, too. I wish it had been there in my time. It would have saved…' He glanced at Ann, clearly sure she was remembering too. 'They didn't want to go to the local one?'

'No, I think they were eager to get away, to spread their wings in the city, be independent. Lucy lived in Canberra before her mother died, and Jess and her dad came to Granite Springs from Melbourne.

'I think this will do.' Gus slowed down and parked close to a river.

Ann had been too caught up in her thoughts to notice they'd driven through a small town, not unlike the one they'd left behind. When she stepped out of the car, a cool breeze ruffled her hair and scarf. She was glad she'd dressed warmly.

Seeing a picnic table nestling under a large tree, Ann retrieved her backpack while Gus unpacked an esky from the car boot.

Settled at the table, both seated facing the river where a pair of black swans were slowly gliding past, Gus opened the esky. As he began to remove first two plastic plates, then a pack of sandwiches, a slab of fruit cake, two bananas, and finally a bottle of white wine and two glasses, Ann realised she'd underestimated him. The Gus she'd known would never have been so well-prepared, he'd have relied on her, satisfied with a packet of crisps and a Mars Bar.

'I guess we don't need this,' she said laughing and unpacking her carefully chosen provisions.

They ate a leisurely meal, in the company of a couple of noisy black cockatoos who'd decided to make their own meal in the high branches of a nearby she-oak. Ann idly wondered if, like the swans, cockatoos mated for life. Her life seemed to be revolving around couples. Maybe she should just *go with the flow* as her mother would have said before she lost her ability to make sense. Maybe fate was sending her a message.

'It's still early. Fancy a walk?' Gus asked when they'd repacked the car.

The breeze had died down, turning into a pleasant autumn afternoon. He took Ann's hand, and they began to wander along the riverbank, arms swinging. As they reached an old wooden bridge well away from the road, Gus stopped, dropped Ann's hand and took her in his arms.

'Thanks for coming today, Annie,' he murmured into her hair, the scent of his aftershave reminding her of the night of love they'd shared. 'I hope we can do this more often. I couldn't bear to lose you again.'

Ann felt a glimmer of hope stir somewhere deep inside. Maybe this time it would work out for them. She felt his arms tighten, then Gus's lips were on hers and she was seventeen again.

*

It was turning dark by the time they reached the outskirts of Granite Springs, having lingered for some time at the spot by the old bridge. Gus drove straight to Ann's house. When the car stopped, they shared a glance, each knowing what the other was thinking. They were too old to have considered making love by the river, but....

'Would you like to come in... for a drink – and maybe some dinner? I can rustle up something without too much trouble.'

Their eyes met.

Gus didn't reply. Instead, he turned off the engine and opened the driver's door before coming around to help Ann out. Together – and hand-in-hand – they made their way up the path and into the house. Unlike last time, there was no awkwardness. This time, Ann pulled Gus towards the bedroom where they quickly divested themselves of their clothes and fell onto the bed.

It was completely dark – had been for some time, but Ann had barely noticed – when she returned an awareness of her surroundings.

'Wow!' Gus stroked Ann's face, his fingers tracing her forehead, her eyelids, before finishing on her lips. 'Was it this good in our twenties?'

Ann didn't reply, content to bask in the aftermath of their lovemaking, to recover from the tumult of passion that had overtaken them.

They lay like this for several more minutes, legs entwined, bodies so close it would be difficult for an onlooker to tell them apart.

'There was some mention of dinner,' Gus said with a grin.

'Hungry?'

'A little. What had you in mind?' He pulled her even closer.

Ann laughed, the sort of gurgling laugh of sheer delight that hadn't escaped her lips for years. 'I have shepherd's pie in the fridge. It only needs heating up, and I can throw some veggies into the microwave.'

'Sounds like my kind of meal.' He released Ann and gave her a gentle tap on the bottom as she got out of bed.

'Hey, don't think just because we've made love, you can take liberties.' But she loved the fact they felt so at ease with each other.

Looking around for something to hide her nakedness, Ann saw Gus's shirt lying in a heap on the floor where he'd tossed it in their rush to undress. She picked it up and slipped it on, rolling up the sleeves to fit her, and inhaling the scent of him which clung to the soft fabric.

Ann hummed to herself as she placed the casserole dish in the microwave and prepared the vegetables, slicing potatoes, carrots and cauliflower and popping them into another casserole dish. She was setting the timer on the microwave when a pair of arms encircled her waist.

'Need any help?' Gus murmured into her hair.

Ann turned abruptly to find herself in his arms, her face against his naked chest. She allowed herself to relax against him for a moment, then, 'If you want dinner, you need to leave me to fix it,' she said, but her tone contradicted her words. She had missed this intimate contact with another human being – with Gus – and was determined to enjoy as much of it as she could before...

She stifled the reminder that this wasn't forever. He would leave and she'd go back to the life she'd lived for so long. But was it wrong to want to enjoy him for however long he stayed in Granite Springs?

Ann realised how much she'd changed in the past twenty-four hours – since Gus had picked her up only that morning. If only Fran and Peta could see her now.

'Mmm, this is delicious. A good cook, too. Is there no end to your talents?' Gus smiled across the table, his fork spearing the last piece of potato.

'Needs must.' Ann felt his bare feet touch hers under the table sending quivers up her spine.

When he'd finished eating, Gus poured them both another glass of the shiraz he'd found on Ann's wine rack and opened earlier. After taking one sip, he leant his elbows on the table, his face serious. 'Annie, I don't want you to think I'm toying with you, that this is a flash in the pan. When I said I'd always loved you and still did, it wasn't a ruse to entice you into bed – even though it did have that outcome. I meant it. I have and I do. Now I've found you again, I don't intend to let you go. I know we live thousands of miles apart and I don't have a solution... yet. But I intend to find one. You do believe me, don't you?' He reached across to take Ann's hands in his.

Ann's stomach lurched. What did he mean? She wanted to believe him – with all her heart. 'I think so, but how...?'

'I don't know. I have a few things I need to work out. For now, I'm here. Cassie needs me and it will give us time... time to find each other again. Though I think we may have just done that.' His lips curled into that familiar grin, making Ann's stomach flutter. 'For a start, you know I've taken office space in that technology park of Danny Slater's. For now, it'll only be to provide me somewhere I can work, but in the longer term, who knows? There are distinct possibilities. I've been intending to spread the interests of CAT overseas. Why not to Granite Springs?'

'You mean… you can't mean you'd move here – permanently?' Ann was afraid to put her wildest imaginings into words.

'Let's just say it's within the realms of possibility. Or you could come to Canada.' He threw out the suggestion with another grin, as if Canada were only a few miles away.

Ann gasped.

'Don't worry. I'm far from figuring out how it's all going to happen, and a lot will depend on you.' He rubbed his thumb across the back of Ann's hand, sending shivers up her spine again.

She knew she had to tell him about the child she'd lost, but how could she do it without losing him again?

Twenty-five

'I hope your Easter wasn't too boring, Dad. You could have joined us,' Cassie said, as Chris helped her into the car to take her to her rehab appointment.

'No, not boring at all. It actually turned out to be quite interesting.' He tucked the wheelchair into the boot and slipped behind the steering wheel.

'It was?' Cassie sounded dubious.

'I do know a few people in Granite Springs, you know.' He chuckled. 'On Sunday, I bumped into your professor while I was out on a run. He invited me to a barbecue where I met another nice couple.'

'Prof Kerr? That was good of him. Did he say anything about me? I want to get back to class, but I don't think it'll be possible until I get rid of the wheelchair. I can't manage to move myself around, and the guys have their own classes to attend. Maybe once I'm on crutches. Don't know when that'll be.' She looked wistful, then grinned. 'I'll ask the therapist person today. Deb says it might only be a few weeks, if that.'

'He did ask after you. And he said they'd try to make it as easy for you as possible. He's one of the good guys. You're lucky there.' Chris swallowed. 'Then yesterday I went on a picnic.'

'On your own? We didn't see you by the river.'

When he didn't answer straight away, she turned to peer at his face. 'Did you go with Ann Baird? I knew it!' she exclaimed when he reddened. 'What gives? Are you and her an item?' She raised her eyebrows.

How he hated that term. It said nothing about the deep feelings he had for Annie, about the pleasure of the tender passion they'd shared. 'I suppose you could call it that,' he said.

'Wait till I get back to campus! The others will freak out.'

Chris blanched. 'I hope you don't intend to spread gossip about Annie and me. It's not... We're not... She's...' He stopped. How could he explain to his twenty-year-old daughter what Annie meant to him? He decided he wouldn't try. 'I think she deserves a bit of privacy regarding her personal life,' he said, knowing he sounded sanctimonious. 'I know what university gossip can be like and I don't want to think of you adding to it.'

'Okay, my lips are sealed.' Cassie made the motion of zipping her lips. 'I won't say a word. But you have to admit, it's weird. I come back to your hometown, have an accident. You come to pick up the pieces and end up with your old girlfriend. It's like a Hallmark movie. In fact, I think there might even be one.' She chuckled.

By this time, they'd reached their destination. Chris unloaded the wheelchair and helped Cassie into it before wheeling her inside the hospital, this time to the outpatient's area on the ground floor.

After a short wait, a cheerful nurse approached them. 'Cassie Thomas? I'll take you through now.' She looked at Chris. 'Do you want to come with her?'

Cassie shook her head. 'I'll be fine, Dad. Go and get yourself a coffee or something.'

The nurse smiled again. 'We'll be around an hour, Mr Thomas. You can come back for Cassie then.' She wheeled her off.

Chris was at a loose end again. An hour wasn't long enough to get any work done and, while he was itching to make a start in his new office space, he knew he would no sooner be there than he'd have to turn around again. Cassie's suggestion of coffee was a good one. He walked towards the hospital café, the one where he and Annie had enjoyed coffee together, then turned. He had no desire to spend an hour here.

Instead, he went back to the car and headed into town. Once there, and about to go to the flat, he found himself outside The Bean Sprout Café. Remembering its excellent coffee and the mouth-watering selection of cakes and slices in the glass cabinet below the counter, he pushed open the door.

The aroma of strong coffee immediately hit him. He ordered a macchiato and a slice of toasted banana bread and settled down at a window table to check the emails on his phone. He hadn't taken time this morning.

After waking up with Annie by his side, he'd been otherwise occupied and hadn't been able to think of anything but her. Thinking of Annie brought back a flurry of memories. He still had trouble believing it was actually happening, that they were together again, a couple or, as Cassie suggested, an item. Waking up beside her had been better than he could have imagined in his wildest dreams. He wanted to wake up there every day.

But he could tell from her manner over breakfast that Annie wasn't quite convinced of his sincerity. He'd said he loved her, not only when they were in bed, but at the dining table last night when he'd tried his best to lay his feelings on the line, to project into the future, and this morning over breakfast when he'd reiterated his intentions. But there seemed to be something holding her back.

His eyes flickered through the emails, deleting many and scanning a few he'd reply to later. Then his eyes settled on one from a Sam Walker, editor of The Granite Springs Advertiser. *What the...?* Wasn't he the man he'd seen having dinner with Annie?

'Here you are. It's Chris, isn't it?' Marie put his coffee and banana bread on the table. 'I hope your daughter is feeling better. Ann Baird told me she's out of hospital. We met at a barbecue on Sunday,' she said, seeing his puzzled look.

'Oh, yes, right. Cassie's recovering slowly,' he said, knowing he shouldn't be surprised to find his daughter's health being the topic of conversation.

'Good. We get a lot of the students in here. They've been talking about her, too. Granite Springs is still a small town and we care for our own. This initiative with Canadian students is important for the university – and for the town. It could result in a tourist boom.' She chuckled.

'In your dreams.' Frank joined them. 'Marie, you're needed in the kitchen,' he said, then turning to Chris, added, 'I'm glad to hear she's on the mend. They can be pretty headstrong at that age. Marie and I have a niece at university in Canberra. Who knows what she gets up to over there! Enjoy your coffee and banana bread,' he said walking away.

How could Chris have forgotten this community spirit, this concern for others so common in his hometown? He'd lived in cities for so long, he'd become accustomed to the isolation, the lack of anything like this caring atmosphere he was rediscovering.

He opened the email from Sam Walker, dismissing the trace of jealousy it provoked. He was the one sharing Annie's bed, not this Sam guy. But the memory of seeing them together still stung.

He read through the email. It was perfectly polite. Sam had heard of Cassie's accident and that she was out of hospital – not difficult in this town. He wanted Chris's permission – as Cassie's father – to approach her for a story. It was a reasonable request, but Chris wanted to check with Cassie before replying. For a moment, he wondered how Sam had got his email address before realising it wouldn't have been difficult. All his contact details were on the CAT website. One of the hazards of being a public figure.

Chris had no idea how Cassie would feel, but suspected she'd be thrilled to be featured in the local paper. He'd check with her when he picked her up.

He closed his phone and settled down to enjoy his coffee and indulge in a little people watching. At this time of day, the café was busy with groups of young mothers with small children and babies. Chris found himself smiling, glad he was here, in this place he once called home. Could it be his home again?

It was soon time to return to the hospital to pick up Cassie. 'Thanks a lot, Frank. This is becoming a home from home for me. Pity you don't do dinner, too, then I'd never need to cook at all,' he joked.

'All good with the flat?'

'Yes thanks. It's ideal for my needs. I was glad to find it.'

'Happy to help.'

Walking out of the café, Chris thought again what a decent man Frank was. Annie's cousin had lucked out there.

Back at the hospital, he had only a short wait before Cassie was wheeled out. This time she was accompanied by a younger woman wearing green shorts and a white cotton shirt bearing the hospital logo.

'Hi, Dad!' Cassie grinned. 'This is Thea. She's the therapist I've been working with. She's given me exercises to do at home and says I should practice on my crutches. Maybe I can get rid of this contraption and get back to class soon.'

'Mr Thomas?' Thea addressed Chris. 'Cassie's making good progress. She's young and fit, both of which are in her favour. But I've cautioned her not to try to do too much too soon, or she could suffer a relapse. Slow and steady is the way to go. But she's right. She should be able to manage on crutches, and you can return the wheelchair on her next visit.'

'See, Dad?' Cassie grinned, her whole face lighting up. 'Deb can help me with the exercises. She'll know what I can do safely.'

'Would you like to have lunch somewhere?' Chris asked when they were back in the car. Maybe they should go back to The Bean Sprout again.

'I'd love a McDonald's McVeggie Deluxe. Do you think we could go there?'

Chris winced, but he had asked, and he did want to please Cassie. She deserved some spoiling. 'Just this once,' he said, matching her grin.

'Come on, Dad. You know you enjoy their burgers,' she teased. 'And I've been dying for a Coke.'

Chris grimaced but did as she asked and soon they were parked in the McDonald's car park.

Inside, Chris left Cassie and her chair at one of the tables while he ordered, choosing a Big Mac and coffee for himself, thinking how he'd have much preferred another of Frank's coffees at The Bean Sprout.

'I had an email from the editor of the local paper this morning,' he said, when they were enjoying their meals, Cassie groaning with delight over her veggie burger. 'Gosh this is good.' He took another bite of *his* burger.

'Did he want to do an article on you?'

'No, on you.'

'Me?' Cassie squealed. 'Why me?'

'It appears he heard about your accident and now you're on the path to recovery, he wants to feature the brave Canadian student who survived a dreadful accident. I imagine he wants to use it to profile the student exchange program, too. It'd be good publicity for the university.'

'Why did he contact you?'

Chris scratched his head. 'I wondered that too, but I suppose, as I'm your dad, he thought it appropriate to ask my permission. Also, I guess it may be easier to find my contact details from the CAT website.' Chris hoped he was right about that. He'd hate to think Annie might have given Sam Walker the story. 'How do you feel about it?'

'Me – in the local paper? Wow! That'd be amazing. Will they want a photo? I can send it back home. Everyone will be so envious.'

'If you're sure?'

'Of course. But I don't want a photo in this wheelchair. When do you think it'll happen?'

'I have no idea. I'll reply and give him your number and email and he can take it from there.'

'Sounds good.'

They finished their meals with Cassie describing in detail the exercises she was to do and trying to calculate how soon she'd manage to return to classes at the university. 'I'm missing so much,' she groaned. 'Some of the guys are taking notes for me, but it's not the same. I miss being on campus. This is such a great university, Dad. It's not as huge as back home, more friendly. Why didn't you go here?'

Chris laughed. 'There was no university in Granite Springs when I was your age. As you know, I studied in Canberra, at the Australian National University. It's an excellent university, too, and Canberra's a lovely city.'

'I know. Miles and I went over there one weekend in the Christmas holidays.' She gave him a sideways glance. 'I didn't say anything to you or Mum. I knew you'd ask all sorts of questions and I wasn't ready to share him with you.'

'Mmm.' Chris wondered when she would have been ready to share information about Miles. If she hadn't been in this accident, and Chris hadn't come to Australia, would he ever have heard his name? 'And now?' he asked.

Cassie's expression became more serious. 'He's important to me, Dad. I don't know what I'm going to do when the exchange finishes. I wasn't going to say anything, but...' She bit her lip. 'Do you think I could transfer... finish my degree here?'

'Whoa! That's a big decision. You need to think it through. I'm not sure it would even be possible.' Chris was stunned, struck by the parallel with his own life. Though in Cassie's case, she wanted to stay with the man she loved.

'Miles is looking into the ins and outs of it. He has a friend who works in immigration in Canberra.'

'Oh!' Chris was at a loss for words. Cassie had it all worked out. What would he do if she did manage to stay here? Was it a sign he should stay, too? It would help resolve matters with Annie and would entail building a larger CAT presence in Granite Springs than he'd intended. And Cassie wouldn't stay here forever. Even if she did succeed in transferring to Willian Farrer University, in a year's time she'd graduate. Then where would she go?

What it all came down to, was how much was he willing to do for the two women who were now his life?

Twenty-six

Ann had been feeling good when she arrived at work. Waking up with Gus had been bliss, something she'd only dreamed about. He said he loved her, and she had to believe him. It was hard to change the habits of a lifetime, to trust what he said, but the euphoria of their night together still cast an aura around her, making her want to sing and dance.

But, once in the office, it didn't take long for the elation to wear off, even if it still sat in a corner of her mind reminding her of the passion they'd shared.

'Ann, can I have a word?'

Ann looked up from checking her emails – her first task every morning. One of her staff members was standing in the doorway. 'Certainly, Kerrie. Come in.' She swung around to face the visitor's chair.

Kerrie took a seat, clasped her hands together and said, 'It's about the new lunch schedule.'

'Yes?' Ann had recently been forced to stagger staff lunch hours to ensure the office was always manned.

'It's not fair that Janelle and I have to go after everyone else.'

Ann sighed. For several days now, she'd caught Kerrie and Janelle whispering together, only to stop when she appeared.

It started when Ann took Janelle and Kerrie to task for using university facilities to do their own photocopying for a community group they belonged to – an obvious abuse of university resources.

Janelle, usually the more vocal one, had been brazen enough to tell Ann she wasn't going to do any more photocopying, saying it wasn't in her job description. As if any job description could itemise every single task that would have to be done. While most of the lecturers did their own copying, several of the older males preferred to dump it into the Education office, regarding photocopying as too menial for their inflated egos.

Clearly today, Kerrie had drawn the short straw to front up to Ann's office.

'You do understand why I had to do it, Kerrie? We can't leave the office unmanned. As you must be aware, lunchtime is when many of the students come to us for help.'

Kerrie had a bullish expression.

'What would you like me to do?'

'Change it. Some of the others could do the late lunch.'

Ann sighed again. They'd already been through this at the last staff meeting with the majority agreeing. She tried to remember if either Kerrie or Janelle had spoken out then. She didn't want to overturn the agreed arrangement on the whim of two disgruntled members of staff. 'How about we leave it for now and discuss it again at the next staff meeting?' she suggested with a forced smile.

Kerrie left, and Ann could see her whisper to Janelle with occasional glances back towards Ann's office.

They were both in their thirties and should have a better understanding of the way an office like this functioned. But they continued to grumble about their hours, about her style of management, and – in their view – her lack of consultation. She'd had to bite her tongue a few times to stop herself telling them if they didn't like it here, they could go elsewhere. That really would set the cat among the pigeons.

Normally, Ann loved her job, but some days she'd gladly have changed her role for one without management responsibilities. This was one of them.

She was glad she'd arranged to have lunch with Fran. She needed to let off steam and her friend was the ideal person to help soothe her ruffled feathers. Perhaps her uncertainty about Gus was making her oversensitive. Fran could always make Ann feel better.

*

'Am I such a bad manager?' Ann asked Fran when they were seated in Banjo's and had been served with roast beef and asparagus rolls and coffee. 'You knew me when you worked with Professor Kerr. Be honest with me.'

'Not at all. Ann. As far as I'm concerned you do a wonderful job against some very difficult odds. I can remember what those two were like, even back when I was Nick's PA. As you know, I didn't mix much with the girls in the office. But I could see what they were doing. They tried to undermine you at every turn, tried to turn the others against you. It didn't work. It looks as if they've now decided to take a different tack – to criticise you to your face. Don't let them get away with it.'

Ann took a drink of coffee and sighed. 'Some days I wish I could throw it all in and fly away.'

Fran's eyes widened. 'I thought you loved your job?'

'I do. And I know I shouldn't let those two get under my skin. All the other staff are wonderful. Most of them would do anything for me. But it only takes two to rock the boat.'

'Don't let them upset you – or let them see they do. It's what I've heard called *the rough and tumble of the workplace* – a bit like the rough and tumble of the playground, I've always thought.' She chuckled. 'I know it's hard to shrug it off, but that's what will irritate them more than anything. What they want is to get under your skin and see you suffer. I bet they'd like nothing better than to think they'd managed to force you to leave.'

'You're right. I knew I could count on you. What makes you so sensible?'

'When you've been through what I have, you're bound to see things differently.' Fran's lips tightened for just a moment.

'Sorry, that was thoughtless of me.' How could Ann have forgotten Fran's past, the loss of her partner and child then, more recently, her mother.

'Water under the bridge.'

But Ann could tell from the way her eyes clouded that Fran hadn't completely forgotten.

'To get back to you.' Fran brightened. 'What's been happening with

Chris Thomas? Didn't you say you were seeing him yesterday? Did you take our advice?'

Ann blushed.

'You did! Good for you! Maybe he's the answer. Maybe he can help you escape from all this.'

'You're as bad as he is. It's all moving too fast. I don't know if I can believe his protestations.'

'His protestations? You mean…? Oh, Ann! How wonderful. It's like a fairy tale.'

'Steady on. I'm still trying to get my head around it all.'

'Well, don't wait too long. That's all I can say. And it sounds as if you're not wasting time talking about things.' She raised one eyebrow.

Ann blushed again. She hated to have her relationship with Gus the subject of speculation, even from a close friend. But she did need to talk to someone, and she knew Fran would understand.

'I never expected to feel this way again, Fran. All those years… I buried my feelings, kept a tight rein on my emotions. How can I have let Gus in again? How can I have risked being hurt? I thought I was safe from the tumult of emotions I experienced as a teenager and young woman and now… I find I'm just as gullible. Tell me I'm not being a fool.'

'You're not being a fool,' Fran complied, making Ann laugh.

'There. We've settled it.' Fran picked up her roll and took a bite. 'Yummy. I love the way they do them here. 'Now, don't you feel better?'

Ann thought for a moment, before realising that she did feel better than she had when she arrived at the café. 'Talking things over with you always makes me feel better.'

'Good. Now enjoy your lunch, because afterwards, you still need to go back and face those monsters, because that's what they are. Maybe you could arrange for them to be transferred?'

'Perhaps one of them, but two would be difficult. Human Resources would wonder what I was doing wrong.'

'Well, as I said, don't let them get you down. You need to believe in yourself. Nick would say the same.'

Ann walked back to the office in a lighter frame of mind than she'd left it. Fran was right. She mustn't let Kerrie and Janelle see how much they'd riled her. She needed to be strong and try to ignore their barbs.

And as for Gus… Her face softened at the thought of him. She'd take what was offered right now and devil the future.

Twenty-seven

Two weeks had passed, two glorious weeks. Chris and Annie had fallen into the habit of spending almost every night together, usually at Annie's house where she'd cook them a delicious meal before they headed to bed.

Chris spent his days in his new office, from where he found he could easily conduct his business. It was peaceful to sit there, the open door allowing him to listen to the birds squawking in the surrounding trees. Danny Slater had cleverly designed the park to retain much of the surrounding bush, and Peta Forrest had capitalised on this in her interior design, just as she had done at *The Springs*.

Cassie's plan to switch universities was still in the air, with Chris trying not to think of it, while his daughter pressed him at every turn. She had already written to the administrative offices in both Willian Farrer University and her university back home to check her options.

'How would you feel about going camping?' Chris asked, twisting a strand of Annie's hair in his fingers. They were lying together in her comfortable bed, the early morning sun peeping through the venetian blinds, the cackle of the resident kookaburras having wakened them.

'Camping?' Annie twisted around and attempted to rise, hampered by Chris's scissor-like grip on her legs with his. 'Are you mad? We're not seventeen anymore.'

'I know that, but doesn't the idea of getting away from it all, spending time in the bush, have some appeal? It's a long time since I set foot in an Australian National Park. It could be fun.'

Annie seemed to consider. 'Maybe,' she said after a long pause. 'When did you have in mind?'

'This weekend?' Chris held his breath.

'So soon?'

'I've been checking it out. We can hire a tent and book a site. We're not likely to bump into anyone we know,' he added, knowing how paranoid Annie could be regarding gossip. Although he was sure her neighbours must have seen his car parked in her driveway and drawn their own conclusions.

When Annie still didn't reply, Chris pulled her close, feeling the warmth of her body and inhaling her unique scent. 'Just think, Annie,' he murmured. 'You and me in a tent far away from those pesky staff members who're stressing you, from your nosy neighbours, away from our computers, our phones. I bet there won't even be coverage where we're going. Doesn't it have some appeal?'

He could feel her weakening, and continued, 'You and me beneath the stars, cooking on an open fire. It'll be a different world.'

'You always did know how to get round me, Gus Thomas.' She laughed, the gurgling laugh he remembered, but which he didn't often hear these days. 'Okay, but if I'm not enjoying it, we'll come straight back – right?'

'Deal.'

'Now, will you let me get up? I have work to go to, and don't you have to take Cassie to her rehab appointment?'

'I do.' Reluctantly, Chris released Annie and followed her into the ensuite and into the shower.

Over breakfast, Chris tried to discuss the proposed camping trip, but Annie was unforthcoming on the subject, merely saying she'd be happy with wherever he chose to go. He had to accept that, instead focussing on how well Cassie's recovery was going. Even that, however failed to draw much response from Annie.

Kissing Annie goodbye, Chris headed off to grab a change of clothes from the flat before picking up Cassie. Each time he did this, he wondered at the futility of paying rent for a place where he rarely slept. But he knew Annie wasn't ready for him to formally move in, even though he spent most nights with her.

He knew from experience what it would be like in the student house at this time in the morning. In term time they'd all be rushing around getting ready to leave and Cassie would most likely still be in bed or just out of it. But this was semester break so he doubted anyone would be about.

There was no need to wait for someone to answer the door. As Chris had learnt on previous visits, the door was never locked. He'd tried to talk with them about it, but his advice fell on deaf ears.

Over the past few weeks, he'd learned to be patient, prepared to wait till Cassie made it into the kitchen. She was fiercely independent and refused the help he wanted to offer. He made coffee for himself and Cassie and sat down.

'Dad!' Cassie slowly made her way into the kitchen, stumbling a little on her crutches but grinning with satisfaction. 'I'm beginning to get the hang of them,' she said, dropping gratefully into a chair and propping the crutches against the table. 'I want to go back when classes start again later this week. I've missed too much already. Deb says I should be good to go.'

'Hmm.' It wasn't Deb who'd make the decision. 'Let's see what Thea has to say, shall we?' He bent to kiss her on the forehead. 'Have some coffee. Want something to eat?'

'Toast and vegemite. Thanks, Dad. You're a lifesaver.' Cassie took a long drink of coffee and yawned. 'We were up late last night watching a movie. Miles is still dead to the world.'

Chris winced as he always did at the reminder his daughter and Miles shared a bed. But it was no different to him and Annie at their age. He busied himself making toast.

'Ready?'

They'd finished their coffee and Chris had joined Cassie with a plate of toast and vegemite. He was surprised she'd taken to the acquired taste which, for him, brought back memories of his childhood on the farm, of his mother in her wrap-around apron chivvying him to get ready for the school bus.

'Just about. I need to let Miles know I'm leaving.' Cassie manoeuvred herself onto her crutches and hobbled out of the room, leaving Chris to puzzle why she felt the need to waken Miles to let him know.

*

At the hospital, it was the same routine he'd become accustomed to. By now, both he and Cassie were familiar figures in the outpatient's area and were greeted with smiles for him, and encouragement and praise for Cassie.

Aware exactly how long Cassie's therapy would take, Chris had come prepared. He'd brought along his iPad and, today, he intended to research camping areas in the surrounding national parks.

A glow of anticipation filled him as he settled in a corner of the hospital café with yet another cup of coffee and opened up the internet.

Before long, he'd managed to both book a camping site and arrange the hire of equipment. By the time he'd read the list of items deemed necessary for what was called the *two-person escape package*, Chris was beginning to wonder if his idea of getting back to nature was a mirage. The hire company was in Canberra so Chris would have to drive over before the weekend to pick up all the gear. He hoped the Subaru would be able to fit it all in.

The prospect of a trip to Canberra brought other memories flooding back, and reminded Chris of the old friend he'd intended to contact. He and Dave Wilson had been good mates all through university. They'd kept in touch but over the years their communication had dropped away to newsy emails at Christmas. Less ambitious than Chris, Dave had stayed in Canberra taking up a position with a local company and marrying a local girl. Several times in recent years, Chris had envied his old friend and wondered what his own life would have been like if he hadn't allowed his ambition to drive him on.

He entered his old friend's number into his phone, chuckling as he imagined Dave's surprise when he learned Chris was in Granite Springs and planning a trip to Canberra.

*

By the time Friday came around, Chris was excited and had managed to instil some of his excitement into Annie.

'Do you do a lot of bushwalking in Canada?' she asked over a breakfast of French toast topped with slices of banana.

'Not as such and not recently. We tend to call it hiking and there are some good tracks. When Gail and I first got together we spent most weekends on them, but as time went on, Cassie was born, we both became busy in our respective careers. It fell by the wayside,' he said, regretting the pun, and how much his life had changed from his earlier more carefree existence. 'You?'

'No.' Annie shook her head as if the idea was absurd. 'It's not something I'd do on my own and there was no one to go with. Oh, I know there are bushwalking groups, but I've never been one for joining those sorts of organised things. I did go on a bush walk with Fran once, but it was ages ago. I am looking forward to this weekend. It'll be good to get away. It's been a fraught week.' She closed her eyes and sighed. 'So, you're off to Canberra today?' she asked, when she opened them again.

'Mmm.' Chris finished chewing his mouthful of toast. 'I'll pick up the gear. If it won't all fit in the car, I can hire a trailer too.'

'I thought we were roughing it. How much gear are you picking up?'

Embarrassed, Chris took a drink of coffee before replying, 'It's what they call *the two-person escape package*. It seemed easier to get the lot.'

Annie chuckled. 'And you said you were catching up with an old friend from your student days?'

'Yeah. Remember Dave? It'll be good to see him again, though it's been a long time…' his voice trailed off as he realised it was the same length of time he and Annie had been apart. 'I should get off,' he said hurriedly. He rose and picked up his plate and mug.

'Leave those, I can do it.' Annie rose to join him and envelop him in a hug. 'Have a good day.'

'You too. Don't let those two women wear you down,' he said kissing her affectionately on the lips.

'It's easy for you and Fran to say, but I'll try,' she said. 'See you tonight. Drive carefully.'

'Will do.' Chris kissed her again and headed out the door. He couldn't remember when anyone last told him to drive carefully. It made him feel cherished.

*

The drive to Canberra passed quickly, Chris's mind filled with visions of the weekend ahead with Annie. Cassie, too, wasn't far from his thoughts. Following a positive report from Thea, she'd started classes again two days earlier and, according to her, was managing pretty well. Chris had offered to drive her there, but independent as ever she refused, telling him she could do this, and Miles would drive her there and back.

True to his word, Nick Kerr had taken steps to ensure her lecturers were aware of her reduced mobility and Cassie reported everyone was being very supportive.

Once he reached the outskirts of the city, Chris's eyes were drawn to the autumnal hues. The deciduous trees lining the streets were a tapestry of colours, their leaves displaying tints of red, gold, russet and crimson. He'd forgotten how the city was plunged into this spectacular display, so different from the eucalypts around Granite Springs. It was one of the things he'd loved about Canberra as a student.

Making his way to the camping store, the car boot was soon filled with more than he and Annie would ever need for the next couple of days. They would have two whole days and nights to enjoy each other without any interruption. Perhaps he could finally put to rest her fears of him leaving her again. She hadn't said so, but from her occasional silences, he knew she still doubted his sincerity.

Dave hadn't changed. Apart from thinning, greying hair, he was still the same lanky fellow who'd shared his study hours and listened to him rave on about Annie over a few beers.

'Good to see you again, mate!' he greeted him. 'Let me buy you a beer. It's been too long.'

Chris looked around the smart city bar, a far cry from the old pub they'd frequented as students. Dave seemed at home here, but to Chris it felt strange, as if it were trying too hard to be fashionable.

When Dave returned bearing two small glasses of craft beer, he said, 'Not my usual watering hole, but one of the guys in the office recommended it. Didn't expect it to be so poncy.'

They laughed, back on the old footing.

'So, what gives? What brings you back to Oz? Must say it knocked me for six to hear you on the phone.'

Chris gave him a potted version of his visit, finishing with, 'So, you see, I'm almost back where I was when I last saw you. Older, but none the wiser.'

'I remember how you used to rush back to that town of yours, to… what was her name?'

'Annie.'

'That's right. So, you didn't marry her? I'd have sworn you'd have been the first of us to tie the knot. How is Canada? I never had the same urge you did to make my mark. I've been happy to stay here. Met Pat at a cricket match and haven't looked back. We have three boys, grown now, of course. The eldest is on staff in our old faculty, would you believe?'

'Wow!' Chris was glad to see his old friend so happy and content with his life. It was a far cry from his own. But he still had hopes it wasn't too late for him and Annie.

Dave picked up the menu and grimaced. 'Finish your beer and let's get out of here and find a decent pub. This stuff's not going to put hairs on your chest.'

Chris laughed. He'd forgotten how down-to-earth Dave was. It was refreshing to know he hadn't changed.

They drank up and left the upmarket bar to settle for a regular Australian pub not far away.

'That's better,' Dave said, when, having ordered shepherd's pie with two veg and schooners of Carlton Draught, they found a spare table, its top sticky with beer.

The next hour was spent rehashing their student days, and it was with regret Chris finally rose to leave.

'Think about what I said,' Dave said as they shook hands outside the pub. 'I never did get to meet your Annie back in the day. Pat and I would love to have the pair of you to dinner. You could even stay overnight. She's a good cook, my Pat. She'd do us proud.'

'Thanks. I'll think on it.'

'Do more than think. I'll give you a bell after the weekend.'

'Okay.'

As he drove back to Granite Springs, Chris couldn't help thinking again what his life might have been like if he hadn't left when he did. He and Annie could have had a good life here – in Granite Springs or even Canberra. Why had he been so bull-headed? Why had he gone ahead when it was obvious Annie had torn loyalties? He could have been like Dave, living here with a wife and children. His parents would have liked that too. What had made him so eager to get away?

Twenty-eight

Ann was looking forward to the camping weekend with Gus. She was beginning to relax in his company, to almost believe him when he said he still loved her. About her own feelings, she wasn't quite so sure. Having spent the past thirty-five years regretting her decision and stifling her emotions, it wasn't easy to let her love for Gus show. She was scared to admit it, even to herself, afraid of being hurt again, even if she was relishing their time together. It had felt so natural to kiss him goodbye this morning after breakfast, but was she storing up future hurt?

When she reached the office and checked the roster, she gave a sigh of relief to discover she wouldn't have to deal with the two troublemakers. It was Janelle's rostered day off which meant there was only Kerrie. As was the norm when there was only one of them present, there were always fewer hassles. As she walked past Kerrie's desk, she noticed the woman was eating what appeared to be her breakfast. Even though Ann's blood boiled at this abuse of work time, she looked the other way, remembering Fran's advice – don't let them get to you.

The day passed quickly, the routine interrupted only by a visit from Cassie in the early afternoon. She stood at the office reception, leaning on her crutches, a wide grin on her face.

'Good morning, Cassie. It's good to see you back. How are you managing?' Ann asked.

'I'm good. Just a bit wobbly on these things sometimes.' She lifted one of the crutches. 'Dad said I should say hello if I was in the building, but I really needed to talk with you about something.'

'You'd better come into my office,' Ann opened the main door to allow Cassie in and led the way to her small office at the back of the room.

'How can I help you?' she asked, once Cassie was settled, her crutches lying on the floor beside her. Ann hoped the girl didn't want to ask about her relationship with Gus. She had no idea how she'd handle it if she did.

To her surprise, it was about something completely different.

'It's like this,' Cassie began. 'For personal reasons, I want to switch my studies to William Farrer – transfer to the course here. I thought it'd be simple and contacted my uni back home and the admin here. I've asked Canada to send me copies of my transcript and I've applied for an extension to my student visa. But I need to work out how my old course fits with the one here, and what subjects I'd need to enrol in. Can you help?'

Ann was stunned. All she could think to say was, 'Does your dad know?'

Cassie gave a wicked grin. 'I mentioned it to him the other day. I think he was surprised, but he's cool. I told him I don't want to leave Miles. He's my boyfriend. He's studying music and has a place in an orchestra. It's a good solution.'

Ann was silent for several moments, moments when she wondered how Gus really felt about his daughter's decision. It must have come as a shock, yet he'd said nothing about it to her. 'Sounds like it,' she said finally. 'If you let me have your transcripts, I can help you work things out.'

'Cool, thanks.' Cassie reached for her crutches and fitted them under her arms. When she reached the door, she turned round to face Ann again. 'About you and Dad... I'm good with it.' She hobbled out, leaving Ann speechless.

*

Ann stretched out in bed feeling the now familiar thrill as her toes and Gus's met. He turned to pull her into his arms, gave her a quick kiss, then said, 'We should make a move if we want to make the most of the weekend.'

Despite an initial disappointment, Ann agreed and leapt out of bed. 'Beat you to the shower,' she said gaily, wondering where her energy had come from. She hadn't behaved like this since… since she and Gus were together before. It was as if he'd infused her with a new lease of life, better than any vitamin or age-defying cream.

Over breakfast, she told him about Cassie's visit to the office. 'What do you think about her plan to transfer?' she asked, watching his reaction carefully.

'It's her life,' he said. 'Miles – her fellow – seems a decent guy.' He rubbed his chin. 'Makes me think of us at their age. Maybe they'll get it right.'

Ann bit on the inside of her cheek. Damn! Was he suggesting it was all her fault – or was he willing to take some of the blame?

'But we have a second chance,' he continued. 'I never thought that would happen. Come here.' He rose, picked her up and swept her into his arms, kissing her soundly. 'This weekend, we need to talk.'

'Sounds ominous.' Ann was trembling, whether from excitement or fear, she wasn't quite sure. A second chance – was that what they had? And would she blow it like she had the first?

Breakfast over, they set off, singing in tune to the radio as they left Granite Springs and drove out along the highway.

It was almost lunchtime when they reached their destination and found a perfect camping spot near a creek. After a few attempts, they managed to erect what seemed like a very small tent. They set up their bedding before storing the provisions Ann had bought the day before and having a lunch of the sandwiches she'd prepared before leaving home.

The afternoon was taken up with a long bushwalk, so it wasn't till after a dinner of sausages and potatoes cooked over an open fire that they talked.

'I've been thinking a lot about us,' Gus said, as they sat in the light of the glowing embers of the fire and the moon, his arm slung around her shoulders.

Ann shivered and moved closer. Was this the time he was going to tell her he was leaving? Was he going to spoil their weekend together?

'I can't let you go again, Annie. You mean too much to me. I was young and foolish. I should have stayed. The job wasn't as important to me as you. I was an arrogant, ambitious bastard. Can you forgive me?'

Ann was stunned. 'That's a bit harsh,' she said. 'There's nothing to forgive. It was me. I chose to stay.'

'For a very good reason.' He removed his arm and clasped his hands, dropping them between his knees and gazing into the remains of the fire. 'I should have been more understanding of your predicament. But I was young, thinking only of myself.'

'No, Gus.' Despite thinking exactly that for over thirty years, Ann put a reassuring hand on Gus's shoulder. 'We were both young. We made different decisions.'

Gus turned back towards her, took her face in his hands, and gazed into her eyes. 'I love you, Annie Baird. I want to spend the rest of my life with you. But there are a few things we need to resolve.'

Ann's heart was thumping so loudly she thought he must hear it. What was Gus going to suggest?

'It's clear we can't go on living so far apart, so...' Gus took a deep breath. '...I propose to set up a subsidiary of CAT in Granite Springs. I'll need to be here to get things going, which fits with Cassie, if she manages to set up this transfer she's so set on. We'll be able to be together, too. Maybe stay for a few years, then we'll need to take stock, decide where our home will be. My business means we can move back and forth between here and Canada, but it's up to you – where you want to live most of the time. I must admit, I'm enjoying being back more than I expected.'

Ann didn't know what to think. *Did he expect her to give him an answer? What was he asking?*

Gus must have seen her indecision. 'Sorry. What I'm asking you is, are you willing to take a chance on me again – to accept I love you, always will, to spend our lives together?'

Ann felt a bubble of excitement well up until she felt she was about to burst. She remembered what that weird old woman had said, something about an opportunity. Was this what she was talking about? How could she have known?

'I want that too,' Ann said, only to find herself enveloped in a hug, Gus's arms around her, his lips on hers, silencing anything else she wanted to say.

The rest of the weekend was wonderful, spent walking and making love. It was late when they drove back to Granite Springs on Monday evening, Ann's head on Gus's shoulder. It had been a weekend to remember, a weekend which had laid all Ann's fears to rest.

Twenty-nine

Chris drew a hand through his hair as he fired up his laptop and sipped the coffee he'd picked up at The Bean Sprout on the way. He'd dropped into the flat for a change of clothes after their camping weekend, when they'd spent their days bushwalking and their nights curled up together in the tent. It had been like being teenagers again, and he felt invigorated. Life was good.

While waiting for the computer to load, Chris took out his phone. During the weekend he'd turned it off to save the battery, but now, he was eager to contact Cassie to see how she was coping with being back on campus. He knew he was fussing, but wasn't that what dads did?

He was surprised to see a number of missed calls and texts from a Canadian number he didn't recognise.

He opened the most recent text.

Chris, it's Stan. Call me. Bee.

Chris felt his gut churn. What could have happened to his right-hand man? Bee was Stan's wife. She wouldn't contact him unless it was something serious. He checked the time. It would be early afternoon back home. He pressed to return her call.

'Chris! Thank goodness. I've been trying to reach you. Stan…' Bee's voice broke.

'Bee, I'm sorry, I was incommunicado. What's happened to the big guy?' Chris cursed himself for turning off his phone. But he hadn't anticipated any kind of emergency. Stan Gray was Chris's age, a fit big man who exercised regularly and played competitive sport every weekend, putting Chris to shame. It couldn't be anything serious.

'He's had a heart attack,' Bee stammered through tears. 'I'm at the hospital now.'

'How bad?' Chris was suddenly alert.

'They say we got him to Emergency just in time. He could have…' Bee broke down.

Chris waited till she spoke again.

'Oh, Chris, I was so scared. They say he's out of the woods now, but I don't know when he'll be able to go back to work.'

'Don't worry about work. The most important thing is to get him well again. Is there anything I can do to help? Is there anyone with you?'

'I'm fine, thanks. I have my sister, and the boys have been wonderful. But, as soon as he could speak, Stan said I must call you.'

Chris had forgotten Stan and Bee's boys were now grown. Unlike Chris, he and Bee had married early. They'd be a good support for her. He was humbled, but not surprised that Stan's first thought had been for Chris and the company.

'Tell him to put all his energy into getting better, not to worry about work. I'll fix something up.'

When he finished the call, Chris sat gazing into space. He cursed under his breath. This was the last thing he expected to happen – and just as he and Annie were getting on so well. But there was nothing for it. He had to go back to Canada to sort things out, find a replacement for Stan for however long it took him to recover. Only then would he be able to return to Granite Springs.

How was he going to tell Cassie? And how was he going to explain to Annie?

*

Cassie was the easier one. He sent her a text asking if he could meet her for lunch.

Sure, Dad. Banjo's at 12? Have an hour free. Cxx.

Chris looked at his phone again, trying to decide. No, he wouldn't call Annie at work. That would be the coward's way. He needed to tell her face-to-face this evening over dinner. Right now, he needed to arrange a flight.

The thought of returning to Canada and leaving Annie again, made him feel as if an enormous weight had descended on him. How could he make her understand?

He was choosing other priorities again, putting his company before their relationship. But how could he do anything else? CAT was his livelihood. He needed to be there, to talk with the staff, to reassure them, to arrange for someone to take Stan's place. They were a young crew, none with the experience of his second-in-command. Who could he trust to take Stan's place?

Surely Annie would accept his need to make the trip to sort things out. This time he wasn't leaving her forever.

He turned back to his laptop to check flights.

*

Arriving at the campus, Chris was struck again by the beauty of the place. Instead of a large brick monstrosity or buildings separated by quadrangles, William Farrer University was composed of a series of single and two-storey light brick and sandstone buildings, set among glades of trees and bushes.

As he made his way to the café Cassie nominated, Chris passed groups of students sitting around on the grass, despite the cool of the day, and others sauntering along pathways bordered by low shrubs and bushes. No wonder Cassie loved it here.

The Banjo Patterson Café, named after the famous Australian bush poet, sat at the end of one of those pathways, this one bordered by bottle brush. *It must look spectacular when in bloom*, Chris thought, as he headed up the path.

Once inside, Chris had trouble finding Cassie. It seemed as if half the student population of Granite Springs had decided to have lunch there and they were all intent on making as much noise as possible. This wasn't helped by the loud thud of background music.

Finally, he saw a familiar hand waving to him from the back corner of the café. He made his way towards it.

'Hi, Dad! You don't mind Miles being here, do you? We always lunch together when we can.' She smiled at the young man sitting beside her looking slightly embarrassed.

'I can go if you want to talk with Cassie in private,' Miles said, starting to rise.

'No, stay.' Chris put up one hand. 'It'll be fine.' While Chris was surprised to see Miles, it might be just as well. Cassie was probably going to be upset he was leaving, and perhaps Miles could comfort her.

'This is great,' Cassie said. 'Lunch with my two favourite men. Did you want to see me about anything in particular, Dad? You need to order at the counter. Miles has already ordered for us.' She beamed at him again.

Had he and Annie behaved like this? Chris pondered as he weaved among the tables to reach the counter. The shock of Bee's call had taken away any appetite he might have had, but he ordered a macchiato and a burger, then forced his way back to Cassie and Miles.

'Okay, Dad. What's up? Why the sudden urge to come to campus?' She took a sip of the coffee which had arrived while Chris was ordering and stared at him, her eyes so like his own.

Chris decided there was no point in beating about the bush. 'I have to go back to Canada.'

'Back home? Why? I thought you were going to stay till I was fully recovered.' Her forehead creased, and Miles took her hand.

Home? Chris wondered why, suddenly, Canada didn't seem like home. Home was here where he'd grown up, where Annie was. It always had been.

'There's an emergency situation. Stan's had a heart attack. I'm needed back at CAT headquarters to sort things out. I will be back as soon as I can. I hate to leave you like this. You'll be all right?'

'Don't worry, Dr Thomas,' Miles said. 'I'll see Cassie is okay, make sure she doesn't overdo it.'

'How awful.' Her lips turned down. 'But...'

'What's the matter?'

'I was wondering about my sessions with Thea. But don't worry, Dad. I'll work something out. Give my love to Uncle Stan. I hope he's okay.'

Chris bit his lip. In the rush to arrange things he hadn't taken Cassie's rehab sessions into account. How could he have forgotten?

'No worries. I can take you.' Miles squeezed her hand.

Cassie turned to him, a smile beginning to appear. 'But your classes?'

Miles shrugged. 'I'll talk to Prof Larsen. He's a cool guy. He'll understand.'

Relieved to have one problem sorted, Chris said, 'Thanks, Miles. I'm glad Cassie has you. I'm flying out tomorrow, so...'

'Can we have dinner tonight?' Cassie asked, seemingly relieved, too, to have this settled.

Chris was torn. A last dinner with Cassie would be perfect – if he didn't have the discussion with Annie hanging over him. 'I'm sorry,' he said. How could he explain to his daughter he didn't want to spend his last night in Granite Springs with her?

There were footsteps behind him, and he heard a voice say, 'Gus, you didn't tell me you were coming to the campus today.'

He turned. 'Annie!' Of course, she worked here. It was no surprise she was having lunch in Banjo's too. She looked as wonderful as usual, dressed in the smart grey tailored suit and white blouse he'd last seen her wearing over breakfast. There was another woman hovering behind her, a woman with short spiky blonde hair.

'Are you going to introduce me, Ann?' she said with a grin.

'Oh! Gus this is my friend, Fran Larsen. Fran, this is...' she hesitated for a moment, '...Chris and Cassie, and... I'm sorry I don't know the young man.'

Before either Chris or Cassie could speak, Fran gave a peal of laughter. 'But I do. Miles is one of our students in Music and Drama. Pleased to meet you, Chris and Cassie. I've heard a lot about you both.'

The tips of Chris's ears turned pink. This was the Fran Annie had told him about. She'd obviously told her about him, too. 'Hello, Fran. Good to meet you. Meeting Cassie for lunch was a sudden impulse,' he said to Annie, daring Cassie to say more.

Annie only nodded, then the two women moved on as Fran nudged Annie towards a free table.

'Are you having dinner with *her*?' Cassie asked. 'Is that why you can't have it with me?'

'I need to tell Annie I'm leaving,' Chris muttered, hoping her table was too far away for his words to be heard.

'Is that who you spent the weekend with – your bush getaway?' Cassie winked.

Chris blushed. He found Cassie's teasing about Annie difficult to cope with.

'Don't worry, Dad. I'm glad you've found someone at your age. And, I told you, I approve. She's going to help me sort out this transfer business. Do you know when you'll be back?' she asked, neatly changing the subject.

'I don't. I need to check where things are at and find a suitable replacement for Stan, hopefully from within the company, but if not...' Chris's shoulders sagged at the possibility he might have to advertise the position, and the time it would take to find a new second-in-command. 'Hopefully soon,' he said, trying to hide his fear. 'I have the office here, and I'll keep the flat on. I'll keep in touch, of course.'

'Okay.'

Chris's meal arrived and they concentrated on their food. As he ate, Chris watched Annie and her friend who were seated some distance away. She looked so happy, almost carefree, occasionally glancing in his direction with a knowing smile. Breaking the news to Annie was not going to be easy.

Thirty

'So that's the man who has you all hot and bothered?' Fran leant across the table to whisper to Ann, a twinkle in her eye. 'Not bad.'

'Shh.' Ann blushed. 'I didn't expect to see him here.' She looked over, caught his eye and smiled.

'Obviously not! I saw how you both turned red.' She chuckled.

'We... I... didn't!'

Fran chuckled again. 'You should see your face. You'd think you'd been caught out in *flagrante delicto*.'

'Stop it!' She risked another glance over to Gus's table, but they were all busy eating. When she looked again, they'd left.

'How was the weekend?' Fran asked when their meals arrived. Today they'd both ordered pumpkin soup served with sour dough bread, plus their usual coffee and tea. 'Camping?' She raised an eyebrow.

'It was good, wonderful.' Ann beamed at the memory. 'I took your advice and decided to trust him – and my gut feeling.'

'And?'

'I think it's going to work out, Fran. I really do. It's not like before. We're older now and hopefully more sensible. Gus plans to set up a subsidiary of his company here and stay for a few years, then we can decide where we want to be.' She had butterflies in her stomach just thinking about it.

'We? So that means...?'

'We're going to be together.' There, she'd said it out loud, the phrase that had been going around and around in her head since Saturday, sitting by the campfire with Gus, gazing up at the stars. It felt right. *But it had felt right before.* She stifled the tiny voice threatening to burst her bubble of happiness. Gus wouldn't let her down again. He couldn't. They were no raw youngsters. They were adults who'd each had their share of troubles, who'd found each other again and intended to stay together.

'I'm glad.' Fran reached to cover Ann's hand with hers. 'He seems like a good guy and his daughter's a cutie. I didn't know she was involved with Miles Sharkey. He's one of Owen's prize students, has already been offered a place in the Canberra Symphonic and been playing with them. He's going places. So, what's next? He's still living in Frank's flat?'

Ann blushed. 'We haven't got that far. But he's rarely there.' It had crossed her mind. She'd be lying if she said it hadn't. But, although they spent almost every night together, neither had mentioned the obvious solution – that he move in with Ann on a more permanent basis and give up the flat. Was that what she wanted? Her mother, a dyed-in-the-wool catholic, would turn in her grave at the thought of Ann living in sin – as she would see it – in her house.

'What's stopping you?' Fran took a mouthful of soup and bit into her bread. 'Owen would have moved in with me in a flash if he hadn't had the acreage – and the goats to look after. It was more sensible for me to move out there.' She peered across the table at her friend. 'You're not worried about what people will say?'

Ann twisted her hands in her lap. She knew it shouldn't worry her but for so long she'd lived in this town, conscious of the wagging tongues, of the censorship of so many women who deemed themselves the arbiters of the town's morals. Then there was Susie. She almost laughed when she considered what her righteous sister might think. Perhaps it would have been different if it had been someone like Sam Walker Ann was involved with, someone Susie had introduced her to, who had Susie's seal of approval. But Gus, the man Susie blamed for Ann's pregnancy – she'd go spare. Ann hadn't even told Susie he was back in town, though she might have heard on the grapevine.

'It's this town,' she said. 'I've lived here all my life. I know what they can be like. And there's Susie.'

'Your sister? What's she got to do with it?'

'She sees herself as my saviour. It was Susie who helped me when I was pregnant, after Gus left. And now, she keeps producing these unsuitable men for me. I've told you about them.'

'I thought the last one – Sam Walker – wasn't as unsuitable as usual.'

'No. He's a nice guy.' *And if Gus hadn't appeared on the scene, maybe she and Sam would have become more than friends.* 'But Susie took my side about Gus. She'd never believe I could forgive him.'

'Well, it's your life. If I were you, I wouldn't want to waste a minute of it. Life's too short.'

Maybe Fran was right. And what was it that woman, Fran's neighbour, had said?

'Remember Magda?' Fran asked, reading Ann's mind. 'She's a wise woman. She got it right about Owen and me. Didn't she say something about not letting an opportunity escape?'

Am flinched. She'd forgotten Fran was there, too. 'Something like that,' she admitted.

'Well, there you are,' Fran said, as if the matter was settled.

*

The conversation with Fran bothered Ann all afternoon, making any issues in the office take second place to the argument going on in her mind. By the time she left to go home, she'd almost decided to bring it up with Gus. Fran was right. It was crazy for him to retain a flat he rarely slept in and only went back to for a change of clothes. What did it matter what the gossips in Granite Springs thought? They probably already knew. His car had been sitting in her driveway every night recently. It wouldn't take a genius to put two and two together.

She decided to cook a special dinner. Gus was due to arrive around six, giving her time to prepare.

When Gus arrived, he looked weary, but he hugged her as warmly as before and his kiss was everything she could wish for, making her long for the end of the evening when they'd be together in her warm bed.

'Hard day?' she asked when they pulled apart.

'Mmm. Tell you later.' Gus drew a hand through his hair.

'Did you have a good lunch with Cassie?'

'Sure. You?'

'Mmm.'

'So that's your friend, Fran? Miles says she keeps the professor in the School of Music and Drama on his toes. He calls it the MAD house.'

'She's good, used to be Nick's PA, before Kay.' It was funny, Ann mused, how all that had come about. Kay was appointed to Fran's position while she was overseas. This had led to her and Nick getting together. Then Fran was appointed to the new school where she met Owen. Maybe there was something to fate after all.

This led her to her own decision. She'd talk to Gus tonight, once they were settled with a glass of wine.

'Something smells good.' Gus followed Ann into the kitchen.

'Roast chicken. I decided we should celebrate.' Her stomach was churning in anticipation of what she had to say. 'Wine?'

'I'll get it.' Gus fetched a bottle of white from the fridge while Ann took two glasses from the cupboard.

'The chicken will be a little while. Let's take it into the living room.'

Once there and seated together on the sofa, Gus poured the wine.

Ann sipped hers, then took a deep breath and turned to face Gus. 'Thanks for a wonderful weekend. I couldn't stop thinking about it all day, and I have a suggestion to make.'

Gus smiled, but Ann thought she detected a hint of something she couldn't identify in his expression – something that didn't match his smile. Was it guilt? What did he have to be guilty about?

'You're spending so much time here, it seems crazy to keep paying rent for the flat over the café. Why don't you move your things here?' She held her breath. Surely he'd agree?

But, instead of the immediate agreement she expected, instead of Gus sweeping her into his arms again, he looked down into the glass he was holding, and cleared his throat. 'I've received some bad news.'

Ann began to tremble. What on earth could he mean? 'Bad news?'

'From Canada. Stan, my second in command, the guy who's been managing the office there while I'm gone – he's had a heart attack. I need to go back for a while to take care of things.'

Ann felt as if her world was falling apart. For a moment, she thought she was going to faint. She had a sense of *déjà vu*. It was happening all over again. Gus was leaving her. 'No!' The word exploded from her lips, and the glass she was holding tipped over, spilling wine on her lap.

'I'm not going for good. I'll be back as soon as I find someone to take over Stan's role. It doesn't change anything, Annie. It's not like before.' Gus took Ann's glass from her and pulled her into his arms, his mouth on her hair. 'I love you,' he murmured. 'I meant what I said on the weekend. I want you in my life. You're everything to me.'

Ann breathed in the now familiar aroma of the man she loved and tried to keep calm, to believe what Gus was telling her. 'Sorry.' She lifted her head to meet his eyes. 'It's a shock.'

'For me, too. That's why I met with Cassie at lunchtime today. I had to tell her, too.'

'When... when do you leave?'

'Tomorrow.'

'So soon?' Ann couldn't believe what she was hearing. She and Gus had just spent a wonderful weekend together. She'd finally managed to trust him, to believe there was a future for them, now this.

Belatedly, she asked, 'Your friend, Stan, how bad is it?'

'Pretty bad, but his wife says he'll recover. She tried to call me all weekend, but I had my phone off. You do understand, Annie? I have to go. But I'll be back as soon as I can – and I love your suggestion. When I come back – yes?'

'Yes,' she agreed, when all she wanted to do was yell and scream about the unfairness of life, of a fate which had given her a second chance with Gus, only to have it whipped away again. But not forever, she reminded herself.

Over dinner, Ann and Gus managed to make conversation, but the knowledge of his imminent departure hung over them like a cloud. It wasn't till they were in bed, their bodies entwined, Gus's lips on hers, that it was forgotten in the surge of passion that overwhelmed them.

Neither of them slept much. It was as if both wanted to fill every one of their last hours with memories, memories which would sustain them until they were together again.

But, in the cold light of morning, when they arose bleary-eyed, there was no escaping it.

'What time's your flight?' Ann asked over breakfast, her cup clasped in both hands to stop them trembling.

'Ten-thirty, then I have a couple of hours in Sydney before the connecting flight. I'll go over to the flat and pack, then I can check the car back in at the airport.'

'Of course.' Ann had all but forgotten Gus was still driving a hire car. Somehow, returning his car made his departure seem more final. She gave herself a shake. There was no point thinking like this. She needed to put on a brave face, give Gus a positive image of his Annie to remember. She forced a smile.

But, once in the car, on her way to work, Ann began to crumble. Gus was gone or would be in little over an hour. How was she going to cope without him now that she'd taken the step of entrusting her future to him yet again?

For some reason the weird woman's words came back to haunt her. This time, she remembered them exactly, as if the woman were sitting in the car with her.

'Your journey has yet to be completed. There will be a reminder from the past, a chance to put right something you regret. Don't let the opportunity escape. It could bring you great happiness.'

Could she trust the old woman was right? Or was she about to suffer all over again?

Thirty-one

It was hard to say goodbye to Annie. At her door, Chris hugged her as if he'd never let her go, then kissed her, storing up the feeling of her lips on his, and inhaling her unique fragrance.

'I wish you didn't have to go.' A tear trickled down Annie's cheek.

Chris wiped it away with one finger. He wished that, too. 'I'll be back as soon as I can, before you know it,' he murmured, pulling her to him again for one more hug, his lips grazing her cheek before searing her lips one last time. Then, reluctantly he let her go and he headed to his car.

At the flat, Chris hastily packed. He hadn't brought many clothes with him, so it didn't take long. He checked the fridge to make sure there were no perishable items, throwing out a half-full carton of milk, the last few slices of a loaf, and an overripe banana.

With time to spare, he decided to pop downstairs for a coffee. He needed to let Frank know he'd be away for a bit, and it would help make up for the lost sleep. He thought back to the night he and Annie spent together, how he'd almost changed his mind about leaving. But he knew he couldn't. There was too much at stake.

'Morning, Chris. The usual?' Frank asked from behind the expresso machine, when Chris walked in.

'Thanks, Frank. I wanted a word. I have to make a dash back to Canada.' Somehow it didn't sound so bad put that way. Perhaps he should have said it like that to Annie.

'That's quite a dash. Trouble?'

'One of my staff – my right-hand guy – has taken ill. I'll be back as soon as I can. I wanted to let you know the flat will be empty for a bit.'

'As long as you'll be back.'

Chris wondered if now was the time to mention he'd be giving up the flat and moving in with Annie but decided against it. 'Sure thing,' he said instead.

He settled himself at a corner table and took out his phone. While he was waiting for his coffee, he sent a message to Bee to let her know his flight plans, and another to the staff to tell them of his return. He'd be there in two days. Then he opened up the CAT website to check out the staff profiles. Although he knew them by heart, he needed to review them to work out who, if anyone, could take Stan's place in the interim.

By the time he'd finished his coffee, Chris had narrowed his option to two. He wanted to be sure the person he chose had both the experience to do the job and the ability to maintain the respect of the rest of the multitalented crew. He thought either Alan Tennant or Cheryl Sherwood were distinct possibilities and planned to spend time with both before making a decision.

That done, it was time to leave. Chris farewelled Frank and set off for the airport.

*

It was a shock to arrive back in Canada after Granite Springs, even though he'd always thought the North American country more similar to Australia than the United States. He'd always felt like a foreigner there.

It was still early afternoon when he arrived so, despite suffering from jetlag, Chris's first stop was the office – located in a tall glass structure close to the centre of town. It had always given him the feeling he'd really made it. He enjoyed standing on the pavement looking skyward to see the building tower above him, knowing his company filled an entire floor.

Today, this feeling of elation refused to appear. All he felt was exhaustion and a sense of loss. He wondered what Annie was doing now. It would be ten o'clock on Thursday morning in Granite Springs. He could picture her, dressed in one of the business suits she habitually wore to work, sitting in front of her computer. Or perhaps she was having coffee at Banjo's with her friend Fran. Maybe Cassie was there, too. He liked to think of his two favourite women in the same place, perhaps even exchanging friendly greetings.

He shook his head and walked through the heavy glass door.

'Welcome back, Dr Thomas,' Mona, the receptionist CAT shared with other inhabitants of the tower building, greeted him. 'Good to see you again.'

Chris smiled and nodded. He didn't have time today for his usual chat when he asked about Mona's extended family who had immigrated there from India several generations ago. She was a marvel at keeping tabs on the comings and goings of all the office staff in the building – a mammoth task, but one which she performed with ease and good humour, managing to keep abreast of everyone's movements.

'The boss's back!' Chris heard the murmur immediately he entered his office floor and was relieved to see so many happy faces.

'Dr Thomas.' Lena, his PA, a woman who'd been with him from the beginning, came out to greet him. 'We didn't expect to see you today.' Her voice held a note of disapproval. The same old Lena, who always tried to run his life, who despaired of keeping him in line, who was loyal to the core. She never changed. It was good to be back.

'Hi, Lena. Can you come into the office and bring me up to speed?' He knew she'd been working closely with Stan while he was away and would have her finger on the pulse of the company.

After chatting with Lena, Chris drew up the personnel files on both Alan and Cheryl and studied them, before setting up meetings with both for the following day. The sooner he could get everything sorted out, the sooner he could get back to Australia, though, after talking with Lena, he'd identified a few issues he needed to handle himself. It wasn't like Stan to have let things slide. He wondered if his old friend had been feeling bad for some time. There hadn't been any indication in their regular calls.

A visit to the hospital was next on his list, but he'd head home first for a shower and change of clothes. He'd checked out the visiting hours with Bee and knew he wouldn't be able to see Stan till early evening.

Maybe he could even catch a short nap. He was beginning to feel the effects of jetlag and the thought of a soft bed was very attractive.

Before he left, he sent a text to Annie telling her he'd arrived and what his plans were, to be rewarded almost immediately with a short reply and a kiss emoji. He grinned, wishing she was with him, to kiss him in real life.

After a shower and a nap, Chris felt a hundred percent better. He was hungry but having emptied the fridge and thrown out any perishable food before he left for Australia, could only find a tin of tuna and some water crackers to snack on. He added grocery shopping to his to-do list, wondering how long he'd need to stay.

Bee was already at Stan's bedside when Chris entered the ward. 'Bee!' He greeted her with a hug and peck on the cheek before turning towards the bed, shocked to see his old friend looking so frail, a shadow of his former self.

'Hey,' Chris said, trying to inject a positive note into his voice, 'so this is what you get up to when I leave you.'

'Sorry, Chris, I've let you down.' Stan seemed to have aged since Chris last saw him.

'Don't be stupid. You couldn't have predicted this. The most important thing now, is for you to get better. Don't worry about me or CAT. We'll cope and be waiting for you when you're back on top of your game again.'

'They say it could be weeks, even months.'

'However long it takes.' Chris patted the hand lying outside the covers.

'Listen to Chris, Stan,' Bee said. 'Thanks, Chris.' She gave him a watery smile. 'I told Stan you'd understand. No job's as important as your health.'

'No,' Chris agreed, realising how, for years, he'd thought CAT was more important than anything else in his life. Maybe he wasn't so different from Gail after all. But he had prioritised Cassie, too. And now there was Annie.

He stayed a little longer but could see Stan was tiring, so made his farewells, promising to return later in the week. As he left, he wondered again how long it would be before he was on the return flight to Australia. No matter how important Annie and Cassie were to him, he couldn't leave till he was sure CAT was in safe hands. It was one thing to tell Annie he could run his business from anywhere; it was only partly true. He needed a steady hand at the helm right here in head office.

The hospital was like any other hospital, the only difference between this one and the base hospital in Granite Springs being the size. Vancouver General Hospital was an enormous multi-level building but had the same distinctive atmosphere and the same sense of urgency permeating the corridors. Chris was glad to leave. He fervently hoped Bee was right when she said Stan was on the mend. He was too young to be so ill.

After shopping on the way home, Chris grilled himself a steak and threw together a salad, before pouring a glass of red wine and settling down in front of the television. But he found it difficult to concentrate on the news programmes he used to devour. He missed Annie. He missed Granite Springs. Damn it, he missed the renewed sense of happiness he'd experienced over the past couple of months.

He needed to speak with her. He needed to see her. He rose, went to have a shower to waken himself up, then to the kitchen to pour another glass of wine. It should be late afternoon in Granite Springs. With luck, he'd be able to catch her.

Pressing speed dial, and setting the phone to Facetime, Chris waited with bated breath as he heard Annie's phone ring. He drummed his fingers on the kitchen benchtop as it rang and rang.

'Gus!' Annie's beautiful face appeared on the screen. He could see shelves of books behind her. She was in her office.

Her voice was music to his ears. Seeing her made him want her even more. 'Annie! I miss you – so much.' He heard voices in the background. She wasn't alone.

'Just a minute.' She spoke to someone else. A door closed. 'That's better. Oh!' She chuckled. 'Did you just get up?'

Chris looked down, realising he hadn't taken time to dress properly after his shower. He was sitting, naked from the waist up, on one of the high stools at his kitchen bench. 'I just got out the shower.' He laughed, feeling better now he could see and hear her, but wishing she'd been in the shower with him.

'It's good to hear your voice, to see you. I miss you too.' There was a pause while she patted her eyes with a tissue. 'Sorry. How was the flight?'

'As usual. I hate those long hauls. And I hate being so far away from you.'

'And your friend?'

'Stan?' Chris sighed. 'He's not looking good. I called in to see him after I'd been to the office. He seems to have aged. He's a husk of the vibrant, energetic man I left back in January.' He bit his lip remembering Stan's face, almost as white as the pillows he was lying on. 'His wife says he's on the mend, but it could be weeks... months before he's back to his old self.'

Annie's indrawn breath made his stomach quiver.

'Do you... will you have to stay till then?'

'No! But I may have to stay longer than I intended. It depends what happens tomorrow.' He took a sip of coffee. 'I plan to meet with a couple of the crew I've earmarked as possibilities to take over from Stan. If they don't work out...' He dragged a hand through his hair.

'Oh, I hope they do!'

'Me, too. I can't wait to get back to you – and Cassie. Have you seen anything of her?'

'She's fine. She popped into the office today. I've worked out a study plan for her if the transfer goes through. She's thrilled with it.'

'Thanks. What's been happening with you since I left?' It had only been two days, but it felt like forever. Now he was back in Canada, Granite Springs and all that happened there seemed like a dream. It felt surreal.

'Not a lot. Nothing's changed here.'

Chris sensed Annie was uncomfortable. Even though she was pleased to hear from him, to see him, and said she missed him, there was a reserve, not unlike when they'd first met again.

'I'm sorry, Gus. I need to...' She looked away from the screen and there was the sound of a door opening and closing.

'Sorry. You're at work. I called at a bad time.' He felt guilty, his need to see and hear her having forced him to call as soon as he woke instead of waiting till she was home, till she was alone and could talk freely.

They both hung up and Chris stared at the blank screen. Then he looked around. This rebuilt and renovated Edwardian house was their family home, the one he and Gail had purchased to bring up the bevy of kids they intended to have – or was he the only one who'd had that dream? It was a far cry from the comfortable Federation home Annie lived in, the one she'd invited him to share.

Why did he still live here? When Gail left, he'd thought it important for Cassie to keep the home she was familiar with and had grown up in. It was close to her school and friends. But was it still so important? Cassie was grown and had clearly demonstrated on his trip to Australia she was independent with a mind of her own. Would she ever want to live here again? Did *he* ever want to live here again, with its reminders of the past?

He meant what he said to Annie. He could easily base himself in Granite Springs. He'd need somewhere here too, of course. But not a place like this. Maybe it was time to sell, to look for something smaller, perhaps a unit or townhouse, something which could easily be locked up when he and Annie were in Australia?

Thirty-two

Ann was missing Gus. She understood his need to go back to fix the problem with his business. Of course, she did. But there was still a little voice inside telling her this had happened before. It had been two weeks now and not even his frequent texts and Facetime calls could completely silence it.

She'd found it best to keep busy. It was what had sustained her over the years, and it would sustain her now. But things weren't the same as they had been before Gus returned, before she'd allowed herself to fall in love with him again. Whatever she was trying to do, whether it was her work at the university, or her various volunteer activities, Ann always found her thoughts wandering to Gus. He also invaded her dreams with visions of searing passion which forced her to suddenly awaken, then have difficulty in getting back to sleep.

This morning, she was feeling tired, the restless nights beginning to catch up with her. Ann had noticed Kerrie and Janelle giving each other smug glances over the past few days but decided to ignore them. She was becoming better at looking the other way in the hope they'd stop whatever they were up to, perhaps even decide to look for employment elsewhere.

She wasn't unduly surprised to receive a call from the Human Resources manager around eleven o'clock. Flora Richards had been with the university almost as long as Ann had, and they'd often collaborated on recruitment panels. Although it was unusual for her to ask Ann to come up to her office, there was nothing in the call to raise her suspicions.

'I'm going over to HR. Won't be long,' she said to Rachel who was manning the front desk.

When she reached the administration building, Ann pushed open the door. 'Flora wants to see me. Okay if I just go in?' she asked the girl at the desk who was a stranger to her.

'You are?'

'Ann Baird, from Education. Flora called me.' Ann tapped her foot impatiently. The girl must be new. Ann was familiar with most Human Resource staff.

'Take a seat. I'll let Ms Richards know you are here.'

'But...' Ann was in the habit of just walking into the office but decided not to make a fuss. The girl was only doing her job, even if she was being somewhat officious. She sat down and gazed into space. It was the first time in days she'd had nothing to do.

Before long, Flora appeared, her lips taut. 'Sorry to keep you. Come in.'

Instead of going to Flora's office, Ann found herself being ushered into a small meeting room, empty apart from two chairs and a table on which lay an open folder.

'This is difficult, Ann,' Flora said, when they were both seated. 'We've had a complaint – two, actually – and I'm obligated to follow them up.'

Ann felt the breath leave her body. Suddenly she saw her two problem staff members, their smug looks, their whispers. She could guess what this was about. She automatically straightened her shoulders. Flora and she had worked together for years. Surely she wouldn't believe the ravings of two disgruntled women?

Flora opened the folder, her eyes scanning the documents. She looked up. 'I'm sorry, Ann, but two of your staff have made what appear to be serious complaints about your treatment of them.' She raised her eyes to meet Ann's. They were filled with compassion. 'I know how difficult it can be, managing a group of younger women.'

Ann stared at Flora. They were close to the same age. What was she suggesting? 'Perhaps you should tell me what they are complaining about.' She could guess. She'd heard their complaints often enough, could probably recite them verbatim.

'Of course.' Flora's voice was icy. She proceeded to itemise a number of instances, most of which Ann was aware.

A cold shiver shot up Ann's spine. This could be serious. She should have done something about those two, set in place formal disciplinary procedures, instead of turning a blind eye and hoping it would go away.

Flora was still speaking. 'Were you aware of their concerns?'

'Ye…es. They complain all the time. It's been difficult, Flora. I probably should have started disciplinary action, but I didn't want to damage their careers with the university. I have had call to speak with them on several occasions regarding their abuse of university equipment and deliberate flouting of protocols, but…' she sighed, '… it only seems to make them worse.'

Flora looked at her with an expression akin to pity.

'What happens now?' Ann couldn't believe this. First Gus left, now it seemed she was being hauled over the coals for her actions – or non-actions – as a manager. She just wanted to crawl away and hide.

'Well,' Flora tapped on the folder with her finger, 'given your longstanding history with the university and the fact there are no stains on your character, I discussed the matter with Professor Kerr…'

'Professor Kerr is privy to this?' Ann was shocked. It was more serious than she imagined. Damn those two!

'As I said, in discussion with Professor Kerr, it's been decided the first, and perhaps the best, course of action is to have a mediation. How do you feel about that?'

'Whatever.' Ann was past caring. At least *she* wasn't going to be disciplined for doing her job. 'When will this take place?'

'As soon as we can arrange it. I have a contact in Canberra – a skilled mediator. I'll check when he's free.' She closed the folder and stood up.

Ann stood, too.

As they were leaving the room, Flora put her hand on Ann's shoulder. 'Sorry about this, Ann, but I have my job to do, too. I don't for one minute imagine you've done anything wrong. But when there's a complaint, we need to be seen to be taking steps.'

'Thanks, Flora.'

Somehow Ann managed to make her way back to the office. She paused outside the door, then climbed the stairs to Professor Kerr's office. She wasn't ready to face the two troublemakers just yet, to see their smug looks, hear their whispered comments.

'Hello, Ann,' Kay greeted her at the top of the stairs. 'Want to see Nick? He's free. Go right in.'

Ignoring the hint of what she thought was pity on Kay's face, Ann cautiously pushed open the door to Nick's office.

Nick was sitting behind the desk. He looked up and rose, taking off his glasses. 'Ann, come in. Take a seat. He moved over to where two chairs were placed by a low coffee table and gestured to one of the chairs, taking the other himself.

'You've been to HR, I take it?' he asked as soon as they were both seated.

Ann nodded. Now she was here, she wasn't sure what she wanted to say.

'It's a rum business, but all too common, I'm afraid,' he said, tugging on his beard. 'I told Flora I didn't want to be part of it. I'm sorry you've been put in this position. I presume they've been difficult to handle – the two who complained?'

Ann nodded again, unwilling to trust her voice.

'You should have come to me.' He looked at Ann for a moment. 'Why do you have to be so stubborn, Ann? It can sometimes help to share a problem. Perhaps I could have done something to help before it got this far.'

Ann knew her independent streak often led to her being seen as inflexible, but that was the person she'd become over the years.

'Anyway, be assured I'm with you on this. If there's anything I can do. Of course, I've given Flora my view on the matter. I don't know the two who complained, but Kay tells me she saw what they were like in the short time she worked with you.'

Ann's stomach clenched. *Kay knew, too?*

Seeing her expression, Nick looked guilty. 'Sorry, I know I shouldn't have spoken to her about it, but...' He shrugged.

'I'd best get back to work.' Ann rose to leave.

'Look, you're upset. Why don't you go and get yourself a coffee? Take some time out. I'm sure you don't do that often enough. The office can get along without you for one morning.'

'Thanks.'

As she went through the outer office, Kay looked up and, seeing her disconsolate expression, asked, 'Want some company?'

Ann surprised herself by agreeing. Although she and Kay weren't great friends, she respected the other woman who had worked for a time in the Education office after her husband died under appalling circumstances. Kay knew what it felt like to have people talking about her.

Once in Banjo's with a cup of camomile tea – Ann needed its calming properties rather than the stimulation of coffee – Kay looked across the table.

'I hope you don't mind Nick telling me about those two,' she said. 'It really made my blood boil. I could see what they were like when I worked with you. I kept pretty much to myself. I'd had enough of the limelight, and the rest of your staff were younger than me. I was glad you gave me the chance to get back into the workforce. Kerrie and Janelle were always carping on about some imagined fault, criticising your management style. I thought you managed very well under what were sometimes very difficult circumstances.'

'Thanks.' Kay's words went a long way to soothing Ann's feelings. When she left the Human Resources office, she felt as if she'd been dealt a blow, but Professor Kerr, and now Kay was telling her she'd done nothing wrong. Of course, she knew that, but it helped to have her position validated.

'Was Flora helpful?'

'Sort of. There's to be a mediation. Evidently Professor Kerr suggested it.'

'Why don't you call him Nick? Everyone else does.'

'I can't. He's... I don't know.' Ann surprised herself with this admission. She'd always retained Nick's formal title, a way of maintaining distance between them. 'He's the boss,' she said weakly.

'He's my boss, too,' Kay said with a chuckle. 'He wouldn't mind. He's not one for formality.'

'I know.'

'About this mediation. How does it work?'

Glad to be on more familiar territory, Ann took a sip of her tea, before replying. 'I've not participated in one before, but I know what happens. A mediator is appointed – Flora says she knows one in Canberra – then he, or she, meets with all the aggrieved parties. I guess that includes me, Kerrie and Janelle. We all give our points of view and the mediator helps us find a mutually acceptable solution. At least, that's how it's supposed to work.'

'Mmm. Wonder how those two will go, I can't see them accepting anything other than the outcome they want.'

'I tend to agree, but I hope I'm wrong. The atmosphere in the office is becoming untenable with them trying to force the other staff members to take sides.' Ann had been trying to ignore what was happening and it was a relief to share it with Kay. 'It was bound to come to a head.'

'What is it that they want?' Kay was puzzled.

'I think they'd love to get rid of me.' Ann shared what had been in the back of her mind, something she hadn't told anyone, not even Gus or Fran.

'No way!' Kay's eyes widened. 'Nick would never let that happen.'

'He wouldn't have a choice if the powers that be decided.' How would Ann feel if it did happen, if she lost the job which had been her lifeline? If anyone had asked her when Gus was still here, she might have said it was for the best, it would leave her free to decide where to live. She might even have linked it to the Magda woman's talk of an opportunity. She gave a wry chuckle. 'Sorry, I was thinking of something else.' She checked her watch. 'I should be getting back. Thanks for listening, Kay.'

'We should do this more often. I've always wished we could get to know each other better, be friends, but...'

'I know. I've been too standoffish. I get that all the time. Some people think I'm snobbish. It's just... I learned to keep myself to myself a long time ago. I think I'm getting better, but I still find it difficult to let go.' She smiled apologetically. 'I'd like to be friends, too.'

Kay squeezed her arm as they walked back to the Education building. 'Hang in there,' she said as they parted at the foot of the stairs. 'Don't let them get you down. Remember, I'm only upstairs.'

Ann took a deep breath before entering the office, pleased to see both troublemakers busy at their desks.

The rest of the day passed uneventfully, but Ann was glad when it was over, and she could go back to the peace of her own home. Gus had promised to call again tonight. After the day she'd had, she couldn't wait to hear his voice.

Thirty-three

Two weeks later Chris was still no further forward in finding a replacement for Stan. Neither Alan nor Cheryl had been willing to take on the responsibility, and in retrospect, he agreed with them. They were part of the crew. It would have been difficult for either of them to switch to managing their colleagues. But what was he to do?

Now he was here, everything was flowing smoothly. He'd been able to restore order to the group, stunned by Stan's heart attack, and the commissions were flowing in. But he couldn't, wouldn't, stay here forever. His life wasn't here any longer.

His phone rang.

Lena.

'Dr Thomas, I have Mrs Thomas on the line.'

Chris cursed under his breath. *What did Gail want? He had enough on his plate without any of her ridiculous demands.* 'You'd better put her through.'

'I heard you were back,' she said, without any preamble. 'Is Cassie recovered? I'm going to be in Vancouver on Friday. I thought we might have dinner,' she continued, without waiting for a response.

'Cassie's improving, but I'm only back here temporarily. Stan Gray's had a heart attack and I needed to see to things here.'

'I heard about Stan. That's how I knew you were back.'

How could Chris have forgotten? Gail still had her contacts here in Vancouver – what he and Cassie used to call her female mafia. He didn't know how they did it, but it was difficult for anything to remain secret from them for long.

'So, dinner?' she asked again. 'I'm staying at the Fairmont Pacific Rim. I can book us a table.'

About to refuse, Chris thought, *What the hell!* He had nothing else to fill his evening. He'd heard The Botanist, the restaurant there, put on a good spread and Gail was always good company, even though her insistence on his presence at dinner probably meant she had another agenda.

'Okay.'

'No need to sound so reluctant. I thought we could talk about our daughter. Seven o'clock.' She hung up, leaving Chris wondering exactly what he'd agreed to.

*

By the time Friday came around, Chris was regretting having agreed to meet Gail. What could they say to each other that hadn't already been said? She wanted to talk about Cassie. Had Cassie told her mother about her plan to study in Australia? That would almost be enough for his ex to find an excuse to fly to Vancouver to bend his ear.

Chris knew there was no way he could get out of dinner with Gail. He could only hope they didn't end up arguing – the common outcome of their infrequent meetings these days.

Trust Gail, Chris thought as he entered the luxury hotel with its spectacular harbour and mountain views. Nothing but the best for the former Mrs Thomas. It had irked him during their divorce proceedings when she told him her income exceeded his, so she had no need of a settlement. He looked around the foyer. CAT might be successful, but he'd never spend his hard-earned dollars on staying in a place like this. In all the years he'd lived in Vancouver, this was his first time to enter these palatial surroundings.

'Well, Chris.' Gail observed him carefully, once they were seated on a peach-coloured bench seat that Gail called a banquette. 'You're looking well. Australia must have agreed with you. But you're back now.' She picked up a menu.

'Temporarily,' Chris said, repeating what he'd already told her on the phone. 'As soon as I can find someone…' He stopped, unwilling to share his frustration with her.

'Ah! I might be able to help you there.' She sent him a sideways glance over the top of her menu.

How could she help? 'I suppose you have an IT manager tucked away in that enormous bag of yours,' he said sarcastically, referring to the large tote bag Gail carried everywhere.

'Now, now. I do have an idea, but later. I think I'll have the duck consommé followed by the roasted maitake mushrooms. You?'

Chris studied the menu. Whatever he chose, the meal was going to cost him an arm and a leg. He couldn't help thinking of the dinners he'd enjoyed with Annie. She was happy with a simple pasta or fish meal; no need for these fancy dishes. 'The tagliatelle and beef sirloin,' he said, putting down the menu and leaning his elbows on the table.

Gail pursed her lips but managed not to say anything about the habit he knew annoyed her. 'I think we should have the Californian cabernet sauvignon,' she said with a smile. 'Okay with you?'

Chris nodded. It was one of the most expensive wines on the menu.

'You said you wanted to talk about Cassie,' he said, when they'd placed their order and the wine had been tasted and served. 'She's doing really well. She went back to her classes before I left, and her housemates are very supportive. You'd have been able to see for yourself if you'd taken the trouble to come over.'

Gail took a delicate sip of her wine. 'You know I couldn't, Chris. It was hectic at the magazine. Even now. If it hadn't been for the meeting I had today, I wouldn't be here. But I do worry about my little girl.'

'She's not a little girl any longer, Gail. I discovered that pretty soon after I arrived.'

But Gail didn't appear to have heard.

'What's this silly idea she has about continuing her studies over there in that tin-pot university in the town you grew up in? You were pretty keen to get away.'

Chris stared across the table at the woman he had once been married to. She was as elegant and well-groomed as ever, her blonde hair intricately fashioned into a deceptively simple style. With her immaculate makeup and designer outfit she was as unlike Annie as could be. What had he ever seen in her?

'It was a long time ago. I was ambitious. Granite Springs has changed – a lot. It didn't have a university back then. Now there's Willian Farrer University, a technology park, a…'

'Oh, is that the attraction? I did wonder.' Gail paused, her wine glass halfway to her lips.

'We were talking about Cassie.' Chris had no intention of discussing his reasons for wanting to return to Granite Springs. 'I think you'll find she's pretty determined. There are a few attractions there.' The image of Cassie and Miles gazing at each other rose in his mind, reminding him of the envy he'd felt for their youthful exuberance and innocence.

'I suppose there's a boy,' Gail said with an exaggerated sigh. 'There always is. But we can't let it ruin her life.'

Chris was amused at her use of *we*. There had been no *we* when Cassie was injured. 'Cassie's not a child anymore, Gail. She's a young woman with a mind of her own and she's in love. Can you remember what that's like?'

'That's a low blow, Chris.' She took another sip of wine. 'Mmm. I do like this one. Have you met the boy?'

'Miles, his name is Miles, and he's a young man. I have met him.' Chris thought it better not to add he and Cassie were sharing a house. 'He's a good guy – a musician. He has a position in an orchestra in Canberra… and he loves our daughter.'

'So, you approve?' Gail raised one eyebrow.

'Of him *and* her desire to stay – to finish her degree in Granite Springs. I've told her I'm happy to continue her allowance and pay her student fees.'

'You what?'

'You heard.'

Fortunately, their meals arrived, preventing Chris from losing his temper. They ate in a silence punctuated only by Gail's occasional comment about the food, which Chris had to admit was top class.

When they had finished eating and had ordered coffee, Chris said, 'So a meeting in Vancouver? What's that all about? I hear there might be a few problems with your management. Were you called into head office to get the bad news?' He raised one eyebrow.

Gail bridled, her cheeks turning pink. 'You'd like to think that, wouldn't you? You've never been pleased for me, always been jealous of my success, that I've become such a big name, that I earn more than you do in your *big* company.' She gave a brittle laugh. 'Of course, there's no problem. I'd be the first to know if there was.'

Their coffees arrived and Gail took a sip before speaking again. 'I told you I might have a solution to your problem.'

Chris stared at her. He'd completely forgotten her earlier comment, assuming she was joking.

'It so happens one of my colleagues has a cousin…' She paused dramatically.

Pretending to have no interest, Chris took a drink of coffee.

'This cousin has recently relocated to Vancouver for family reasons and is looking for a management position.'

'Oh?'

'Did I mention he has been working for a major software company in the US and specialises in those… things you develop.'

'Really?' It was so like Gail to forget CAT's products.

'Interested?'

'I could be.' Chris didn't want to let Gail see how interested he was. He wouldn't put it past her to refuse to pass on this guy's details.

She dived into her enormous bag and fished out a card. 'This is him.'

Chris took it from her. *Bernard Adelman, BA, MSc.,* a phone number and email address. He turned it over but there was nothing else. 'Very anonymous,' he said, tucking the card into his pocket. He'd call him tomorrow.

He farewelled Gail with relief, refusing an invitation for a nightcap in her room. All he wanted to do was get home and call Annie, get the bitter taste of the evening out of his mind and feel normal again.

Thirty-four

Ann clutched the phone to her chest, a wide smile on her face. It must be almost midnight in Canada, but Gus had called her, and somehow, sharing her worries with him had made them shrink. Even though she knew Kerrie and Janelle would still be there tomorrow, the complaint would still exist, the mediation be planned, for now she could luxuriate in the glow of Gus's call and the reassurance both of his love and that things at the university would work out in her favour.

His report of dinner with his ex had initially concerned her, but as he described their conversation, her annoyance about Cassie's choices, she'd simmered down. She hoped he'd find a replacement for Stan soon. Otherwise, who knew when he'd be able to get back... if at all. As she thought about a future without Gus, all her old insecurities threatened to return, making her decide to do something to stop thinking about it.

She was saved by her phone ringing again. Seeing Fran's face on the screen, Ann relaxed and settled down for a chat.

*

Ann's heart was pounding as she walked across campus to the administration building, to the room where the mediation was to be held. Before entering, she breathed in deeply for a count of five, held her breath for a count of three, then out again for a count of five. It was a technique she'd learned some time ago and it usually helped her relax, but it didn't seem to be working today. She took another deep breath and walked in to find the room empty apart from a young man with a beard who was wearing dark-rimmed glasses.

'Hello. You must be Ann Baird. I'm Doug Gray.'

'Good morning.' There was nothing good about it, but at least he didn't appear threatening. Ann drew out a chair and sat down. Almost immediately, there was the sound of footsteps and Kerrie and Janelle walked in together. They glared at her and took their places opposite.

Doug introduced himself again, took a seat, and outlined the conflict as it had been described to him by Flora Richards, before explaining the process. Each side would be given time to state their case, with the other side given time to respond. He'd act as a go-between to attempt to find a resolution agreeable to both parties. He emphasised he was not there to find the solution for them, only to facilitate the communication, promote understanding, and assist them to identify their needs and interests to reach an agreement.

First, he asked Kerrie and Janelle to speak.

As Ann expected, it was Janelle who elected to be spokesperson for the pair. 'Ann isn't treating us fairly,' she said, hotly, 'and she's asking us to perform activities which are not in our job description.' She flourished several sheets of paper which Ann recognised as the standard job description for administrative staff within the university.

Kerrie nodded in agreement, adding, 'And she's not allowing us to take lunch when we want to. She's a hopeless manager.'

It all sounded so petty.

'Right,' Doug said, making a few notes. 'Ann?'

Ann took another deep breath, then said, 'Firstly, the university job descriptions are generic, designed to fit a number of different positions, to ensure each office functions efficiently meeting the requirements of the academic staff. It's a fact of life that many of our male staff don't want to bother with doing their own photocopying. In relation to the lunchtimes, it's important the office is manned at all times so we agreed, at a staff meeting, to draw up a roster.'

'But…' Janelle began.

Doug held up a hand. 'This is Ann's turn.'

She subsided, looking mulish.

'Thanks, Ann. Is there anything you'd like to add?' Doug asked.

'There is.' Ann took a deep breath. 'Both Kerrie and Janelle have become a disruptive element in the office, complaining about minor matters and refusing to comply with university protocols and procedures.'

'Is this correct?' Doug looked at the two women.

'Ann is always unfair towards us,' Kerrie complained.

'Do you have an example, Ann?'

The mediation continued back and forth with Doug trying to help them reach agreement. But the pair were being their usual difficult selves. When asked what they would like to see happen, both Kerrie and Janelle fell silent, while Ann stated she'd like them to recognise her management, and for the office to continue to be able to work efficiently.

Finally, Doug asked Ann if she was willing to continue to work with them on her staff. 'Of course,' Ann said in surprise, although she'd love to be able to dismiss them. But when he asked the two woman a similar question about continuing to work with Ann, their response was a resounding, 'No.'

'I think we're done here,' Doug said.

When Kerrie and Janelle left, Doug met Ann's eyes and shook his head. 'They're living in a fantasy world,' he said. 'They don't want a manager at all. Seems to me they just want to do their own thing. They're not going to be happy wherever they are.'

'What happens now?' Ann asked, glad it was over.

'I write a report for Flora, then it's up to her. But I don't think you need to worry. I can't honestly see what all the fuss is about. They have no real reason for complaint. Their claims are merely what we'd call vexatious. Maybe you can get rid of them,' he said with a grin.

'Maybe.' But Ann doubted it.

Instead of heading straight back to the office where she'd have to face them again, she sent a text to Fran and made her way to Banjo's where they'd arranged to meet for coffee and a post-mortem. Coffee and an infusion of Fran's positivity was exactly what she needed.

*

'How did it go?' Fran asked.

They were seated in Banjo's with their coffee, the café quiet at this time of day as most of the students were in classes.

'It could have been worse.' Ann spooned up the chocolate from the top of her cappuccino, then took a sip. 'The mediator was a nice guy. I felt he was on my side. We all said our bit, then he asked if we felt we could continue to work together.'

'And?' Fran leant forward, her cup clasped in both hands.

'I said yes. They said no. I'm not sure where we can go from here. At least I know for sure they don't want me as their manager.'

'It was pretty clear before now. But that explains it.'

Ann was puzzled.

'I had a call from Flora in HR, just after your text. That's why I was late. She wanted to know if I could find work for an assistant.'

'An assistant?'

'She's not wasting any time. Your mediator must have gone straight in to see her and she's trying to find places for them.'

'What did you say?'

'I managed to discover who she was talking about before I told her there wasn't enough work for another bod. All lies. I'd love an assistant, but not one of those two.'

'Sorry. But they might be okay in the MAD house. Maybe it was just me that's the problem.'

'I doubt it. Those two are poison. I pity any school or department that takes them on. But it does look as if you'll be rid of them.'

And down two staff members, Ann thought. But that was a problem for another day, and the office would certainly be a happier place without them. Her spirits rose. Maybe this mediation had been a good idea after all.

'What's happening with your Gus?' Fran asked. 'Any word of his coming back?'

'No.' Ann's sprits plummeted again.

'You need something to take your mind off him and the stuff in the office. Why don't you come along to the choir tonight? We're between performances, so it's more for fun than anything else. I don't know why you stopped coming.'

Ann didn't know either. She'd enjoyed her time with the choristers, enjoyed singing. But somehow, over the years, as she became more involved in her other volunteer activities, singing for pleasure had seemed self-indulgent. But right now, the thought of singing again did have some appeal. She remembered how she'd been able to lose herself in the music, forget everything in the joy of singing.

'Go on, you'll love it. It's different with Owen. George was good, a great conductor, but Owen seems to bring out the best in everyone all the time – and it's fun.'

There was that word again! It had been a long time since Ann did anything for fun – until Gus reappeared, she reminded herself. 'Okay, I'll come along tonight, but I'm not sure I want to become a permanent member again.'

'You will,' Fran said optimistically. 'Just wait till you see Owen in action.'

*

If Ann hoped she would be able to sneak into the choir without any fuss, she was wrong. Many remembered her from when she had been a member before, and those who didn't, knew her from one or other of her various community activities. She was welcomed and forced into smiling to everyone as she took the spot Owen pointed to among the contraltos, placing herself between Fran and Kay Kerr.

Fran was right. As the rehearsal progressed, Ann discovered Owen certainly had his own style, and it was one which took the entire choir along with him on the journey. Starting with melodies from West Side Story and progressing to more classical pieces, Ann found herself transported to another world. It was impossible to think of anything other than the joy of being part of this wonderful band of choristers.

'I was right, wasn't I?' Fran asked, when the evening was over.

'It was… different,' Ann said, about to add more when she was aware of someone coming up behind her.

'Good to see you again. You're a hard person to pin down.'

Ann turned abruptly, almost bumping into Sam Walker's broad chest. 'Oh!' She moved back quickly, but not before he'd grasped her gently by the wrist. Looking around for Fran to rescue her, she discovered her friend had melted away and was now talking with Owen and another man she didn't recognise.

'I didn't know you were a member of the choir,' she said, wondering how to move away without appearing rude.

'This is only my second time. Are you new, too?'

'No…yes… I used to belong but haven't been for ages. Fran…' she looked around again, fruitlessly, '…persuaded me to come again. She's Owen's wife. We're good friends. We work together at the university.' Ann knew she was babbling, but didn't seem able to stop herself.

'Have you time for coffee, or perhaps a glass of wine?'

Ann hesitated. She didn't want to go anywhere with Sam, but she did remember he was good company and she needed something to keep her mind off Gus and today's mediation.

Gus hadn't called before she left, and she'd almost stayed home to wait for his call. Why hadn't she? She'd told herself she was tired of waiting by the phone, but that wasn't the real reason. The mediation had disturbed her, making her realise how easily things could change. This time the mediator had sided with her, seen how ridiculous the two women's claims were. But what if he hadn't? What if Flora Richards had chosen someone else, someone more easily swayed by the two women? What would happen to her?

'Friends – remember?'

She did. They'd agreed to be friends, then she'd ignored his calls, declined his invitations. Embarrassed and feeling guilty, she said, 'Friends. And coffee would be good. Thanks.'

They left separately to meet outside Pavarotti's. On the way out of the room and walking across campus to where they'd parked, Sam admitted he hadn't eaten, intending to take advantage of the Tuesday pasta deal at the restaurant.

Once inside, they settled at a table in a quiet corner. Ann looked around. It was ages since she'd been here, not since… She stifled the memory of coming here with Gus to celebrate her twentieth birthday. It had seemed the height of sophistication. Now it was just a family restaurant, one which had been in the Pavarotti family for several generations.

Sam ordered the pasta dish of the day, which was linguini with shrimp and roast vegetables, while Ann settled for coffee.

'So, what's been happening with you?' he asked, as he made inroads into the large bowl of pasta, then without waiting for a reply continued, 'I've been doing a feature article on the university – the exchange programme it has with Canada. The student who had the accident proved to be a good way to promote it.'

Ann remembered Gus telling her about this, how Cassie was so excited to be the focus of a newspaper article. 'Cassie Thomas,' she said.

'That's right. A plucky girl. Makes good copy, too. Of course, you'd know her.'

'Yes.' *And her father.* Suddenly, the image of Gus appeared in her mind. *What was she doing here with Sam Walker?* But a tiny voice was telling Ann Gus had left her again, with no indication of when he'd be back. According to him, it was all dependent on his finding a suitable new manager to handle the Canadian side of the business. Meantime, she was to survive on phone calls, emails and texts of which there were many. But it didn't make up for the empty space in her bed.

'When will the article be published?' she asked, determined to show an interest in her companion.

'Probably Friday. It'll capture the interest of our weekend readers. Then, depending on how much it generates, we might do a follow-up. *Where next for our plucky Canadian student?* You know the sort of thing.'

Ann didn't, but she supposed Sam knew what he was talking about. The paper had certainly changed its focus since he took over. There were more human-interest stories and reports on international affairs. It had changed from the farming broadsheet it used to be.

Sam had almost finished his pasta when she asked the question that had been puzzling her. 'What brought you to Granite Springs? I'd have thought you'd prefer to work on a city newspaper.'

Sam's normally open face clouded over, making Ann wish she hadn't asked.

He pushed away his empty plate and leant his elbows on the table. 'It's simple. I burnt out. I was a political reporter on one of the majors for many years, but Canberra and all the intrigue around it started to get to me. It never stopped. I had to either give up journalism altogether or find something less stressful. When I saw the job here advertised, it was like a lifeline.'

'And you're enjoying it – living in Granite Springs?'

'Immensely.' He grinned. 'I've found it easy to become part of the community and it's close enough to Canberra for me to keep up with old friends. My son lives there, too. I'm divorced,' he added, perhaps seeing the question in Ann's eyes.

She looked down. His personal life was none of her business. She didn't want him to think she was interested in more than friendship. 'I should be getting home,' she said, to cover her confusion.

'You're right. We both have work tomorrow.' Sam placed his credit card on the bill which had appeared as if by magic. 'We should do this again.' He met her eyes, a question in his. 'Unless…' He raised one eyebrow.

Ann knew what he was asking. So much for *only friends*. But what was she to say? She didn't want to be rude, and Gus was so far away with no sign of an end to his absence. 'Maybe, but I don't want you to get the wrong impression. I'm not in the market for a… I'm sort of involved.' She looked down again. 'We did say friends only.'

'We did.' He gave a sigh. 'But a guy can hope.' He put both hands up defensively. 'Okay, friends it is. Can I at least call you?'

Ann nodded. But as she drove home, she began to wonder; was she being fair to Sam, was she being fair to Gus, was she being fair to herself?

Thirty-five

Ann couldn't wait to pick up the paper on Friday morning. She took it to the breakfast table and opened it with one hand, a cup of tea in the other. She flicked through a few pages. 'Brave Canadian student,' she read the headline aloud, before skimming the rest of the article silently, then reading the by-line – Sam Walker, Editor. He'd done a good job, presenting a fair picture of Cassie and the exchange program. Professor Kerr would be pleased.

She finished breakfast and sent Cassie a text, suggesting they have lunch, remembering how she'd promised Gus to check on her while he was gone. *She must be thrilled*, she thought. *It's a good photo, too.* She held the page up to get a better look at the picture of Cassie sitting at her laptop, her crutches propped up beside her.

Cassie's answering text arrived almost immediately, suggesting Banjo's at twelve o'clock. Smiling, Ann replied.

Next, she sent a text to Gus, then tried to call him, but there was no reply. It was close to midday in Canada, so he must be busy working. Disappointed, Ann scanned the article and emailed it to him with the news she was meeting Cassie for lunch.

By the time she arrived at the office, Ann was feeling good, though she had some regrets about agreeing to meet Sam Walker for a drink after work. He'd been persistent, pretending he wanted to get her reaction to the article on Cassie, which she knew was a lie. Why should she feel guilt when she had no idea what Gus was getting up to in Canada? Their call last night had left her feeling frustrated, and she'd had a quiet cry when she hung up. Gus was as loving as usual, but still didn't know when he was going to make it back. It seemed he had an interview lined up with a possible replacement for Stan, but how long was it going to take? Ann knew she should be patient, trust Gus, but the fear was still there, the fear he'd stay away like he did before. Had she built up her hopes only to have them torn down again?

As soon as she entered the office, Ann's mood changed. She was early, but both Kerrie and Janelle were there before her, sitting at their desks chatting while eating breakfast and drinking coffee. She could feel her chest tighten as they fell silent when she walked past.

'Good morning,' she said with a tight smile.

'Morning,' they chorused.

Ann could hear them whisper as she opened her office door. Taking a deep breath, she fired up her computer and took a drink from the bottle of water she'd brought with her. Checking her emails, she found one from Flora Richards. Flora stated that she had received Doug Gray's report and would endeavour to find alternative positions for the two women who had made the complaints. But she emphasised it wouldn't be easy, as all other schools in the university were fully staffed. '*They would have to be supernumerary*,' Flora said, '*and you wouldn't be able to replace them.*'

It was as Ann thought, but anything to be rid of their continual grumbling and disruption to the smooth flow of the office.

The rest of the morning passed without incident, apart from a flurry of texts from Gus who was thrilled with the article and hoped she and Cassie enjoyed their lunch. *Wish I could be there with you*, he texted, with a line of emojis. Ann smiled at this. She wished it, too. And she wished she'd refused Sam's invitation. What had possessed her to accept?

*

Banjo's was alive with students when Ann pushed her way inside to see Cassie sitting towards the back. She'd forgotten how noisy students *en masse* could be, and ordered a quiche and salad before weaving her way towards her.

Cassie was flourishing a copy of The Granite Springs Advertiser. When she saw Ann, she waved it in the air. 'Hi, Ann. Did you see it? A half-page spread and a big photo. Do you think I look okay?'

'You look great and it's a good article. You must be pleased. Your dad is.'

'I am. I spoke with him, too. And guess what, my transfer's come through. Thanks so much for all your help. Prof Kerr says I can enroll in the extra subjects you identified as an external student, so I can graduate with the others. It'll be a lot of work, but worth it.'

'I'm so glad for you.'

Ann's meal arrived, along with the cappuccino she'd ordered and an acai bowl for Cassie. They were halfway through their meal, when Cassie said, 'Mum's not happy about it.'

Ann was puzzled, then realised what Cassie was talking about. 'Your transfer?'

'Mmm.' She forked up another mouthful. 'Dad told me, then Mum called to try to get me to change my mind. As if… She's even trying to persuade Dad to change his mind about paying my fees.'

Ann felt a cold shiver run up her spine. 'She's still in Vancouver?'

'Oh, didn't you know? She rang last night to say she and Dad…Oh dear, have I put my foot in it?'

'No. Your dad told me she was there, and he'd had dinner with her.' *Over a week ago.* Suddenly Ann didn't feel so bad about having a drink with Sam Walker. Why hadn't Gus mentioned his ex was still in town?

'Anyway, she hasn't managed it. I think Dad told her where to get off.' Cassie grinned. 'I plan to try to find a part-time job, once I'm free of those.' She pointed to the crutches which were propped against the table.

'I might be able to help you there, too.' Ann spoke without thinking, something she rarely did.

'You can?' Cassie's eyes glowed.

When she was excited, she looked so like Gus, the younger Gus Ann had fallen in love with. Ann's stomach lurched. 'Maybe, maybe not. But my cousin's partner is Frank Beattie who owns The Bean Sprout Café on Main Street. It's possible he may have an opening.'

Ann had a vague recollection Frank's young Italian relative – the one who'd been working in the café – had either just left or was about to. The conditions of his visa meant he could only work there for six months. Ann was a bit hazy about the timing but couldn't remember seeing him there recently. 'I'll ask him.'

'Would you? I'll do anything. Perhaps I could do work in the kitchen even now.'

'I wouldn't recommend it, and I doubt your father would agree. But when you've recovered.'

'Cool. It's a great café. Miles and I go there a lot.'

Just then, a tall skinny young man, with long blonde hair and a wispy beard arrived, lugging a large black case which he dropped beside Cassie's crutches. 'Hey, Cass.' He gave Cassie a peck on the cheek. 'Wow! Prof Larsen was on form this morning,' he chuckled. 'You must be Ann. Cassie has told me about you. You and her dad, huh?' He winked.

Ann blushed. So much for keeping her relationship with Gus secret. 'I should go,' she said, rising. 'I'll check with Frank and let you know.'

As she walked off, Ann heard Miles ask, 'Who's Frank?'

*

Was she doing the right thing? But it was only a drink, Ann told herself as she prepared for her meeting with Sam, and she felt guilty for her rudeness to him earlier. He was a nice guy. It wasn't his fault he wasn't Gus, and they'd been introduced just as Gus came back to town. She owed it to him to at least be friendly.

They'd arranged to meet in the lounge bar of *The Springs*, the new hotel on the outskirts of the town, which was becoming a popular venue for a certain section of the Granite Springs business community. It was one which Ann felt somewhat proprietorial about as her cousin had been the interior designer contracted to create the décor. When Peta set up *Forrest Interiors* a year earlier, no one had imagined how it would take off. Ann's cousin now had almost more commissions than she could cope with and was considering taking on a trainee.

Dressed in a pair of tailored black wool pants and a grey sweater, with a red wool jacket to add a touch of colour, Ann was finally ready.

Gus had called earlier, not long after Ann arrived home. She'd waited for him to say something about his ex, disappointed when he didn't mention she was still in town. Instead, he sounded tired, telling her about what he'd been doing. But when Ann asked if he'd be back soon, he was non-committal saying it would depend on a few things. He still had to interview the potential candidate. She'd finished the call with a tightness in her chest and headed off to shower and change.

Arriving at *The Springs*, Ann was surprised to discover several people she knew milling around in the foyer. She'd hoped to arrive unrecognised but was immediately cornered by one of the local doctors who had treated her mother.

'Here for the fundraiser, Ann?' he asked, gesturing to the function room where many of the group were heading.

'No.' She shook her head. 'Meeting a friend for a drink.' Managing to avoid any further conversation, she moved towards the lounge bar, just as Susie and Adrian walked in. She slipped through the doorway, hoping her sister hadn't seen her.

Sam was waiting in a corner booth studying a wine list. He stood up when she arrived. 'Ann, good to see you.'

'Hi, Sam.' Ann slipped into the seat opposite before he could initiate any physical contact. She wished she hadn't come.

'What would you like to drink? The Margaret River Chardonnay looks good, or would you prefer red, or a spirit?'

'The chardonnay sounds fine.' Maybe she'd feel better after a glass of wine. She glanced around surreptitiously, hoping Susie hadn't seen her. Her sister would be surprised she was here and, if she knew she was meeting Sam, would no doubt read something into it. This was one of the reasons she'd chosen to lead such a private life.

'So, what did you think?' Sam asked when they'd been served, and a full bottle was sitting on the table. Ann looked at it in dismay. She had only intended to have one glass with him, then leave. 'The article,' he added.

'It was excellent. I had lunch with Cassie today and she's thrilled to bits about her foray into the media. Her mother works on a magazine in Canada, so I suppose she knows a little about...' Her voice trailed away. What was she doing talking about Gus's ex-wife? But the woman was preying on her mind.

'Really?' Sam leant forward. 'You know the girl well, or are you familiar with the family lives of all the students?'

'I know her father.' Ann hoped Sam wouldn't inquire any further.

He nodded and gave a rueful grin. 'You did say you were involved with someone. But… a Canadian?'

'Gus is from Granite Springs. I… we knew each other when we were Cassie's age.'

'He must be quite something to make you blush so prettily just talking about him.'

Ann put a hand up to her cheek. Was she blushing?

'He's not here now?'

'He had to return to Canada to fix a situation there. But he'll be back.' Suddenly, Ann was sure of it. Regardless of where his ex might or might not be, what she might or might not be up to, Gus was a man of his word.

'My loss. I'd like to meet him, when he does get back. He's a lucky man.'

Ann blushed again. 'I'm sure it can be arranged.'

They chatted on for as long as it took to drink another glass of wine, then Ann said, 'I must go. Thanks so much for the wine and the company.'

'Thank *you*. I've enjoyed our chat, even if it has meant I've been well and truly defeated in the romance stakes.' He grimaced, then smiled. 'Still friends?' He held out a hand.

'Of course.' Ann shook his hand gratefully. He was a nice man. She hoped he could find someone who'd appreciate him.

Thirty-six

It was one of those days that made you glad to be alive, Chris thought, as he drove to the office. His interview with Bernard Adelman was this morning and he was hopeful. Bernard – or Bernie, as he'd insisted – had sounded very professional on the phone, and the CV he'd sent through was certainly impressive. If he was as good as he seemed on paper, Chris's problems were over.

'Morning, boss,' Lena greeted him and handed him the cup of Starbucks she was in the habit of picking up for him each morning on her way to work.

'Thanks, Lena. Give me a few moments, then can you come in.'

Chris settled at his desk and fired up his computer, checking the emails which had accumulated overnight and deciding which ones to keep, which to delete and which to pass on to Lena for action. It occurred to him he'd need staff in Granite Springs if he intended to work from there – at least a PA to take care of all the mundane tasks. He took a mouthful of coffee, enjoying the caffeine buzz.

There was a tentative knock at the door.

'Ready?'

Chris looked up and gestured Lena to come in. 'I have an interview today with a possible replacement for Stan – temporarily, at least. I expect him to be back on board when he recovers.'

'How *is* Stan?' Lena asked, her face filled with concern. 'We all miss him.'

Chris sighed. 'The doctors say he's making a good recovery, but he still has a long way to go. I doubt we'll see him back this side

207

of Christmas.' He visualised his old friend as he'd seen him only the evening before. Despite good reports from the doctors, Stan still looked extremely ill. It would be a long time before he'd be back to his full strength.

'Oh dear. Poor Stan, and poor Bee. The crew were wondering… do you think it would be okay to send flowers?'

'I think he'd like that.' Why hadn't Chris thought of it?

'Okay.' Lena paused for a moment then said, 'Do you want to use the interview room or your office?'

Chris thought for a moment. There were advantages to both, but if he used his office, Bernie would be able to see the main office setup, and the crew could check him out. He decided. 'I'll do it here. Maybe you can organise coffee for us? Eleven o'clock.'

'Will do. Anything else?'

'There are several emails you can take care of for me, and can you check the diary for next week?' He was tempted to ask her to look up flights to Australia, too, but decided he should wait. Bernie Adelman might turn out to be a dud and he'd have to start all over again.

A new email came in as Lena left – from Gail. His ex-wife was turning into a nuisance, not content with inviting him to dinner, she'd been plaguing him with invitations to drinks, art openings and a magazine launch. Her initial *few days* in Vancouver seemed to have expanded into what was now close to ten days. He had no intention of seeing her again – that first evening had probably been a mistake, even if it had resulted in the contact with Adelman. He had no idea what she was up to, what she wanted of him, but he didn't want a bar of it. On the one occasion he had answered her call, she'd been insistent they meet again for dinner – or even breakfast or lunch, an invitation he'd refused. When he'd asked her again about the rumour he'd heard that her magazine was in trouble, she'd dismissed it in her usual fashion accusing his informant of jealousy.

Meeting Annie again had shown him how superficial Gail was, always had been. He'd been vulnerable when they met, blown away by her undoubted elegance and charm. But what had she seen in him – an ambitious young man in a growing industry who'd be a good meal ticket? That was before her own career took off. He deleted the email as he'd done the others.

At exactly eleven o'clock, Lena showed a tall, dark-haired man into Chris's office. Chris knew he was thirty-five, but he looked older, perhaps due to the limp he was trying to disguise.

'Welcome, Bernie. Please take a seat.' Chris swivelled his office chair so the desk was no longer between them. He shook the man's hand.

When Lena had reappeared with coffee then left, closing the door behind her, Chris outlined Stan's role in the company and the nature of the position. 'Before we start, I should emphasise I don't anticipate this being a permanent position,' he said, 'but there may be other possibilities within CAT.' It had occurred to him, when he was thinking about staff in Granite Springs, that it could be helpful to have additional management staff here in head office, if he did intend to spend most of his time in Australia.

The interview progressed with Bernie outlining his experience and asking intelligent questions about the future direction of CAT. Chris was pleased the younger man had done his homework on the company and even had some suggestions for future projects. He began to relax. This could work, as long as Bernie was able to gain the respect of the group.

Seeming to understand what Chris was thinking, Bernie asked diffidently, 'I wonder if it would be possible to meet some of your senior staff. You didn't consider them for the position?'

'I did, but they chose to decline, feeling too much a part of the crew to move into the role. That's why I've had to look outside the company. It's a good idea for you to meet them. It's almost lunchtime. Why don't I organise something to be brought in, and a group of us can gather in our meeting room? It can be quite informal.'

'Thanks, but I didn't intend to put you to any trouble.'

'It's no trouble. I should have thought of it myself.' Chris picked up the phone to call Lena. He instructed her to arrange some platters from the café downstairs and to inform everyone food would be available in the meeting room. It was something he'd done from time to time, often as a means of celebration when they'd been working to a tight deadline.

Chris was pretty sure Bernie would fit in, and this would give him a chance to see how he could relate to the others. This was almost as important as being able to do the job, as it would allow Chris to get back to Granite Springs and Annie with a clear conscience.

*

'They're a good bunch, I think we'd work well together, I look forward to your decision.' Bernie took Chris's outstretched hand as the staff gradually filtered back to their desks.

'I'll let you know early next week,' Chris said. 'You mentioned you could start immediately?'

'I can. Be glad to get back to work. The family…' He rubbed a hand across his head. 'It's been difficult. It would be good to get out of the house, as well as finding employment. You're doing good things here and have a good crew. I'd be thrilled to work for you, with them, to be part of CAT.'

The men smiled at each other and parted. Chris was ninety-nine percent sure Bernie would work out. He just needed to find out the opinions of his staff, especially those of Alan and Cheryl who were his longest serving members.

'Senior staff meeting at three,' he said to Lena, before entering his office again to find yet another email from Gail – this time to a gallery opening. He deleted it. What was wrong with the woman?

The meeting with senior staff reinforced Chris's own opinion, with several saying how impressed they'd been with Bernie's attitude.

'I liked how he didn't try to be too familiar or to lord it over us,' Cheryl said.

Alan's contribution was, 'I checked with a mate who knew his previous company. He had only good things to say about him, said we'd be lucky to get him.'

Chris was happy to have his own opinion confirmed. He'd be able to return to Granite Springs leaving CAT in good hands. But not yet. He'd need to spend a couple of weeks with Bernie to bring him up to speed.

He hummed to himself as he drove home. He couldn't wait to tell Annie the good news. When he arrived there, he picked up the phone.

Thirty-seven

It was going to be a cool clear Saturday, perfect for gardening. As she drank a cup of tea with breakfast, Ann planned her day. Over the past few weeks, she'd let the garden go, distracted by Gus's presence. But no longer. After last night she needed something to take her mind off herself, off Gus and off the business at the university.

She dressed in an old pair of trousers and a warm shirt and went out to examine what needed to be done. She had returned to the house to fetch her pruning shears when the phone rang. Seeing her sister's number, Ann sighed.

'Hi, Susie, you just caught me. I've been in the garden.' She waited, sure Susie had something on her mind. Hopefully not another of her dreaded dinner parties.

'Ann, yes, lovely day for the garden. I was telling Adrian he ought to get into ours. I called because a little bird told me you were at *The Springs* last night. We attended a fundraiser there, but I didn't see you.' Her tone implied it was somehow Ann's fault. 'You weren't alone,' she continued. 'In fact, I hear you were with Sam Walker. I thought I saw you leave my dinner party together back in March. Have you been seeing him all this time? You've kept it very quiet. Why didn't you tell me, at least thank me for introducing you?'

Oh dear, exactly what Ann had been afraid of. Somehow, she managed to stop Susie from making plans to have them both to dinner, despite her sister refusing to believe there was no relationship. Ann was so incensed, she almost told Susie about Gus, but stopped herself in time. That really would have sent Susie off on a tirade. She'd blamed Gus for Ann's pregnancy, and had never forgiven him for what she saw as him abandoning Ann in her time of need.

By the time she came off the phone, Ann was shaking. She picked up the shears and went back out to the garden, using the energy from her anger with Susie to prune more ruthlessly than was necessary. Then she raked the leaves into a compost pile before doing some much-needed weeding and working out which plants would benefit from repotting.

It was almost lunchtime when she finished. Having worked off her annoyance, Ann drew off her gardening gloves and went back inside, pleased with her efforts.

She was finishing a spartan lunch of sourdough bread and cheese washed down with a cup of tea when her phone rang, and she saw Gus's face on the screen. Wishing she had time to at least pull a comb through her hair, she answered.

'Annie, it's so good to see you. You're looking lovely as ever.' Gus's warm voice made Ann want to weep. She was feeling tender after Susie's call, and if Gus thought she looked lovely when she'd just come in from the garden, he must really love her. She'd washed her hands at the kitchen sink before making lunch but hadn't taken time to look in the mirror. She must look a fright.

'You can't mean it. I've been in the garden.'

'I can see that.' He chuckled. 'There are twigs in your hair and you have a streak of dirt on one cheek.'

Ann put a hand up to her hair where a leaf was attached. She pulled it free with a grin. 'Good to see you, too.' Gus looked as immaculate as usual, his fading chestnut hair falling over his forehead, his eyes sparkling. She remembered. 'The interview. It was today, wasn't it? Have I got the day right?'

'It was. I met with Bernie Adelman this morning.'

'And?' Ann held her breath and crossed her fingers, but from the grin on Gus's handsome face, she knew the news was good.

'Looks like I've found someone who can take Stan's place.'

Ann exhaled, all her suspicions of Gus and his ex spending time together forgotten. 'Oh, Gus, that's great news. Soon, I hope?'

'As soon as I can, and it can't be soon enough. Give me a week or two to get the new guy settled and I'll be there. I've missed you, Annie. So much.'

'I've missed you, too.' Ann almost wept with joy. Her lonely nights would be over. Gus was coming back.

*

Deciding she'd done enough in the garden for one day, Ann took a shower and changed into her jeans and a warm sweater. She made herself another cup of tea and took it into the living room where she settled down in a comfortable armchair with the copy of Di Morrissey's latest book she'd picked up from the library.

She was lost in the stirring tale when she heard a car draw up, followed by the sound of running footsteps and a loud knock at the door. As she reached the door, she could hear Lily's voice, saying, 'Do you think Auntie Ann is home?'

'Hi Ann,' Peta said, when Ann opened the door to be almost bowled over by Lily's hug. 'It's been too long. I'm sorry I haven't been around before now.'

'Not at all. It's good to see you both.' Ann hugged Peta, while Lily disappeared through the house.

A few minutes later, Ann and Peta were seated at the kitchen table, and Lily was busy in the dining room with an old jigsaw she'd unearthed from the hall cupboard.

'What's been happening with you?' Peta asked, taking a sip of the liquorice spice tea. Ann made. 'Mmm, this is delicious.'

Ann didn't know where to start. When Peta arrived to stay with her a year earlier, her life had been a dull routine, never changing from one week to the next. But it had been safe, predictable. Now she sometimes felt she was on a roller coaster.

When she hesitated, Peta filled the silence. 'Is Chris still away? I saw the article about his daughter in the local paper. It was excellent, should be good for the college too. Is she happy with it? Have you spoken to her? What's been happening at the university?'

Ann felt overwhelmed with the barrage of questions. Since Peta's life had undergone such a mammoth change and she and Frank had got together, she'd become much more assertive and confident. Ann barely recognised the grief-stricken woman who'd arrived on her doorstep with her shy, withdrawn granddaughter. 'He's still in Canada, but should be home soon.' She grinned, remembering their call. 'It'll probably take him another couple of weeks to tie things up there. And, yes, Cassie's delighted with the article and her fifteen minutes of fame.'

'And what about you? Have you decided to listen to your heart? I know how difficult it can be when you've been used to being on your own. But, speaking from experience, with the right man, life can be wonderful.'

'You *and* Fran!' Ann pretended to be annoyed but was glad to have such good friends. While their advice hadn't always been welcome, they meant well, and she'd finally taken it to heart. Then she relented. 'But yes. When Gus comes back, he's going to move in here.' She followed Peta's gaze, seeing the house through Peta's eyes, remembering how she felt the first time Gus was here. 'What? Don't you think he should? Do you think we're moving too fast?'

'Of course he should, if it's what you both want. But…' She frowned as she met Ann's eyes.

'What?'

'Have you told him – about the baby?'

Ann felt her knees go weak. Peta had hit on the one thing Ann was afraid to mention to Gus. It was her guilty secret, the one that held her back from total commitment. So often she'd been on the brink of mentioning it, only to draw back for fear of ruining this second chance at happiness. 'Not yet,' she admitted.

'Don't you think you should?' Peta asked gently. 'If he loves you as much as he says, he'll be understanding. The baby was his too. Don't you think he deserves to know?'

Ann sighed. She knew it was something she must do, if she and Gus were to have any sort of future. 'I'll do it,' she promised.

Peta glanced around. 'And… I was just thinking…'

'I know. This place. It looks as if time stood still. I haven't changed anything since Mum passed. You probably felt like you'd stepped back in time when you and Lily walked in a year ago.' Ann remembered how she'd asked Peta to remodel a house for Susie, when she should have been asking her cousin to do the same for her.

'Well, I don't want to offend you, but it could do with a bit of an... improvement. Not a lot,' Peta hurried to say. 'It's surprising how a few small touches can make a difference.'

'You're right. After Dad died, it was just Mum and me for so long. I'm afraid we let some things go. And I didn't care enough to make any changes,' she said regretfully.

'You say he won't be back for a couple of weeks. That would give you time to have the place painted, replace or recover some of the furniture, freshen things up. It wouldn't take much. What do you say?' Peta's eyes twinkled.

'You don't think I'm stupid, do you? Neither of us is getting any younger.'

'Only if you start thinking that way. Look at Fran and me, Jo and Col Ford, Magda and George Turnbull.'

'I suppose.' Ann bit her lip. When she was talking to Gus, everything seemed wonderful. It was only when she was alone the doubts crept in, doubts about him, about his ex, about Ann herself. Was she really meant to have a second chance at love, a love she'd managed to destroy so effectively first time around?

'Now, why don't I pop round tomorrow evening with some colour charts and swatches of material? I'm really looking forward to this.' Peta glanced around the kitchen. 'Maybe not in here, but the living and dining rooms, and perhaps your bedroom?'

Ann flinched. Peta had never seen the inside of her bedroom, the one that had been her parents', and she'd moved into after her mother went to the nursing home. It still had the old floral wallpaper her mother had been so proud of, though Ann had added her own touches with new bedlinen and a doona to replace the old candlewick bedspread. But it still had an old-fashioned appearance. What had Gus thought of it? She smiled to herself. Gus had been more intent on her than on the bedroom. But it would be nice to have it modernised. 'Nothing too drastic,' she warned.

Lily joined them before any more was said, Peta merely mouthing, 'Tomorrow,' before Lily said, 'I'm hungry, Auntie Ann. Do you have any biscuits?'

'I can do better than that. I made some chocolate brownies. Fetch me the green tin from the pantry. And perhaps you'd like some milk to drink.'

'Yes please.'

'You spoil her,' Peta said with a smile as they watched Lily run to the pantry, bring back the tin, then a carton of milk from the fridge.

'Have one, too, Peta. I should have opened them earlier. They're not as good as those Marie makes for The Bean Sprout but... Oh, that reminds me. I promised Cassie I'd talk to Frank.'

'About?'

'She's looking for a part-time job, or will be when she can move without her crutches. I wondered if Frank had found anyone to replace his Italian cousin.'

'Not yet. Cassie would be perfect. Al and Tina have both found work on a resort up in Queensland and headed off a few weeks ago. Frank has been muttering about how he'd become used to having an extra pair of hands and is missing Al. Would you like me to talk to him?'

'Would you? Thanks.' Ann was relieved to have one more matter taken care of.

After farewelling Peta and Lily, Ann looked around the house with fresh eyes. A new look was exactly what was needed to blow away the cobwebs of the past years. She was entering a new phase of her life, making a new start, and she couldn't wait for it to begin.

But first, she had to keep her promise to tell Gus. Perhaps it would be easier in an email. She settled down at the computer, determined to do just that. Tears streamed down Ann's cheeks as she relived those dreadful days and weeks, setting out exactly what had happened all those years ago, starting with the discovery of her pregnancy, through the discussion about an abortion to the miscarriage and her subsequent guilt.

But, having written it all down, Ann couldn't bear to send it. It was too harsh to let Gus know this way. Regardless how difficult it might be, she knew she had to tell him face-to-face. She closed the computer and went to bed.

Thirty-eight

Chris felt so happy when the plane finally touched down in Granite Springs. Unlike his previous arrival, this time, it felt like he was coming home. He couldn't wait to see Annie again. And Cassie told him she was walking without the aid of crutches, though she did need the assistance of a stick at times.

As he walked across the tarmac, he could see Annie waiting for him, her hair blowing in the breeze. He quickened his pace, eager to hold her again, to feel her familiar body against his.

'Hey!'

'Hello, you.'

They stood looking at each other, drinking in the sight, then Chris moved forward and took Ann in his arms. For a moment she resisted then, as if suddenly throwing caution to the winds, she returned his hug.

'Welcome back!' Ann's face split into a wide smile. She linked her arm in his and they strolled together to the baggage carousel.

'It's so good to be here,' Chris said, as they waited for the luggage to be unloaded. 'There were times when I thought it might never happen. No,' he corrected himself, 'I knew it would, but worried it might take a lot longer. It was lucky Gail suggested Bernie to me, or I could still have been trying to find a suitable candidate.'

Chris thought he detected a slight withdrawal from Annie at the mention of Gail.

'You didn't tell me he was your ex's suggestion.'

'Didn't I?' Chris drew a hand across his hair. Maybe he hadn't. There had been no need. He'd told Annie he had dinner with Gail, but not the specifics. He didn't want to dwell on the way Gail manipulated him into the meal, or how she'd continued to harass him for another meeting. 'He's related in some way to a colleague of hers and was looking for work in Vancouver. Pure serendipity that he had exactly the skill set I was looking for and the rest of the guys can relate to him. I was happy to leave CAT in his capable hands. Now I can get on with setting up properly here.'

'Cassie's eager to see you, too,' Ann said, as they began the drive back into town. 'She wants to show off how well she can get around.'

'Sounds as if you and she have been getting to know each other.'

'Sort of.' Ann hadn't seen a lot of the girl, but they'd met for coffee a couple of times and developed some rapport. 'We have you in common.' She smiled at Chris. 'Where would you like to go? I'm afraid I need to get back to work.'

Of course she did. What had he expected? That Annie would drop everything because he was back? She had a life, a job. 'Drop me at the flat,' he said. He wondered if now was the time to confirm his moving into Annie's home, to give Frank notice he'd be vacating the flat. He glanced sideways at her, but she was concentrating on the road ahead. He leant back, his eyes closing. It had been a long flight.

*

Chris awoke with a start when the car stopped. He must have fallen asleep almost as soon as they left the airport. He kissed Annie goodbye and was about to head upstairs to the flat when he changed his mind. He'd love a decent cup of coffee.

'Surprise!'

Chris blinked at the smiling girl who delivered his macchiato and rose to give her a warm hug and kiss. 'Cassie, what are you doing here? Are you sure you should be...?' He glanced down at her legs.

'I'm good. This is only my second shift here. Ann helped organise it, and Frank and Marie have been wonderful. I'm supposed to be stuck in the kitchen and there's a chair for me when I get tired, but when

Frank said you were here, I decided to surprise you.' She slid into the seat opposite Chris. 'It's good to see you back, Dad. I missed you, I think Ann did, too,' she said with a twinkle in her eye.

'But what are you doing working here? Doesn't your allowance cover all your expenses?'

'Dad! I'm not a baby. I can't stay dependent on you forever. It's time I learned to earn my keep – or some of it. This is a great café. I'm going to enjoy working here. And, before you say anything, it won't affect my studies.' She grinned.

Chris laughed. 'How are your studies going?'

'Very well.' Cassie launched into a description of the course of study Ann had helped her put together, finishing with, 'Prof Kerr's been really helpful, too. Though he says if any more of us decide to stay, it may ruin the exchange programme.' She chuckled.

'And Miles?'

'He's good, too.' She beamed, then her eyes clouded. 'No doubt you've heard what Mum had to say about him. I'm not going to let her ruin my life. She's obviously forgotten what it's like to be young.'

Chris coughed. It was almost exactly what he'd told Gail. But his former wife had a mind of her own. Cassie was a bit like her in that respect. 'Your mum is… she has her own opinions.'

'I'm glad *you* don't think the same way. Ann doesn't either,' Cassie surprised him by saying. 'I like her, Dad. Is she the reason you're setting up a division of CAT here in Granite Springs? Are you and she planning to stay together?'

Chris shifted uncomfortably. This wasn't a conversation he wanted to have with his daughter.

'Sorry, Dad. I should get back to the kitchen. It's great to see you. Catch you soon.'

As she moved off, Chris could see she still had a slight limp, but she'd made remarkable progress in the time he'd been gone.

'Good to see you back. Your daughter's a hard worker, very determined. I'd say she gets it from you.' Frank came across to join Chris. 'I hear you may not be needing the flat for much longer.'

Chris looked at Frank in surprise. 'How…'

'Sorry. As you know, my partner, Peta, is Ann Baird's cousin. She may have let slip a comment about you and her. Sorry if I spoke out of turn.'

Granite Springs with its small-town gossip mill. But Peta was Ann's family.

'Not at all. I suppose the whole town knows.'

'I doubt it. Ann's always been a very private person. I wouldn't have heard anything but for Peta.'

'Right. Well, I do expect to be moving out. But I only returned to Australia this morning and Ann and I haven't had time to discuss things. I'll be sure to let you know when I have something definite.' Chris couldn't wait to bring up the subject with Ann again. They hadn't spoken again about his moving in. He hoped she hadn't changed her mind. The thought of living with her, the memory of her sweetness, had kept him going over the past few weeks, encouraging him to put his house in Vancouver on the market. Had he been too hasty?

Thirty-nine

The day seemed to drag for Ann after she returned from picking up Gus. She couldn't wait to see him again, but she had matters to take care of in the office. It was over two weeks since the mediation and there was still no sign of Kerrie and Janelle being redeployed. Flora had been in touch, but so far, she hadn't managed to find anywhere to move them to. It would be so much easier if they'd decide to resign. But they appeared to have no intention of doing so. Meanwhile, they continued to make her life a misery with their eternal whispering, disregard of office procedures and blatant refusal to accede to her requests.

Ann sighed as she walked past the desks of the two women, wishing she could persuade one of her colleagues in another school to offer to take them. But it was a Human Resource issue, not up to her to take unilateral action, much as she'd like to.

At her desk, Ann found a list of the practice teaching placements for the coming semester, along with lists of accommodation for the students. One of the attractions of the School of Education at Willian Farrer, was the way they not only placed the students in schools for their teaching practice, but also arranged their accommodation. Over the years, Ann had been instrumental in developing a list of places where the students could live relatively inexpensively, and each semester, it was the job of her staff to match up students, schools and accommodation.

She picked up the lists and took them into the main office. Despite everything else being digitised, she still preferred this be done manually and, on one wall of the office, there was a large board designated for this task. Checking all the schools were accounted for on the board, Ann looked around the office. This was a routine task, which could be boring, but several of her staff normally volunteered to do it, choosing ways to make the dull task fun. It was a two-person job, one filling the board, while the other entered the data on the computer.

Today, it seemed almost everyone was busy, all except Kerrie and Janelle who were chatting quietly.

'Kerrie. Janelle.' Ann chewed the inside of her cheek, afraid they'd ignore her. She hated how the two women had succeeded in undermining her confidence in herself as a manager.

They looked up with their now customary mulish expressions.

'The prac board needs to be done. How about you two make a start on it?' she asked, trying to sound as pleasant as she could, pretending there was no ill feeling between them.

'Why us?' Janelle asked. 'Why not…' She gestured to the other staff who were clearly fully employed.

'Are you busy with another task?'

'No, but…'

'Come on,' Kerrie said, to Ann's surprise. 'It needs to be done. We can at least make a start, can't we?'

Janelle stared at her for a moment, before agreeing, and Ann handed them the lists she was carrying.

'Thanks. It would be a big help, and our students will be grateful to know their placements before the semester break.' She smiled and walked back into her office with as much dignity as she could muster. Once there, she leant her head on her arms. How long was she going to have to suffer this?

*

'It's been too long.' Gus pulled Ann into a tight embrace, his lips finding hers and stopping her from speaking. He'd been waiting for her to come home and she barely made it through the door before his arms enfolded her.

It felt so good, so right. The worries of the day disappeared. This was where she belonged.

'Did you catch up with Cassie today?' she asked sometime later, when they were seated side by side on the sofa enjoying a glass of wine.

'I did – at The Bean Sprout. I believe I have you to thank for that, too? Cassie likes you.'

'I like her, too. She's a lovely young woman, a credit to you. I was glad to be able to help.'

'You haven't changed your mind? About me moving in here? You've done something to the place, haven't you? I like it.' He gazed around approvingly.

'You can thank Peta. She made me realise how I'd let the place go. I hadn't changed anything since Mum left. It was time. It's handy having a cousin who's an interior designer.'

'Thank you, Peta. But I bet the colour scheme was your choice.'

Ann nodded, smiling and gazing around the living room which was now decorated in her favourite autumn tones. It worked well, giving the room a restful ambiance. She realised she hadn't replied to his question. 'And of course I haven't changed my mind... if you still want to.'

'Of course. I can be packed up in no time. I'll have to give Frank notice, but it doesn't mean I have to stay in the flat. He guessed I was going to leave. Your cousin...'

'Oh! Not many secrets in Granite Springs.'

'Or in your family. She's okay about us?'

'Delighted. It's Susie who could prove the stumbling block.'

'Your sister? I remember her. She was always a bit protective of you.'

'She still is. I told you about her dinner parties.' Ann took a deep breath. Gus was bound to find out, so she knew she had to tell him. 'She's still intent on matching me up with Sam Walker.'

'The editor guy, the one who wrote the article about Cassie?'

'Yes. You thought I was interested in him till I told you I wasn't. And I'm not, but...'

Ann wished she hadn't mentioned Sam. She stole a glance at Gus. He was rubbing his forehead.

'I met him again at the choir.'

'I didn't know you were a member of the choir. The Granite Springs Choristers?'

'I'm not... I wasn't... Well, I was some time ago, and Fran persuaded me to attend a practice – only as a way of distracting me. I was missing you. There was all this stuff at work.' She took Gus's hand. 'Sam Walker was there and… we had a coffee together afterwards.'

'So, you had a coffee with Sam Walker. Should I be worried?'

'Of course not. You know you're the only man for me, always have been, but…' She bit her lip.

'There's more?'

'He invited me for a drink – to talk about his article on Cassie.' Even as she spoke, Ann knew it sounded crazy. Why would the editor of the advertiser want to talk with her about an article he'd written? 'It was only a glass of wine at *The Springs*. But a friend of Susie's saw us there – there was a fundraiser on that night.'

'And your sister got the wrong idea? I suppose it *was* the wrong idea?' Gus pulled his hand away and peered into Ann's eyes as if he'd be able to see the truth of her words.

'Don't you trust me?' Ann couldn't believe she might have ruined Gus's homecoming.

'Of course I do. Come here.' He pulled her to him again. 'I'm just jealous to think I missed out seeing you all that time when I was in Canada,' he murmured into her hair. 'We have a lot of time to make up. Thanks for being so honest with me. You always have been. One of the things I've always loved about you is your honesty, even if sometimes you made things difficult for yourself – and others. It's a trait not many people have. Even I fall short at times.' He looked down.

Ann felt a rush of guilt that she was still keeping a secret from him but decided it would serve no purpose to reveal it now when everything was going so well.

Then, unbidden, the memory of Cassie's reference to her mother's presence in Vancouver came back into Ann's mind. She knew she shouldn't mention it, but she did. 'Cassie said her mother was in Vancouver for some time.' It was Ann's turn to look down at the table.

'She's right. Gail told me she was only there for a few days. We had dinner. I told you about that.'

Ann held her breath.

'The damn woman stayed on. I don't know what she intended. She kept calling and emailing me, inviting me to one event after another. As if I'd be interested in socialising, especially with her. I was there to work, to tie things up, to visit Stan. I didn't contact any old friends. I ignored all Gail's messages. I didn't see her again.' He paused and stared at Ann. 'Did you think I did? Did you think I was seeing Gail in Vancouver and not telling you?'

Relieved, Ann let out the breath she'd been holding. 'I might have,' she admitted.

'Annie, you have to help me out here. Is that why you accepted Sam Walker's invitation? Were you jealous, too?'

Silently, Ann nodded. That was exactly why she'd agreed to have a drink with Sam Walker – twice.

'We're a pair of fools. Come here.' Gus rose and picked Ann up, twirling her around and around before setting her down and kissing her firmly. 'Now, let's carry on to where we should have last night. I want to see if you've remodelled the bedroom, too.'

Ann squealed with pleasure as Gus picked her up and carried her into the bedroom kicking the door closed behind him and placing her gently on the still unmade bed.

*

They were lying together, still in each other's arms when Gus had finally took time to admire the new décor in the bedroom. 'This all looks less feminine. It's really nice, Annie,' he said.

On Peta's advice Ann had the cabbage rose wallpaper which her mother had loved – and her father hated – removed, to be replaced by having the walls painted in a pale green. The heavy oak furniture had been replaced by a light, white-painted bedhead and bedside tables, and the old carpet removed to be replaced by a thick pile wool blend. It was more of a change than Ann planned but, she reasoned, they'd be spending a lot of time there.

'You do still intend to move in?' Ann asked.

'Try to stop me.' Gus murmured, pulling her back towards him. 'I can't wait. And, as I think I said, Frank is expecting me to vacate the flat. I've hardly been there anyway. It won't take me long. I don't have a lot to move – clothes, a few books, my laptop. There isn't even any food in the fridge and the pantry is pretty bare.'

'Why not do it this weekend?' Ann turned her face up to his. To think it was finally going to happen. After all those years of loneliness, after all those sleepless nights, the regrets, the guilt, she and Gus were finally going to be together.

*

Next morning, they surfaced slowly, bleary-eyed after only a few hours' sleep. 'It's so good to be back,' Gus said, his lips on Ann's. 'I missed you. I don't intend to go anywhere without you ever again.'

Ann snuggled into his embrace. It was so good to have him back again. Peta and Fran had been wrong. There was no need to tell him about the baby.

'Sorry, I need to take this,' Gus said as his phone pinged with a text. 'It's work.'

While Gus was responding to his text, Ann popped into the shower. When she emerged, a towel around her hair, Gus was slipping into his pants and pulling on his shirt.

'I need to get back to the flat to send an email to Vancouver,' he said. 'Bernie needs some information urgently. Sorry.'

'Oh!' Ann was disappointed. She'd been expecting them to spend the whole weekend together. 'Is the information on your computer or could you use mine?'

'Good idea. It's all on Dropbox.'

'It's in the study. I can...'

'I can find it.'

Stopping only for a swift kiss, his fingers trailing down her still damp shoulders and sending shivers down her spine, Gus headed for the study, while Ann rubbed her hair dry and made her way into the kitchen to brew coffee and make a start on breakfast.

*

In the study, Gus found Ann's laptop already turned on, and made a mental note to suggest she always close it down to save her battery. He found the information Bernie had requested and opened up the email application. He was about to open a new email when he saw one on the screen addressed to him. Curious, he began to read.

My dear Gus,

I'm missing you so much. These past few months with you have been like a miracle. I never thought I'd see you again and I do want to spend the rest of my life with you.

But there is something I need to tell you, something that happened almost thirty-five years ago, something that changed my life, something I've never been able to forget. I know that, before I can commit to living with you, you need to know the truth.

After you left, even though it was my decision to stay, I was miserable, so miserable I was sick. At first, I thought it was missing you that made me so sick then I discovered I was pregnant. You'll remember how religious my mother was and, in her frail state, I didn't know how I was going to tell her. Then Susie stepped in.

She said she'd help me arrange an abortion, that it was the only way. She managed to persuade me how impossible it would be for me to have a child here in Granite Springs, on my own, with an ailing mother, what people would say, what mother would say. At first, I rejected the whole idea, but the more I thought about it, the more it seemed to me to be the only way out. Despite my misgivings I agreed to...

Gus didn't want to read any more. He pushed himself away from the computer as if he'd been stung, his eyes filling with tears, a red-hot anger consuming him. Annie, his Annie had been pregnant. They had made a child together and she'd killed it. She'd killed their child. He stumbled through to the kitchen where Annie was humming to herself as she made breakfast.

'How could you?' he yelled. 'So much for honesty. I thought you believed in the sanctity of life. Now I find...' Lost for words, he raced out, slamming the door behind him.

Forty

Ann gazed at Gus's disappearing back in horror. The noise of the front door slamming echoed in her ears like the of crack of doom. What had happened? Gus's words rang in her ears. He hadn't... He couldn't have... Ann rushed into the study, the bacon and eggs she'd been cooking for breakfast forgotten. She stared at the computer screen, at the email she'd intended to delete. She gasped, her hands going up to her mouth in disbelief.

Gus had read her email. But only the top part was showing on the screen, the part where she talked about the abortion. He must have read that and thought... Ann wanted to run after him to explain, but it was too late. The damage was done. How would he believe anything she said now? She sank to the floor and wept.

*

The sun was peeping through the curtains heralding a fine winter's day. Ann had lain awake most of the night berating herself and, as she rolled over to see the empty spot in the bed beside her, all she wanted to do was hide under the covers.

Why had she been so stupid? She'd waited so long for Gus to come home, to be with him again, to enjoy his company in bed as well as out of it. And what had she done? Why hadn't she deleted the email? She'd put off telling Gus for so long, then to have him find out this way. He didn't know the whole story, but did it matter? He'd seen enough to make him go off in a rage.

Was there something wrong with her that she managed to ruin things with Gus for the second time? She wouldn't get a third chance. She was doomed to remain single and without love for the rest of her life, at the mercy of Susie with her dire dinner parties. For some reason, the memory of Magda popped into her mind. The old woman had talked about an opportunity. Well, she'd certainly let that one escape.

Ann pulled the covers over her head, glad it was Sunday and she didn't need to show her face at the office. She could hibernate here all day. This was what she deserved, her true punishment for even considering getting rid of her baby. She hadn't been able to go through with it, but she'd allowed Susie to make the appointment. She'd always believed the miscarriage was her punishment, but it seemed fate wasn't done with her and had decided to deliver one more blow. And it was all her fault again.

But Ann knew she couldn't stay here, much as she wanted to. Sluggishly, she arose and stumbled into the shower, the force of the water beginning to bring her to life. Maybe coffee would help too she thought, making her way into the kitchen which still held the reminder of the previous day's breakfast. What had she done after Gus left? She couldn't remember. All she knew was that her eyes were sore from weeping, and the house was a mess. Had she spent all Saturday in bed weeping? Was she losing her mind?

Her phone rang as she was taking her first sip of coffee. She grabbed it in the faint hope it might be Gus, that he might be willing to listen to her, but was disappointed to see Fran's face on the screen.

'Hi, Fran,' she said, dispiritedly.

'Ann, I didn't want to disturb you, I know Chris will be back by now. But I wondered…'

'Oh, Fran!' Ann broke into tears.

'What's the matter?'

'It's me. I'm the matter. I've ruined everything. Gus has gone,' she sobbed, dropping into a chair.

'Are you at home? I'm in town. Owen wanted to attend the church service. I was going to get myself a coffee, I'll be right over.'

'Fran…' But Fran had ended the call. Ann wasn't sure if she wanted her friend to see her looking like this. She had only glanced in the mirror when she came out of the shower and she wasn't a pretty sight, her eyes swollen from crying, her face red and blotched. At least she should get dressed, she thought, looking down at the old towelling robe she'd dragged on.

Dressed in jeans and a sweater and wearing a smidgeon of makeup, Ann felt slightly better by the time the doorbell rang to announce Fran's arrival. She was even feeling glad her friend hadn't given her time to snub her.

'Ann!' Fran threw her arms around her and drew her into a warm hug.

Ann felt herself melt into the embrace, the other woman's presence providing her with much needed comfort but bringing her to tears again. 'Sorry,' she said. 'I can't seem to stop. I've been such a fool.'

'Let's have a cup of tea and you can tell me all about it. Chamomile, I think.' Fran drew Ann into the kitchen and forced her into a chair, while she filled the electric jug and fossicked in the pantry for mugs and teabags.

'Now,' Fran said, when they both had mugs of soothing chamomile tea, 'what happened?'

'I've been so stupid, Fran,' Ann said. 'You and Peta both advised me to tell Gus about how I lost the baby. I promised I would, but it was too difficult, so I thought I'd write him an email. I did write one, but knew it was the wrong way to tell him. I meant to delete it. I was going to tell him after he arrived back. But...'

'He saw the email?'

'Right. But he didn't get all the way through it. I think he only saw the part about Susie talking me into an abortion. He said some hurtful things and stormed out.'

'Oh, my dear! But why not just tell him the truth?'

'I can't, Fran. You didn't see his face, hear him yell at me. I doubt if he'll ever speak to me again. He loves children, wanted a big family. And he thinks I...' Ann stifled a sob. 'No, there's no way I can fix this. I have to live with my mistake. That's my punishment.' Ann looked down into the mug she was clutching with both hands then up to meet her friend's eyes. 'It's over, Fran.'

'Maybe...' But there was no conviction in Fran's voice.

'No.' Ann shook her head. 'If I hadn't been so afraid to tell Gus the truth in the first place, I wouldn't be in this situation. I have to take responsibility for it all. Thanks for listening. It helped,' she sniffed, her eyes still wet with tears. 'I'll get over it. I did last time. But this time it'll be even harder, I really thought we could have a future together. How foolish. As if I could have any sort of happy ever after, after what I planned to do.'

After Fran left, Ann moped around the house, washing up and setting things to rights. Then she tried to settle down to read, but Gus's face kept coming between her and the page, his angry voice ringing in her ears. Would she ever be able to forget it?

Forty-one

Chris had been in a daze ever since leaving Annie's house four days earlier. He couldn't believe Annie had been so cruel to have killed their child. He'd never forgive her.

He didn't stop to wonder why the email had never been sent. It was obvious. She hoped to keep him in the dark to ensure they could continue their relationship. Fat chance of that now. With Cassie on the mend, there was nothing to keep him here.

This morning Granite Springs was looking its best as Chris rose and started to make plans for his departure. It was a cool, clear morning with just a touch of frost on the grass behind the café as he headed downstairs for his morning caffeine hit. Then he had arranged to take Cassie and Miles to lunch at *The Springs*, where he'd stayed when he first came to town.

Frank was his usual cheerful self when Chris walked into The Bean Sprout, a bit too cheerful for Chris who was still smarting from the discovery of Annie's deceit.

'Macchiato?' he asked as usual.

Chris nodded, took what he now considered to be *his* table by the window and picked up a copy of The Granite Springs Advertiser which was lying there. He read the editorial in which Sam Walker was espousing the case for renewing the old bridge across the river. In one corner of his mind, he wondered if the editor would make a play for Annie when he'd gone, before dismissing it.

When he finished his coffee, Chris wandered aimlessly up Main

Street feeling he might be seeing it for the last time. He'd be sad to leave. He'd enjoyed returning to his roots much more than he'd expected but, he acknowledged, much of his pleasure had been in reconnecting with Annie. Now that was gone, there was nothing left.

*

It felt odd to walk into *The Springs* again, like coming full circle. When he checked in here three months earlier, he had no idea what life had in store. If he had, he might have turned around and left again. He sighed and, seeing Cassie and Miles waiting for him in the foyer, knew that would have been a mistake. Cassie had needed him, and he was delighted to see how happy she was, to meet Miles and to be assured of her future happiness. Unlike his own ruined romance, he felt sure theirs was set to last.

'Dad, this place is amazing!' Cassie greeted him with a hug.

'Thanks for inviting us.' Miles shook his hand.

'No problem. I've booked a table for lunch, but why don't we have a drink in the bar first?' He led the young couple into the bar which was beginning to fill up. It appeared there was some sort of event being held in one of the function rooms and groups were beginning to gather, people greeting each other noisily.

Leaving the two young people at a low table, Chris made his way to the bar. He was about to place his order when the woman in front of him turned around. She looked as if she was one of the crowd here for the function in her smart tweed suit and low heels – a typical member of the Country Women's Association which was hosting the charity luncheon.

'It's you!' she said, glaring at him. 'Gus Thomas! How dare you show your face here. You've broken my sister's heart a second time!'

'I don't...' Chris began, then he looked more closely, suddenly realising that, despite the older appearance, the different hairstyle, the unfamiliar style of dressing, he was looking at Susie Baird. This was Ann's sister.

'How dare you!' he said, uncaring of the others standing at the bar. 'It was you who encouraged Annie to have the abortion. It was my child she murdered. Did you ever think of that? How dare you take the law into your own hands and…' He ran out of words, realising by this time the others at the bar were moving away from the two of them. He knew this was neither the time nor place to have this conversation but was too upset and angry to care.

He was aware of Susie looking at him strangely.

'What?' he asked, sounding belligerent.

'She didn't have an abortion. Yes, I encouraged her to have one. It was her only solution, but the silly girl backed out at the last minute, said she couldn't do it, that she wanted her baby, *your* baby.'

'But…'

'Ann miscarried. She almost bled to death. It was the most frightening experience of my life. She's always felt it was God's punishment for her even contemplating the abortion. I don't think she's been inside a church since – unless with the choir.'

The blood drained from Chris's face. He'd wronged Annie. But the email… He shook his head in an attempt to remember. He'd definitely read about an abortion, but had there been more? He'd seen red and rushed out of the study to confront Annie, to tell her… He'd been so angry, so upset, he had no idea what he had said.

'Are you all right?' Susie was still looking at him strangely. She was carrying a glass of wine and, now that she'd sent his world into a spin, seemed to be eager to leave.

'I'll be fine,' Chris muttered, wondering if he would be. He needed to see Annie, to find out exactly what happened, to apologise for jumping to conclusions. But… he looked across to where Cassie and Miles were waiting for him, totally engrossed in each other, oblivious to everything and everyone around them. They reminded him so much of how Annie and he had been at their age, it made his heart ache.

'Can I take your order, sir?' The barman interrupted his thoughts. When he looked up, Susie had gone, walking across the bar to join a large group of similarly attired women.

In a daze, Chris ordered a glass of white wine and two beers, before carrying them over to where Cassie and Miles were seated.

'Thanks, Dad. This is special. Did you have a reason for treating us here today?'

Chris was stuck for an answer. He had intended to break the

news he was returning to Canada, but Susie's revelation had sent him reeling. Now, he didn't know what he was going to do – other than see Annie as soon as he could. He didn't know how he was going to make it through the meal with this on his mind.

Forty-two

Each day was very much like the last as Ann tried to function efficiently with the knowledge Gus was lost to her forever. *It put her worries about Kerrie and Janelle into perspective*, she thought, as she walked through the office oblivious now to their machinations.

While there was still no news on new positions for Kerrie and Janelle, Ann no longer cared. It was as if her life had ceased to exist when Gus walked out. She was just going through the motions. She idly wondered if Gus was still in town or if he'd already returned to Canada, left her, left Granite Springs, just as he'd done thirty-five years ago. At least this time she wasn't going to discover she was pregnant. But she still broke down again from time to time, helpless to rein in the despair that flooded her.

It had only been a few days, but it seemed like weeks. Maybe Fran was right when she'd suggested what Ann needed was a complete change of scene. She'd even gone so far as to hand Ann copies of the Sydney Morning Herald and the Canberra Times, open at the employment sections.

Five o'clock came around. Another day gone. Ann packed up and made her way to her car, anticipating another evening of boring television, accompanied by several glasses of wine in an attempt to get the good night's sleep that proved so elusive these days.

Back home, she took a pre-cooked meal from the fridge, ashamed she'd resorted to those, but unable to find the motivation to cook. She, the Ann Baird who'd always been so proud of her meticulous habits, her cooking skills and her determination not to give in to emotion, was an emotional wreck.

She had poured herself a glass of wine and was peeling the plastic lid from the top of the unappetizing-looking chicken teriyaki noodles when the doorbell rang.

'Damn!' she said, as the hot steam from the noodles burnt her fingers. She didn't want to see anyone. It had to be someone trying to sell something, or Peta wanting to know how she was. She was tempted to ignore it, pretend she wasn't home, but knew the hall light shining through the front door was a dead giveaway. Placing the offending meal on the kitchen bench and taking a gulp of wine before setting it alongside, she went to answer the door.

The figure outlined on the stained-glass panel looked familiar, but it couldn't be. Her stomach clenched and her heart raced as she opened the door to see Gus standing there.

What did he want? Had he come to berate her further? Ann didn't think she could take any more.

'Annie, can we talk?'

Behind him, Ann could see her next-door neighbour taking out his garbage bin and looking at them curiously. 'You'd better come in,' she said, standing aside to allow him to pass, and catching a whiff of his aftershave as he walked by. It brought back such painful memories, she felt dizzy.

'In here.' Ann gestured to the living room.

Gus stood in the middle of the room looking awkward.

'Well?' she asked, eager to get this over as soon as possible.

'I met your sister today.'

'Susie?' *What did Susie have to do with anything?*

'She shot me down for breaking your heart again.'

'So?' Ann hadn't made any secret of her feelings.

'She told me… well, she said you didn't have an abortion.'

Ann collapsed onto the sofa, her eyes filling.

'Why didn't you tell me, Annie? Why did I have to find out from Susie in the middle of the bar at *The Springs*?'

Ann swallowed the lump in her throat. She could barely speak, but she finally managed to force out, 'You didn't give me the chance.'

Gus's forehead creased. His mouth turned down. He dragged a

hand through his hair. 'I'm sorry, Annie. I was so upset, so angry. I couldn't think straight. I thought you'd...' He sat down beside her on the sofa with a thump, his hands clenched on his knees.

'How could you?' But Ann knew how close she'd come to doing exactly what he accused her of. 'When Susie suggested it, it seemed the only way out. You'd gone. Mum wasn't capable of accepting it. I knew what the gossips in this town were like – they'd have a field day. I gave in to her urgings, even allowed her to make the appointment. But I couldn't go through with it. The baby was the last little bit of you I had, I wanted to hang on to it, to her. I was sure it was a girl. Our little Annabel,' she murmured almost to herself.

'I knew if I did go ahead with it, it would be something I'd regret all my life. So, I cancelled the appointment. Susie was furious.' Ann would never forget how her sister had yelled at her, telling her what a stupid bitch she was, and that she wouldn't be there to help her bring up her bastard. But when Ann did need her, Susie had been there for her.

'It was only a couple of weeks later I lost her,' Ann said in a low voice. 'I don't remember much about it, but Susie says I almost died. Maybe I should have. It was my punishment for even having considered an abortion. I knew it was wrong. It went against everything I believe in – or did back then. But it meant there was no gossip. I suppose Susie was grateful for that. But I've never forgotten the child I didn't have, our child, Gus. Can you ever forgive me?' She raised her eyes, still filled with tears, to see tears sliding down his cheeks, too.

'Annie!' Gus moved closer and took the sobbing Ann in his arms. 'It wasn't your fault,' he said, his voice breaking. 'You have nothing to feel guilty for. Damn Susie!' he said, his voice becoming stronger. 'You were vulnerable, on your own, and she took advantage of that to try to push you into doing something you'd never have considered. A miscarriage isn't a punishment, Annie.'

They sat silently for several minutes, comforting each other for the child they had lost, finally able to grieve together.

Then, Gus stroked Ann's hair and wiped away the tears from her cheeks with his finger. 'It's over. Of course, I forgive you. But there's nothing to forgive. You did nothing wrong. I can't believe you've blamed yourself for all those years.' He kissed her eyelids, his lips moving down to her cheeks, then her mouth.

For the first time in thirty-five years, Ann felt as if a burden had been lifted, a burden she'd forced herself to carry, a burden of her own making. Was Gus right when he said losing Annabel hadn't been her fault? Had she been blaming herself needlessly? But his words did make her feel differently about things. And it was so good to feel his lips on hers again, to be back in his arms.

Forty-three

It was two weeks since Chris moved in with Annie – two glorious weeks when it seemed they'd never been apart. Annie's disclosure about the miscarriage had sealed their relationship, bringing then closer than ever. The pair were so in tune with each other, they often thought of the same thing at the same time. It was as if they could read each other's minds, a bit spooky.

Chris was in his new office, busy on his computer, when there was a knock at the door. It swung open.

Gail! What on earth was she doing here? He blinked, unable to believe his eyes.

'Surprised to see me?'

Surprised didn't cut it. Gail had always disparaged the town Chris grew up in, had tried to dissuade Cassie from coming here, from choosing to stay. 'What are you doing in Granite Springs?'

'That's not a very nice welcome when I've come all this way. We have a daughter here, as you've been at pains to point out to me on numerous occasions.'

She perched on the edge of his desk, her elegant outfit and immaculate grooming looking out of place in this country town. Chris had reverted to more casual attire. He hadn't worn a tie since returning from Canada. Today he was dressed in jeans and a sweater.

'You've come to see Cassie? How did you find me?' he asked, curious how she'd managed to find her way to his office.

'It wasn't difficult. I asked at the hotel where the technology park was. The receptionist was happy to enlighten me, even gave me a map. And, yes, I've come to see our daughter. You should be pleased.'

'You won't change her mind.'

'Maybe not.' Gail gazed around the small office space with disdain. 'This is a bit of a comedown from CAT headquarters in Vancouver. Anyway, about Cassie. The article she sent me from the local paper. It got me thinking. I put up a proposal to my editor. He agreed, and here I am.'

What was she talking about? He wished she'd leave, at least get off his desk. The cloying scent of her perfume was filling the room. To think he'd once been in love with this woman.

'I'm going to write an article about how a Canadian student from a city university finds life in a small country town university in Australia. It'll to be a feature article about the differences – highlighting Cassie, with photos. I presume there's a photographer in this one-horse town.' She finally slid down from the desk. 'Now, are you going to take me to lunch?' Gail looked at him expectantly, daring him to refuse.

Chris sighed. He knew Gail. Now she was here, it was going to be difficult to get rid of her. 'Okay, lunch.'

'Could we have it with Cassie?'

Chris sighed again, more heavily this time. Cassie would be at the campus. Annie was there too. What were the chances of her seeing him with Gail and getting the wrong idea? He was aware she'd harboured suspicions about his seeing Gail in Vancouver, suspicions he'd managed to avert. And he remembered his own jealousy of the newspaper editor. 'I should check if she's free. I'll text her.'

Cassie's reply came back immediately.

Mum? Here? Meet U in Banjo's. Cass x

*

Banjo's was crowded. It took Chris a while before he spotted Cassie sitting at the far end of the café with Miles. He took a deep breath, wondering how Gail would react to meeting their daughter's boyfriend.

'Cassie, darling!' In her customary effusive manner, Gail rushed up to the table to enfold Cassie in a warm hug. Chris grimaced as several tables of students stopped their conversations, twisting around to see what was happening.

'Mum, good to see you. This is Miles,' she said proudly, putting an arm around the young man beside her.

Gail's eyes widened as she took in the overly long blond hair and unshaven chin. 'Hello,' she said coolly and held out her hand.

'Good to meet you, Mrs Thomas,' Miles said to Gail, taking her hand. 'And to see you again, Dr Thomas.'

'Hi, sweetie. Miles.' Chris nodded to them both, took a seat and pulled out a chair for Gail. He glanced around, hoping Annie wasn't lunching here today. There was no sign of her, but a woman who looked very like her friend, Fran, was standing at the counter.

'How does this work?' Gail asked, looking around to find a waiter.

'You need to order at the counter, Mum.' Cassie stifled a grin. This wasn't the type of place her mother usually ate lunch.

'Chris?' Gail looked towards him for help.

'I'll do it. What would you like?' He pushed back his chair.

'I suppose they can do a salad? And a skim milk coffee.' She leant back. 'Now, Cassie. Tell me how you are.'

Shaking his head, Chris made his way to the counter to order salad for Gail and a burger for himself, along with two coffees, one skim milk latte and his usual macchiato.

'It's Chris, isn't it?' Fran was about to leave, a carrier bag of lunch in one hand, her purse in the other. 'Is Ann lunching with you?' She looked across to where Chris had come from.

'Not today. I'm lunching with my daughter.'

'Oh!'

Chris hoped she hadn't noticed Gail was at the table, too, though how could she miss her? In this café filled with students, she stood out like a sore thumb.

'Well, nice to see you. Take care.' She walked off, leaving Chris wondering exactly what she meant.

Back at the table, he found Gail was interrogating Miles about his background and his prospects, while Cassie fumed.

'Why are you here, Mum?' she asked when Gail paused for breath. 'If you came to try to take me back to Canada you can just turn around and go back again. I'm staying.' She took Miles' hand and squeezed it.

'I need to go to class. See you later, Cass.' Miles rose, gave Cassie a peck on the cheek and left.

Gail watched him go with distaste. 'What do you see in that boy, Cassie? You could do a lot better than him. He...'

'That's enough, Mum. Now why *are* you here? You didn't come when I was in hospital. Why now?'

'I thought you'd be pleased to see me.' Gail pouted. 'But you will be when I tell you. I'm here on behalf of the magazine. I read the article you sent me. It was quite well written for a country newspaper. But we can do a lot better. How would you like to be the focus of a feature article in the winter edition?'

Cassie looked as if she was going to throw up. 'You came all this way to use my story for your magazine? No way!'

Chris was surprised. Even though he'd thought Gail's idea was exploitative of their daughter, he assumed Cassie would be thrilled.

'You'll change your mind when you see what I intend to do. It'll be a full double page spread, with photos. Better than that tinpot rag.' Gail wasn't easily dissuaded. 'Now,' she looked around the café which was beginning to empty, 'can we go somewhere to have a good chat? I need to catch up with what you've been up to since you came here.'

Cassie sighed and met Chris's eyes over her mother's head. 'I suppose we can go home – to where I live. There'll be no one else there right now. They're all in class – where I should be. Can you drive us, Dad?'

'Sure, then I need to get back. Work to do.' *And I need to talk with Annie before Fran does.*

Forty-four

'You're not going to like this.' Fran's voice sounded tentative.

'What?' Ann wasn't paying attention. She had been reading an email from Flora Richards when the phone rang, and had just reached the part where Flora listed possible alternative employment for Janelle. Ann was scanning the email to see if Kerrie was also mentioned, when Fran spoke again.

'Guess who I saw in Banjo's a few minutes ago?'

Ann stopped scrolling. 'You're going to tell me.'

'Chris Thomas.'

'Gus? Was he having lunch with Cassie? I didn't know he intended to be on campus today.' Ann's mind went back to their hurried breakfast that morning. Both had been sleepy after a late night of movie watching, then they'd become sidetracked in the shower. She smiled, remembering how his skin had felt against hers, how they'd lathered each other with shower gel before turning the shower to a power jet. They had eaten breakfast quickly and without much conversation.

'Cassie, yes.' She paused. 'And a very elegant woman. What does his ex look like?'

'His ex? Gail? I don't know. But it's not likely she's in Granite Springs, in Banjo's.' Ann started to chuckle, then stopped. If Gus was having lunch with Cassie and a strange woman, what was more likely than the woman was Cassie's mother? 'Oh!'

'I just thought I'd let you know. I was picking up a couple of wraps for our lunch when we met at the counter.'

'Thanks.'

'If you want to talk…'

'Maybe later.' Ann's eyes glazed over when she put down the phone, the email from Flora forgotten. It must be Gail, but what was she doing here? Gus hadn't known she was coming – or had he? Ann tried to remember if he'd mentioned anything, but her mind was annoyingly blank. In the two weeks since he returned, apart from their initial misunderstanding, life had been idyllic. Gus had moved his belongings into her house, cancelled his tenancy of the flat, and had cheerfully set off to work in his new office each morning. They'd met up with Cassie and Miles a few times, but most evenings were spent with the two of them making up for all those lost years. Surely he'd have told her if he knew his ex was coming to town?

A commotion in the office pulled Ann out of her thoughts. As usual it was Janelle, but this time, she appeared to be gloating about something. Ann forced her eyes back to the computer screen and reread Flora's email. The HR manager had managed to relocate Janelle in the School of Viticulture. That was what was causing the disturbance. She was telling anyone who would listen how she'd be no doubt organising wine tastings for the staff and be able to buy her wine at a discount.

Ann walked out. 'So, you'll be leaving us, Janelle?'

Janelle only gave Ann a cursory, gleeful glance and nodded, before turning back to Kerrie. 'You'll be next,' she predicted. 'See, I knew it would work.' She threw another glance Ann's way and resumed her seat, burying her head in her mobile phone.

Resisting the temptation to wrench it from her hand, Ann took a deep breath and returned to her desk. She wouldn't have to put up with her for much longer. Flora still hadn't found a place for Kerrie, but Ann hoped that, without her partner-in-crime, Kerrie would be easier to deal with.

She picked up her phone and was debating whether to call Gus when it rang, and she saw his face on the screen.

'Gus, where are you?' Fran's news had robbed her of what would be her normal loving greeting. She heard a loud sigh.

'You've spoken to Fran.'

'What makes you think that?'

'None of the, "Hello, Gus, lovely to hear your voice" you usually greet me with. My guess is Fran beat me to the phone and told you the news.'

'So, it's true. Your wife's here? In Granite Springs?'

'Ex-wife. Gail and I haven't been man and wife for years. But, yes, she's in town. She's with Cassie right now, having a motherly chat.' He groaned.

'Why is she here now?' Ann's stomach dropped. Was she seeking a reconciliation with Gus? She'd stayed in Vancouver when he was there, made all sorts of attempts to see him, if he was to be believed. No, she wouldn't go there. She believed him. But why was she here? Why now?

'She says she plans to do a feature article on Cassie – a more in-depth version of the one your friend wrote.'

'Cassie?'

'She's not interested. I'm in the doghouse for supporting Cassie. We had lunch with her and Miles. Of course, you know that. I'm afraid Miles didn't meet her standards either. I don't know how long she intends to be here,' he added, pre-empting Ann's next question. 'She just turned up in my office this morning. I think she's staying at *The Springs*.'

Ann could visualise Gus sitting at his office desk, dragging a hand through his already dishevelled hair, pushing back that unruly lock which always refused to stay in place. She wished she was there to run her fingers through his hair, to tell him she loved him, that everything would be all right. She looked out into the main office where Janelle was still holding court. Her departure couldn't come soon enough.

The rest of the day passed in a blur. The sandwich which Ann bought earlier lay uneaten on her desk, the bread curling at the corners. She wasn't hungry, couldn't face food. All she could think of was that Gail Thomas was in Granite Springs.

*

It was a relief for Ann when Gus arrived home at his usual time, pulling her into a warm hug as he did every evening. The feel of his arms around her went some way to reassuring her of his love. But there was still a niggle in the back of her mind.

'Have you found out any more?' she asked, then they broke apart.

'About Gail's plans? No. Cassie called me when her mother left. She's agreed to have dinner with her at *The Springs*. Miles isn't invited. Cassie's not happy about that.'

Ann's stomach clenched. Was Gus intending to join them?

'I won't be there either. You don't need to worry about that.' He could read her mind. 'I saw Gail's number come up on my phone a couple of times, but I ignored it. I'm glad it's the weekend and I won't be in the office. She can't find me here.'

'Is she likely to try?' Ann gazed around in dismay. What would she do if Gus's ex-wife turned up?

'I don't expect so, unless Cassie told her where I was living. But don't worry,' he repeated. 'I can handle her. Though I have no idea how her mind works.' He shook his head. 'I have enough trouble working *you* out.'

'How are things at the university?' Gus asked, when they were settled on the sofa with glasses of red wine, a chicken casserole bubbling away in the oven.

'Better.' Ann regaled him with the latest news from HR, finishing with, 'So, one down, one to go.' She could hear the note of despair in her voice.

'It'll work out. You'll see.' Gus pulled her towards him. 'From now on, life is going to get better. I've been talking with your Professor Kerr and it looks like we can come to some sort of arrangement between CAT and the school of education. Maybe we can even end up working together. Wouldn't that be something?'

'I don't doubt it.' But it was a good thought, and it blew away all the worry of his ex-wife and her unexpected arrival.

'But, for now, what we need to decide is if we can leave that delicious smelling casserole in the oven for longer while we...' Gus put down his glass, took Ann's from her hand, and pulled her towards him.

Everything else was swept out of her mind as she was lost in his embrace.

Forty-five

Ann was heading back to the office from a meeting with Flora Richards to finalise the transfer of the two staff members, although only one of them had been confirmed. She had a spring in her step, glad to have finally rid her office of the two troublemakers, and had even received permission to advertise one of the positions. On the home front, Gus and she had settled down into a comfortable routine and although, as far as she knew, Gail was still in town, she hadn't tried to contact him again. Life was good.

As she walked along one of the pathways which crossed the grassy area where students liked to congregate, Ann noticed a girl sitting alone, bent over in distress. As she drew nearer, she recognized Cassie, her eyes red from weeping, a bunch of tissues scrunched up in one hand.

'Cassie, what's the matter?' Ann joined her on the bench.

The girl looked up. 'Ann. Sorry.' She sniffed. 'I'm fine.'

'You're certainly not fine. What's wrong? You can tell me.' Ann hoped she was right. Although she still didn't know Cassie very well, they had found common ground in their love for Gus, and Ann hoped the girl would feel able to confide in her.

The eyes meeting Ann's contained a glimmer of hope. 'I'm pregnant.'

Ann's stomach dropped. She'd been around Cassie's age when she discovered she was pregnant. 'And you're not happy about it?'

'Oh, I am!' Cassie scrubbed her eyes with the damp ball of tissues. 'Miles is, too. We want kids. We've talked about it. It's a bit sooner than we planned, but we can cope. We want to get married.'

'Then…?' Ann's stomach lurched again. She was struck with the parallel. This could have been her story – hers and Gus's. If he'd stayed in Granite Springs, or she'd gone to the US with him. For a few seconds she felt envious of the tearful girl.

'It's Mum. I met her in town between classes. She was furious. She wants me to have an abortion, says it'll ruin my life.'

'No!' The word erupted from Ann's lips. She couldn't help herself. Cassie's eyes widened.

'I'm sorry, Cassie. But you're so lucky to have Miles to support you, and your dad will, too. I know he will.'

'How do you know? How do you know he won't take the same view as Mum, want me to finish my degree first, get more experience of men, find someone more… worthy of me?' She screwed up her face as she spat out the last few words.

'There's something I want to tell you.' Ann took a deep breath and gazed into the distance. She knew this was the right time to share her story with Cassie, the secret she'd kept bottled up for so long. 'I was around your age when the same thing happened to me. Your dad and I planned to marry, but… life got in the way, and when he went to the US I stayed here.' She continued with her sorry tale, finishing with, 'I've had to live with the guilt and regret all my life. I don't think I could have lived with myself if I'd gone ahead with it. As it was, I've lived with the guilt that my miscarriage was my punishment. Don't listen to your mum, listen to your heart.'

When she finished, Cassie was staring at her in amazement. 'You were pregnant with Dad's baby? Far out! And you really think he'll be supportive of me and Miles?'

'I'm sure of it.'

'But, Mum…'

'I think your dad can probably cope with her, don't you?'

Cassie turned and hugged Ann who, surprised to feel the young girls' arms around her, returned the hug. 'Thanks,' Cassie said, drawing back. 'It's been good to talk with you. Thanks for sharing your experience with me. It must have been dreadful for you. How did you manage?'

'My sister helped me.' And Susie was still trying to help her, Ann realised with a shock. In her own way, Susie was doing her best to try to improve Ann's life in the only way she knew. The dinner parties, the dreadful men, they were all Susie's way of helping. 'Will you be all right now? I should be getting back.'

Cassie nodded. 'Miles will be finished his class soon and we'll go home. I thought we could celebrate together with Mum, but...' She swallowed. 'Why don't you and Dad have dinner with us tonight?'

Ann thought quickly. She and Gus had no plans for the evening, other than a quiet dinner and early bed. 'We do have something to celebrate. I'll call your dad and ask him to book a table at The Riverside. How would that be?'

'Really? It would be great. Can you tell him about...' She glanced down at her flat stomach. 'Telling Mum was hard. I don't want to have to go through it again.'

'Of course, I can.' Ann gave Cassie another hug and walked off with a spring in her step again. What wonderful news. A new life!

*

'And I told her we'd take them both to dinner at The Riverside tonight to celebrate,' Ann finished, when she rang Gus a short time later.

'I can't believe it! My little Cassie's going to be a mother. She's...'

'Don't you dare say she's too young,' Ann warned.

'I wasn't going to. But it's a shock. How will she manage her studies?'

'I'm sure she'll work something out, and Miles is being very supportive. They want to get married.'

'Wow! Takes a bit of getting used to. No wonder Gail overreacted.'

'Overreacted? She wants Cassie to have an abortion. How could any mother suggest such a thing?'

'That's Gail. When something she doesn't like happens, her first impulse if to get rid of it.'

'But her own grandchild?' Ann couldn't hide her rage. Cassie's situation reminded her so much of what her own had been. And her mother was acting just like Susie had.

'A grandchild. We'll be grandparents,' Gus said in awe, then chuckled. 'It's probably what spooked Gail. She'd hate the idea of being a grandmother.'

'I think it will be wonderful,' Ann said.

*

'What do you think, Dad? Ann did tell you?' Cassie held Miles' hand tightly and gazed at her dad, oblivious of the busy restaurant.

'She did, and I'm delighted. Though I thought you might have waited for longer before making me a grandfather. I take it your mother isn't pleased?'

'No.' Cassie's face crumbled. 'Did Ann tell you Mum wants…'

Miles patted her on the shoulder.

'It's not what your mum wants, it's what you want.' Ann couldn't help herself. She saw so much of herself in Cassie. How she wished she'd had Gus's hand in hers when she discovered she was pregnant.

'I'm with Annie on this, sweetheart. It's your decision, yours and Miles'.'

'We want to be married, Dr Thomas,' Miles said, Cassie's hand still firmly clasped in his. 'As soon as we can.'

'What about your studies?' Gus looked across the table at the two young people.

'We've talked about that.' Cassie met Miles' eyes before turning back to her dad. 'The baby is due in the summer break and, if necessary, I can take an extra year.' She smiled at Miles with so much love, Ann felt tears come to her eyes.

'You seem to have worked it all out.'

Ann looked at Gus. She knew exactly what he was thinking. She could read his mind. They seemed so young to be parents. But it could have been them, if he hadn't been so pigheaded, if she hadn't refused to join him.

Ann felt Gus grasp her hand in his.

Forty-six

The elegant blonde woman who stood at her door needed no introduction. It couldn't be anyone else. Before Ann could speak, Gail broke into a wild tirade, at odds with her immaculate and elegant appearance.

'How dare you encourage Cassie to have this baby. It'll ruin her life. I know what a child does to a career. Who do you think you are? Just because my misguided husband is experiencing a bout of nostalgia doesn't mean he's going to settle back in this godforsaken dump. His life is in Canada.'

Ann flinched, taken aback by such a torrent of abuse. While one part of her brain recognised this was Gus's ex-wife and Cassie's mother, another wondered how any mother could behave like this. And what was she saying about Gus?

By this time Gail seemed to have run out of breath and invective and stood breathing heavily.

'Have you quite finished,' Ann asked, as calmly as she could, trying to subdue the anger which threatened to engulf her. How dare she come here like this – to Ann's home. How dare she think she could intimidate her.

Gail glared at her.

'I think you should leave.'

The woman didn't move, but began repeating what she had already said, and adding insults which made Ann want to curl up into a ball. 'Cassie told me about you and Gus. He doesn't love you, you know.

He's only using you,' she said finally, her words silencing Ann's instinct to repeat her demand she leave.

Ann was well aware she couldn't compete with this woman in the fashion stakes, nor did she have a high-powered career, but she was sure Gus loved her, and she knew she'd have made a better mother to Cassie than this fashion plate. So why couldn't she bring herself to answer back, to tell her a few home truths?

'Have you finished?' she asked at last, just as a car drew up and Gus came up the front path, a shocked expression on his face.

'What the hell are you doing here, Gail?' he asked, a vein throbbing on his forehead. His eyes softened. 'Are you all right, Annie?' He looked from one woman to the other, then back out to the road. 'I think we should all go inside, don't you?'

Reluctantly, Ann stood aside to allow Gus and Gail to enter, then took a deep breath before following them through the hallway and into the kitchen which was redolent with the roast dinner she was preparing. She looked sadly at the table set for two, the bottle of red wine carefully opened and ready to be poured. Gus had only been gone an hour, to pick up the laptop he'd left at the office by mistake.

'Now, Gail, what's this all about?' Gus stood in the middle of the kitchen, legs astride, arms folded. 'You have no business coming here and disturbing Annie. Anything you have to say about Cassie you can say to me. I presume this is about Cassie?'

'Well, this is cosy,' Gail said, her eyes darting around the kitchen taking in every little detail.

The hairs on the back of Ann's neck lifted. What if what Gail said was true? All her old insecurities came to the fore. She held onto the back of a chair for support. She couldn't believe what was happening.

'Gail?' Gus prompted.

'Sorry to disturb your little love nest. That's what this is, isn't it?' she asked Ann, her eyes swivelling towards her. 'You really thought you could turn back the clock. Oh yes,' she said, when Gus's mouth fell open, 'Cassie told me all about your childhood sweetheart here in Granite Springs. What a sweet story.' She sneered. 'But hardly realistic to think you could recapture it – how many years later? Come on, Chris. Look at the two of you. This isn't your life now. Your life is back in Canada. I've been thinking it was rash of me to leave you the way I did, that perhaps it's time for us to have another go. We were always good together, weren't we?' She moved confidently towards Gus who backed away.

Ann cringed, feeling the blood drain from her face. She wished she was anywhere but here. She didn't want to hear Gus's response. What if he agreed with Gail? What if it had all been a mirage? What if he did intend to go back to Canada, even back to Gail?

'What planet are you living on, Gail?' Gus's voice broke through Ann's wild imaginings. 'We were finished long before you left, had been for years. We both knew that. We only stayed together through a misguided sense of responsibility to Cassie. But she's been happier since you left, too. And now she's making her own life here with Miles, as I am with Annie.' He stretched an arm around Ann's shoulder and gave it a reassuring squeeze. 'If that's all you've come to say, I think you should leave now.'

'I'm going, but you haven't heard the last of this.' With a glare at them both, her head in the air, Gail turned and made her way toward the front door. Gus followed her, and Ann heard something being said in a terse tone before the door closed.

Ann collapsed into the chair she'd been clutching, glad Gail had finally left. She couldn't believe what had just happened.

When Gus returned, ignoring the opened wine bottle, he poured them both a glass of brandy. 'I think we need this. I'm so sorry you were subjected to Gail on the rampage. Now tell me what happened before I arrived.' Gus joined her at the kitchen table, throwing an arm around her shoulders again.

Ann sank back against his broad chest with relief. 'She wanted to tell me to back off, that Cassie was none of my business, plus a lot of other things I can't repeat. Oh, Gus. She made me feel… dirty.'

'My poor baby.' Gus drew her to him in a tight hug, his chin resting on her hair. 'I do love you. You know that. I wish Gail would go back to Canada and leave us all alone.'

'Why is she still here?'

'I'm damned if I know. I don't believe she wants us to get back together. I'd drive her mad in a week. But she's up to something, I wonder…'

'What?'

'Something I heard when I was in Vancouver. A rumour about the magazine she works for. She laughed it off, but if… I'll check it out but not right now. Something smells delicious.'

*

It was early afternoon on Monday, Australian time, before Chris was able to follow up on his suspicions, and even later by the time Alan sent him a copy of a news article which reported the imminent demise of the magazine Gail had been so proud to be part of, the one she'd poured her time and effort into. The article stated the management were bankrupt, and the magazine was about to fold, the final issue having just gone to press. He whistled when he read that. There would be no article about Cassie, never would have been. So, what had prompted Gail's trip to Australia? He couldn't believe her when she said she wanted to get back together with him. But he knew his ex-wife. She never did anything without a motive and her strongest motivation was money.

'That's it!' he exclaimed, wondering why it hadn't occurred to him before now. Of course, Gail hadn't come to Australia to see Cassie, or to seek a reconciliation with him. She was after money, the settlement she had shunned when they divorced. He chuckled to himself. This was something that could be easily fixed, could have been fixed without Gail resorting to the tactics she had. But that was Gail all over. She never took the direct route if she thought she could make more waves by going in a circuitous direction. Chris picked up his phone.

*

'So, it's sorted,' he told Annie, as they sat together on the sofa enjoying a glass of wine after their meal. 'I told her I'd talk to my lawyer back in Vancouver and arrange a one-off amount to tide her over till she finds something else. It shouldn't be difficult for her. She's pretty well-known and is good at what she does. I have to say, it did give me an inordinate amount of pleasure to be able to say the equivalent of "I told you so". She's already booked her flight home.'

'Poor Cassie. So, her mother didn't come to see her after all.'

'You're a much better mother to Cassie than Gail will ever be. All she ever thinks about is herself.' He hugged Annie tightly. 'Now that's enough about her. Let's concentrate on us.'

Annie smiled and snuggled up to him, relieved Gail was out of their lives and their future was secure.

Forty-six

It was a small wedding, held in the Botanic Gardens beneath an old fig tree which had been growing there for over a hundred years. Although disappointed her mother wouldn't be there, Cassie bravely told Chris he and Ann would make up for her.

On a beautiful spring day in early September with only a slight breeze, the small wedding party made their way through the gardens, accompanied by a fanfare of music from Miles' friends. The bride was dressed in a flowing dress of white cheesecloth which hid her baby bump, and the groom was wearing a white shirt with a pair of black pants, his hair neatly trimmed for the special day. It was a joyful occasion, most of the guests being students.

Ann and Gus stood hand in hand and watched as the pair repeated their vows and a couple of rainbow lorikeets flew overhead. Ann was almost moved to tears at the thought this could have been her and Gus.

After the ceremony, they all piled into cars and drove out to The Haven where Owen and Fran had offered to host the reception. They, along with Ann and Gus, were the only people at the wedding who were over twenty-three, though Fran was quick to point out that Owen had never shed his student personality.

As the younger members of the party became more and more boisterous and Miles' fellow music students provided music for dancing, Gus drew Ann aside.

'What do you say, Annie?' Gus gazed at her with a twinkle in his eyes. 'Shall *we* make it legal, too – finally? No more regrets?'

For what might have been the first time in her life, certainly the first time since she was twenty, Ann threw caution to the winds. 'I love the idea. And I love you, Gus Thomas.' She wrapped her arms around his neck. 'Let's do it!'

As her lips touched to his, Ann she knew she was saying goodbye to all the regret and guilt she'd lived with for so long. This was the beginning of a new life, a life with Gus, a life without regrets.

The End

If you've enjoyed Ann's story, I'd really appreciate it if you could leave a review. A few words will suffice, no need for a lengthy review. It will mean a lot to me and help other readers find my books.

Look out for the next book in the
Granite Springs series, *The Life She Dreams*.

Can the past ever really be left behind?

Liz Pender has lived alone since her dreams for the future were shattered by the death of her husband. She retreated to Granite Springs where her life now revolves around her bookshop, The Reading Corner, and her cat, Marmaduke.

Newly appointed editor of The Granite Springs Advertiser, *Sam Walker*, recently moved to the small country town to seek a quieter life.

When Liz's bookshop comes under threat, Sam and Liz are brought together causing sparks to fly. But a summons for help from overseas threatens to ruin Sam's country idyll and reignites the past for Liz.

Can Liz put the past behind her and face a future with Sam, or are her dreams destined to remain just that?

Another feel good second chance romance set in the small country town of Granite Springs where it's never too late to fall in love.

You can order it here getbook.at/TheLifeSheDreams

From the Author

Dear Reader,

First, I'd like to thank you for choosing to read *The Life She Regrets*. I hope you've enjoyed discovering Ann's story.

Having spent seven years teaching university and living in an Australian country town, and don an acreage, I've enjoyed writing a series with a rural setting and drawing on my experience of living in the country – with goats – and teaching in university. This is the eighth book in the series set in the fictional country town of Granite Springs and I'm thrilled by the response of you, my readers, to this series, how you tell me my characters are real people you'd love to have as friends. I feel they're my friends too, and they've become a part of my life.

If you'd like to stay up to date with my new releases and special offers you can sign up to my reader's group.

You can sign up here
https://mailchi.mp/f5cbde96a5e6/maggiechristensensreadersgroup

I'll never share your email address, and you can unsubscribe at any time. You can also contact me via Facebook Twitter or by email. I love hearing from my readers and will always reply.

Thanks again.

Acknowledgements

As always, this book could not have been written without the help and advice of a number of people.

Firstly, my husband Jim for listening to my plotlines without complaint, for his patience and insights as I discuss my characters and storyline with him, for his patience and help with difficult passages and advice on my male dialogue, and for being there when I need him.

John Hudspith, editor extraordinaire for his ideas, suggestions, encouragement and attention to detail.

Jane Dixon-Smith for her patience and for working her magic on my beautiful cover and interior.

My thanks also to early readers of this book —Helen, Maggie and Louise, for their helpful comments and advice. Also to Annie of *Annie's books at Peregian* and Graeme of *The Bookshop at Caloundra* for their ongoing support.

And to all of my readers. Your support and comments make it all worthwhile. I'm thrilled you enjoy my more mature characters and that the situations they find themselves in resonate with you.

About the Author

After a career in education, Maggie Christensen began writing contemporary women's fiction portraying mature women facing life-changing situations. Her travels inspire her writing, be it her trips to visit family in Scotland, in Oregon, USA or her home on Queensland's beautiful Sunshine Coast. Maggie writes of mature heroines coming to terms with changes in their lives and the heroes worthy of them. Her writing has been described by one reviewer as *like a nice warm cup of tea. It is warm, nourishing, comforting and embracing.*

From her native Glasgow, Scotland, Maggie was lured by the call 'Come and teach in the sun' to Australia, where she worked as a primary school teacher, university lecturer and in educational management. Now living with her husband of over thirty years on Queensland's Sunshine Coast, she loves walking on the deserted beach in the early mornings and having coffee by the river on weekends. Her days are spent surrounded by books, either reading or writing them – her idea of heaven!

Maggie can be found on Facebook, Twitter, Goodreads, Instagram or on her website.

https://www.facebook.com/maggiechristensenauthor
https://twitter.com/MaggieChriste33
https://www.goodreads.com/author/show/8120020.Maggie_Christensen
https://www.instagram.com/maggiechriste33/
http://maggiechristensenauthor.com/